*A collection of stories that celebrates
the many faces of erotic love . . .*

The writer-heroine in Natasha Tarpley's story wants to give "All of Me" to a man whose art will always come first.

Reginald Harris's "The Dream" unwinds as a sexy film noir fantasy shared by two unlikely lovers.

"Nadine's Husband" is having an illicit affair with his wife's sister in Preston L. Allen's tale of loyalty, betrayal, and impossible love.

The dressing room of a bridal salon is the setting for "Click," Chris Benson's erotic story of a photographer who gets the picture on the eve of his lover's wedding to another man.

The woman who lives with her longtime partner in "Alpine County" has an unexpected epiphany in Sapphire's haunting tale of love and loss.

CAROL TAYLOR is a former book editor now working as a freelance writer. She co-edited and contributed to *Sacred Fire: The QBR 100 Essential Black Books*. She lives in New York City.

Brown Sugar

A COLLECTION OF
EROTIC BLACK FICTION

EDITED BY
CAROL TAYLOR

A PLUME BOOK

PLUME
Published by the Penguin Group
Penguin Putnam Inc., 375 Hudson Street, New York, New York 10014, U.S.A.
Penguin Books Ltd, 27 Wrights Lane, London W8 5TZ, England
Penguin Books Australia Ltd, Ringwood, Victoria, Australia
Penguin Books Canada Ltd, 10 Alcorn Avenue, Toronto, Ontario, Canada M4V 3B2
Penguin Books (N.Z.) Ltd, 182–190 Wairau Road, Auckland 10, New Zealand

Penguin Books Ltd, Registered Offices: Harmondsworth, Middlesex, England

First published by Plume, a member of Penguin Putnam Inc.

First Printing, January 2001

20 19 18 17 16 15 14 13 12 11

 REGISTERED TRADEMARK—MARCA REGISTRADA

LIBRARY OF CONGRESS CATALOGING-IN-PUBLICATION DATA

Brown sugar : a collection of erotic Black fiction / edited by Carol Taylor.
    p. cm.
    ISBN 0-452-28224-1
    1. Erotic stories, American—Afro-American authors. 2. Afro-Americans—
Fiction. I. Taylor, Carol.
    PS648.E7 B76 2001
    813.008'03538—dc21   00-061161

Printed in the United States of America

PUBLISHER'S NOTE
These stories are works of fiction. Names, characters, places, and incidents either are the
product of the author's imagination or are used fictitiously, and any resemblance to actual
persons, living or dead, business establishments, events, or locales is entirely coincidental.

Brown Sugar is dedicated to lovers
and lovers of fiction everywhere.

CONTENTS

ACKNOWLEDGMENTS

Many thanks to my assistant Audrey; this book could not have happened without you. Thanks to my agent Marie Brown for her guidance and Rosemary Ahern for her editorial wisdom. Thank you Tracy Sherrod for being a good friend. Thanks to my mother Carol and sister Leila to whom I can talk about anything. Thanks Ellis and Marcela for the phone calls, support, and mostly good advice. My deepest thanks to all the writers who worked so diligently to create the original stories in *Brown Sugar*; you are on the cutting edge.

"Brown Sugar, Babe, I gets high off your love
and don't know how to behave."

—D'Angelo, *Brown Sugar*

INTRODUCTION

The Blacker the Berry . . .

Silken sheets, jazz playing softly on the stereo, chocolate pudding licked from a thigh, black silk against brown bodies in warm sticky embraces. Eroticism has always played a role in the lives of blacks, yet these images are rarely ever portrayed. African American sexuality is not only of an erotic fashion but also a romantic and a playful one; it's warm sighs as well as heavy breathing. The many moods of black Eros have only just begun to be explored in movies, music, and literature with stimulating results. Obviously we're onto something.

As Sonia Sanchez wrote, we are definitely *A BaddDDD People*, both inside the bedroom and out. And although attempts have been made, we cannot minimize the potency and urgency of our African roots. In *Brown Sugar* we're here to represent, to show the real souls of black folk, our own particular ardor and passion. Our soul has been on ice enough; it's time to heat it up. Erotica has long been the domain of white America. But it is no secret that we are a passionate people, from our walk to our talk. So why is black sexuality thought of as pornography, or dirty, instead of sexy? Why is it downplayed instead of uplifted? Why is there shame in the full lips, the white teeth, against black, black skin? The hair unruly, reaching up to the sky. The strong muscles in the legs, back, ass, hips, thighs, and calves, straining, the kiss of silk against hot, wet flesh.

While *Brown Sugar*, a cutting-edge collection of original erotic fiction, is definitely for adults only, it is not pornographic. Some of the stories are lyrical and some earthy, some funny, others downright startling. What they share is the goal of reclaiming and redefining black sexuality—in its myriad forms—which has so often been defined for us but less often by us. Black sexuality, sensuality, and eroticism are in the language, the objects of the affection, the whispered words, and the breathy sighs. It is the movement in the half-light of the flickering candles near the sweat-soaked bed. White cotton sheets against berry brown skin, a touch, a caress, a smile, a laugh. Or as Nas so eloquently put it, "Caramel kisses, for Jezebel sisters."

We are an extraordinary people, disciplined by our backbone and uplifted by our spirit. But it is our mind that first delivers us into the realms of erotic entanglement. Our experiences, what we see, feel, taste, and smell: the sensual curve of a shoulder, a lover's scent on our fingers and taste on our tongue. The disturbing ache of desire, the magnetic pull of one body inexplicably, inextricably to another into erotic entanglement. Desire cannot be explained because it starts in the mind shaped by words, phrases, and images. We know only that it exists or that it does not. Sometimes even then we falter, our wits dulled, as our senses are heightened. No one is immune.

We All Have Our Erotic Stories

We are all in a state of wonder and confusion about who we are sexually: gay, straight, bi, vanilla, Dom, Sub, into S/M, top, bottom, and on and on. The bookshelves are laden with self-help books on finding Mr. or Ms. Right and then shaping them to our needs. Because it teaches by experience, the demand for erotic literature grows constantly, proving that variety truly is the spice of life. This is why we read erotica, to lose ourselves, though we often find ourselves within the story. That is why, though I am straight, I can be turned on by homoeroticism. Though I don't crave S/M sex, I can be aroused by it in well-written literature. *Brown Sugar* brings you the myriad forms of erotic entanglement—only this time, you will be able to find yourself in these stories.

Of course we all have our erotic stories. How could we not? It is what makes us who we are. It is why we are with the people we are with, or not with the people we thought we'd be with forever. And it is why we are with the people we never ever dreamed we'd be with. In the same way that every book I've ever read has changed me, every lover I've ever been with has taught me something—whether I've wanted them to or not. I've learned something not only about them but about myself as well. These experiences have been invaluable. I'm old enough now to know that. We should be inspired by the endless possibilities available to us: the infinite combinations and variations on a theme. But we limit ourselves to what we think we like or think we will dislike.

This is a lesson I learned that has stayed with me: that you shouldn't judge a book by its cover, a story by its teller, or a relationship by its beginning. And that you shouldn't think you know yourself so well that you have nothing left to learn.

A Story of My Own

Not long ago, on a beautiful late spring, early summer kind of day, I was strolling through the Union Square market. The weather had just turned and the unseasonably balmy Thursday afternoon had everyone playing hooky. I'd taken my favorite path west across Ninth Street then turned north up University Place to Union Square. As I passed the flower vendors and bakery stands, I clocked him hawking me as he headed across the park with a friend. It was a full clock.

The weather and spring fever had coaxed me into a pair of skintight beige, cropped pants and leather platform sandals. He later told me I'd been strutting, which is not unusual for me. But it was his unrepentant pimp roll and flawless half-naked body that caught *my* eye: one not necessarily more potent than the other. I thought, my eyes are watching God.

A Leo—from his mane of drop-dead dreadlocks, and fuck-me swagger to the lick-me look he gave me—I knew it as soon as I saw him. He was hot. And I felt his heat the minute he turned it on me. I watched him a bit through my shades, but I wanted to give him shit for his bravado, for the look he'd given me. So I kept going. I passed him, ignoring his vibe, but at the last minute I turned and looked long enough for him to see me looking. I smiled. He smiled. When I saw him put his arm on his friend's elbow, I turned away. It wouldn't be long now. I was feeling him and he was feeling me. It can often be as simple as that. And it was.

"Hello."

I turned to find a smile, almost as beautiful as the day, on a face that was just as perfect up close and a body that made me want to stop and talk. He was a deep chocolate dream, his slanted cat eyes and sloping cheekbones set off by full luscious lips. I was in lust.

"Hi," I breathed. Giving away nothing but my time.

"I saw you walking," he said, stating the obvious while making eyes.

Uh-oh, not the sharpest knife in the drawer.

"Yeah, I saw you see me." I turned to him and took off my shades.

"You've got pretty eyes," he said on cue.

"Thanks. So do you." Hey, I knew the script. I knew that he knew I thought he was hot and I knew that he knew that he thought so of me too. But we were drawing a crowd of stares standing in the middle of the market trying desperately to keep our clothes on.

"My name is Trevor."

"I'm Carol."

"All right."

Then silence.

And more silence.

"All right then," I repeated, but my sarcasm was lost on him. He just stood there smiling stupidly, beatifically. The sun was going down on my brilliant day. I was about done, I told myself. Nothing to offer, a waste of time. A candy-coated cutie more delicious than satisfying.

I smiled distractedly, already walking away in my mind.

He snapped out of it.

"You've worn braces, right?"

"No. Not that I know of."

Again it was lost. I sighed.

"Oh. You've got perfect teeth."

He was a face man, all right. Model/Actor/Dancer.

"And you've got a perfect body," I replied, speaking his language.

He smiled, used to it. He moved around a lot on the balls of his feet gauging things about me. My body had been what had gotten him over to me. My height: the same as him, but I was wearing four inches of platforms. Good. My face: he liked it, I could tell. I was lighter than he was, always a good thing. Should we have children they'd be milk chocolate and not bittersweet. My eyes: check. We'd already gone there. My face: I knew it was good—check.

I cut to the chase.

"How old are you?"

"Twenty-five." Silence.

"How old are *you*?" he asked.

"I'm thirty," I answered. Silence.

More silence. Then:

"You got a man?"

"Yes I do," I lied, smiling, covering my ass.

Trevor looked at me, returning my smile. "Is he here?" he asked, arms spread wide to encompass the market.

"Nope." We had an understanding.

"Can I get your number?" He was already going through his pockets.

I reached into my bag and pulled out my wallet.

"Why don't you take my card."

"Your card?" He looked quizzically at the small cream square I offered to him.

"Yeah. *My card*. It has my *phone number* on it." I didn't know how much longer I could keep my brain on pause. Not only was I a baby snatcher, I was snatching them from remedial school.

"Okay. Cool."

A breakthrough.

"All right," he said, fingering the card. Carol Taylor. Editorial Consultant. He looked up at me. "E-di-torial Consul-tant *huh*?"

I was getting a headache.

But at that moment he stepped back and folded his arms under his biceps and gave me a look all over that made me so hot that I knew I had to fuck him. I weighed my options; he was hot but slow. But that was okay, 'cause I was fast enough for both of us. He was more gym than library, more take-out than restaurant, and I knew he'd take almost as long as I would to get ready, probably longer. What the hell, a guilty pleasure. A spring fling and I certainly deserved one. I decided to go with the flow but I would keep a low pro. I put my hand on his arm and smiled. "Yeah. Editorial consultant, call me and I'll tell you what it means." Then I turned on my sizable heel, put one foot in front of the other and walked away.

Careful what you wish for.

Trevor surprised me with a call that evening. I wasn't even thinking about him. But he was hyper and fun and we talked for about two hours. "What did you do after you left me? What do you do for fun? What are you wearing? What does your bedroom look like? Yo', you rollerblade? That shit is mad cool. I'll teach you. You've got the legs for it." And on and on and on. I was tired just holding the phone up to my ear. Is this how he fucked, I wondered?

He lived in the Bronx. Two hundred and thirty-four blocks away from my place, F to the D to the end of the earth. The *very* last stop and then walk even farther uptown. I was *not* going to become a bridge and tunnel girl. I managed to blow him off five times; I simply didn't have time to waste, I told myself. But he was persistent and I finally let him talk me into going to his house. I was pleasantly surprised. He lived in a charming neighborhood in the Bronx—an oxymoron, right. But not only that, homeboy had body *and* a huge old-fashioned bathtub. My place had only a shower. I was in love—with his tub. I immersed myself in our relationship.

I'd never ridden the train so much in my life. Bought a fucking metro card, even. Carried my Diskman like a good-luck charm to ward off the train stupor that seeps into your brain unless it is otherwise engaged. I knew the *Poetry in Motion* ads by heart.

"Love buries itself deep inside me, to the hilt."
"He had only one idea and it was wrong."

A pattern was emerging.

I became a bridge and tunnel girl, spending more time in the Bronx than in Manhattan proper. Quite honestly I didn't mind getting out of town, intent as I was on hiding him from my friends and colleagues. But he taught me a thing or two about judging people according to my expectations and prejudices. I'd assumed anyone as beautiful as he was would be self-involved and vain, and at twenty-five he would be, well, too young. All true. But he surprised me in many ways. He came from a whole different world, one of deeds and not words. A *Gladiator* gym boy, he dwelt in the physical: "I'll just do a quick workout, abs, shoulders, and back, 100 reps each, then I'll meet you later. Okay, Baby?" He was straightforward and dependable, completely lacking in malice and subterfuge. I knew that he would do whatever he said he would do and he did. Innocent, he lived in a world of poetry readings, performance art, and Sundays at Body and Soul. Though Trevor wasn't book smart, he definitely wasn't stupid. I've learned more from him than he will ever know or I could have ever imagined.

One night I arrived at his door for dinner after making up lame excuse after lame excuse as to why I wouldn't eat out with him in Manhattan. I was super-crabby from the trip, which had taken almost two hours door-to-door. He let me in, took one look at my face, took my bag off my shoulder, got down on his knees and took off my shoes. He'd run a bath for me, lit candles and incense, and set up the futon on the floor to catch the cross breeze that didn't reach his bedroom. Then he slid his hands up to my hips and pulled my thong down over my thighs and to the floor. He then pulled my dress over my head, and picked me up and carried me into the bathroom. He didn't say a word as he set me down into the steaming fragrant bath, as though I weighed nothing close to my 140 pounds. Then he stood up, smiled and left, closing the door behind him. I was in love; his tub was so big, a perfect fit.

When he came back twenty minutes later he was naked except for a piece of African fabric he'd tied in a sarong around his waist. He tied his dreadlocks up off his face and pulled on the loofah gloves I'd left in his bathroom and soaped them up. He leaned and whispered against my cheek, "Stand up."

When I did he started to massage me with his soapy hands, paying special attention to my breasts, thighs, and ass. He'd intersperse my bathing with wet kisses wherever his hands had missed, on my cheek, my neck, my forehead, my throat. He then opened up the drain and switched on the showerhead to rinse me off. He maneuvered me under the shower, keeping the water comfortably hot. He told me to close my eyes and when I did he ran the shower massage over my close-cropped hair, down my back, over my ass, and down my legs. Then he reversed the route, coming back up in front and lingering between my legs. With one hand he sat me on the edge of the tub next to him. He coaxed my knees apart and directed the shower massage between my legs, moving the jets of water slowly first over my pubic area and toward my ass then up to my vagina and finally down to my clit, keeping it there as he alternated the stream of water from spray to jet then leaving it on pulsating.

My head shot back and if he hadn't been supporting me I'd have fallen out of the tub, not even caring as I fell. As wave after wave of pleasure shot through me he nuzzled my neck and shoulders licking gently at the corners of my mouth before moving up to breathe into my ear, "Mmmm. Feel better?" Then he laughed deep in the back of his throat. "I bet you're glad now, that you came."

I was.

Waiting to Exhale

Writing about sex has always been an honorable tradition. Just like good sex, good sex writing is in the details, the images, the picture, the scenario, the scene, the wonder of what is real and what is fantasy. Good sex writing paints a picture; it shows as well as tells, and it connects your mind to your body. This is the reason why I cannot have an orgasm without playing out—either mentally or physically—a fantasy. When I've connected my mind and my body. It's the only way I can get off. There, I've said it. Talk about exhaling. Though it sounds straightforward enough, it took me thirty-three years to figure it out and as with all things miraculous it happened quite by accident.

I was with a new lover who playfully slapped me on the ass. I jokingly told him "that wasn't a real slap"; that he should go ahead and "spank me." So he did. He gave me a harder slap, then another, then another, each harder than the last until we were both drenched in sweat and panting. Revelatory for both of us, we'd lucked out and managed to stumble blindly into each other's sexual piece of the puzzle. I'd found someone who not only wanted to please me, but also got off doing it. Sadly we have people who are willing but not able. And here he sat, a beautiful half-naked woman draped across his lap, who was quite excited about what he was doing to her.

My life turned a corner.

So why, I asked myself, had I had the best sex when I was *thinking*, when I was *aware* and in the moment? When my lover comes he moans my name over and over and over and over. He hangs onto the moment, keeping me as firmly in his mind as he is in my body. I don't have to wonder who he's thinking about when we fuck. Though I have asked in the moment, "What's my name, baby?" No hesitation.

"Carol Angelee Taylor
Carol Angelee Taylor
Carol Angelee Taylor
Carol Angelee Taylor
Carol, Carol, Carol, Carol, Carol."

When he asks me whose cock is this I already know the answer because he's told it to me: it's mine. Do you see? Instead of fucking with my mind, he connected my mind with the fuck. Not unlike erotica, because reading erotic fiction connects the mind with the act. This is what I hope *Brown Sugar* will do by sharing our fantasies and our experiences and by showing you many different worlds. In almost all of these stories, literature, both poetry and prose, plays an important role in seduction and attraction. Whether it sets a mood, paints a picture, or simply gives insight, we come to it again and again and again, in these stories.

Don't Judge a Book . . .

As I leapfrog through my thirties many things are becoming clearer, more sharp and in focus. One thing is that far too often the yearning for the fucking is more thrilling than the fucking itself. Unfortunately, we confuse the two. The other is the realization that the men who've made the best love to me are the ones I didn't expect to. Was it because I thought I had nothing to lose by the encounter and was rather casual about it? Or had they asked me the right questions, done the right things at the right times? Did they surpass my expectations because I didn't have any? Was it because I'd connected mentally as well as physically?

I had a lover who surprised the fuck out of me, almost quite literally. Let's call him Brian. No, not Brian, that's his real name. Okay, forget the name. Now we'd run into each other a hundred times moving in the same circles as we did. I never looked twice at him, barely looked once even. He wasn't my "type"; he was a little too mild-mannered. Looked like a company man, all button-downs and oxford wingtips. I'd seen him all over the place, at openings, signings, parties, and events. Then one day while I'm visiting a brother who had invited me down to listen to his band, I run into him. We're both there alone. We'd drift together, say hi, exchange names, then drift apart, instantly forgetting each other, busy looking around as we were. But we kept ending up in the same space, laughing, talking, and dancing. During one of those moments we'd drifted together, he asked if I wanted to get coffee. I said okay before I'd even thought about it. Five minutes later we were in a cab, my tongue down his throat and his hands up my shirt. I spent the next three days in his apartment in a fuck stupor.

He was a full body, sweating, no-place-is-sacred, nothing-is-too-funky, kinky, pinching, spanking, full-on-fucking kind of guy. And definitely a stamina-Daddy with a big hard dick that kept on keeping on. Normally you worry just a bit about fixing the hair, brushing the teeth. Trying to regain some semblance of respectability the next morning. I never even got there, pulled out of my sleep as I was at 7 A.M. for more full-on, fuck the morning breath, moaning, wailing, screaming in places, banging. We barely talked. We barely ate, just enough to keep our strength up. We barely left the apartment except for condoms, Pellegrino water, carrot juice, and food. This was not a man I had ever thought I would be attracted to, but we connected in every sense. We had the same interests and listened to the same music. We talked about theater, dance, and books. And we read to each other. Sure, he'd blown my body—but he blew my mind along with it.

Practice What You Preach

Even though it took me over thirty years to achieve orgasm during lovemaking, I consider myself lucky because now I know what I'm looking for, and I know how to get it. Now my lover makes sure I come every time and knows me well enough to know if I have or haven't. We talk to each other, read to each other, make up scenarios and stories. We will not stop until we each get off. We have an understanding; I let him do whatever he wants to me and he returns the favor.

You know, ladies, we've fucked ourselves with this whole hard-to-orgasm thing. Now men are like "Well, dag, since she ain't never gonna come no how, I'ma get off myself. My dick 'bout to fall off anyway." We've given them an easy out as well as an easy in and out. But what is done can be undone. Work with me. In the middle of twenty minutes of hard-core fucking if you *know* you're nowhere near coming and homeboy is hard on the finish line, tell him to stop. Yeah, just like that. Stop.

Breathe together for a while then ask him to talk to you—not talk "dirty" to you, just to talk to you. Have a conversation. So what if you're naked? Ask him how it feels to be fucking you. What does it feel like inside you? If he's smart you won't be able to shut him up. Or ask him to spank you, or eat you, or pinch you, or lick you all over; or ask him to stop and read to you. Whatever it takes to get you to that mind-body connection.

Susie Bright was right when she said, "A good book is on par with a good fuck." Hopefully *Brown Sugar* will give you a little of both.

The Whole Nine

The first of its kind, *Brown Sugar* is reflective of our myriad histories, experiences, and complexities as black people. As such the stories here set the stage for seduction with a distinctly new flavor and they are as insightful as they are sexy. In "Hail Mary Full of Grace," Marci Blackman's gender-bending role-playing and candid sexuality is as funny as it is startling. "Movie Lover" is a hip-hop video track on paper. Michael Gonzales's staccato prose and Technicolor imagery surrounding "the Bustelo-hued" Romeo Blue will raise your temperature and keep you off kilter. In "Nadine's Husband," Preston Allen's sexy prose will make you start over at the beginning the minute you turn the last page, unwilling to say good-bye to his all too familiar characters. Reggie Harris's hot and horny imagery in "The Dream" will make you catch your breath and keep it caught right up to the last page. In "Never Say Never," Diane Patrick's home-girl musings strike a chord as she dates not only across the color line but under the height line as well. In "Peeping Tom," Pamela Sneed's strong and unerring sense of herself will unnerve you even as it excites you as she allows you to see the things that have shaped her. The sheer beauty of Leone Ross's writing will intoxicate you every time you read "Drag," finding something fresh and startling each time. RM Johnson's insight and perception will have you nodding in agreement in "Slipping and Falling" because we all have, or loved someone who has and lived to regret it. After reading the story you might understand why we sometimes have to slip and fall to realize what is really important to us. Lisa Teasley's haunting "8 Hours of Mina and Stan" will bring you closer to the page to hear the half-whispered words told between the lines by lovers who know each other far too well, and themselves almost not at all. Kwame Dawes's "Deecy and Pheo" is awash with the music and people of Jamaica and is almost as hot as its island setting when two lifelong would-be lovers finally consummate the act. I know you'll want to linger, but *settle* for a while in Robert Fleming's atmospheric and beguiling Paris of music, literature, and love in "Responding to Her Touch." The author himself, at one time, was a musician. Immerse yourself in Sapphire's mesmerizing prose and unsettling imagery in "Alpine County." Her narrator though at the end of her life is not ready to give up living. In "How I Became a Writer," Lois Elaine Griffith tells her story almost to herself, but the silence speaks volumes and will resonate with anyone who has ever had a lover "who quit them," only to find something far more precious. "White Girl Blues" is both funny and sad, as Jervey Tervalon shows how hard it is to understand and sometimes avoid attraction. Chris Benson's "Click" crackles with energy and dark humor and portrays perfectly the obsession that comes with lost love. Jabari Asim's "Rocket Love" shows how vulnerable we all are when we fall in love and open ourselves to something that can be alternately heaven and hell. In "All Of Me," Natasha Tarpley sweeps you up in her sweet, sexy, and sad story as she illuminates the reality of a casual relationship and the inherent pain of proximity without intimacy. "Random Acts of Violins," Tony Medina's performance piece on paper, moves along with a hummingbird-like beauty and speed. His verbal dexterity and acrobatic prose meld together in a love story that alternates between sexy, sarcastic, and sincere. This is no cookie-cutter collection.

The voices here are all diverse—wicked and wise, hot and cool, hard and soft, from staccato rhythms to lyrical mesmerizing prose, from Day-Glo imagery to spartan, eerie landscapes—yet they converge and coalesce, are distinct and original. These writers are all part of the new black literary diaspora, and although divergent, they are bound by their common African heritage. Parts of the same whole, they represent the past, present, and future of black literature. This fresh and sexy collection is an unprecedented assortment of fiction written by an eclectic yet cohesive group of well-established, well-known, and up-and-coming black writers. They prove that though we may not share experiences, we share images. These images are what transport us—with only a ripple of silk and a last happy sigh—out of our bedsheets and into the arms of a lover.

So if you're ready let's explore and revel in all the rich and varied dimensions of sexuality and sensuality in every color and hue—in fact, the whole nine. In *Brown Sugar* is something for everyone; and you never know, you might learn something. What you hold in your hands is a signal achievement and a cause for joyous celebration of unity in sensual diversity; 'cause it's time to finally come correct.

Brown
Sugar

PRESTON L. ALLEN

Nadine's Husband

W HEN Johnny reached to change the radio station, his shirtsleeve receded, exposing a muscular forearm the color of slate, glistening with sweat despite the cold, cold air conditioner. Johnny switched stations until TLC's "What About Your Friends" came on. The truck pulled to a stop. Already we had arrived, again.

"Same time tomorrow," he said, something distant in his voice.

"I'm off tomorrow," I said. "My car should be ready then."

"Oh." Was that disappointment in his voice? "They must be charging you an arm and a leg."

"A whole paycheck."

"Mechanics are such a rip-off."

"Here. Thanks," I said, passing him two dollars for gas.

"No, Pam." Johnny shook his head. "Don't even try to offend me."

Our hands touched once as he said good-bye. As always, I moved away from his truck hoping that Johnny watched me with longing. But when I whirled expectantly, he was looking straight ahead, leaving only his sensuous side view to my inspection: the easy sweep of his forehead, the broad promontory of his nose, his thick lips and strong chin, one heavy-lidded eye focused on something, but not me. I stared at his handsome, impassive profile with longing, and then I remembered that Johnny was Nadine's husband, and regardless of what I thought about Nadine, she was still my sister.

I waved and the truck crunched through the gravel and pulled away with a noise like rocks in the engine. Johnny would have to fix his muffler soon. Maybe next week I would be giving him rides home.

I kissed him once, back when I was thirteen. My breasts had come in that summer, fleshy like the rest of me was quickly becoming.

We were in the toolshed Johnny had built for Daddy. Sunlight seeped through the wooden slats in a swath of light that highlighted the pucker of his lips, the twin swells of his chest, the nipples. His belt buckle hung too low, revealing his washboard-tight stomach and the top of his Calvin Klein briefs. Every part of him the slanted light touched seemed to glow. He should have worn a shirt with a ripe thing like me following him around.

He was irresistible. I kissed him. Once. He pushed me off, wiped my surprise from his lips with a T-shirt he used as a rag. That stung more than his words. "I love Nadine. I'm a one-woman man. You're like a sister to me. A kid sister."

"But I love you, Johnny!"

"That's so sweet, little sis."

"Stop treating me like a child." I gave him my best pose, with my head flung back seductively, my lips pouting, and my hands akimbo so as not to block his view of my budding chest. "I'm only four and a half years younger than Nadine." I caught him looking at my chest. "They're almost as big as Nadine's."

"Bigger," he said.

"Really?"

"I think so." He glanced at them again. When he looked up, his face was awash in embarrassment. "But that's not her best quality. Her best quality is that I love her."

"Are they really bigger than Nadine's?"

"You are such a silly little thing." He showed his even white teeth in a broad smile and threw his arms around me in a hug. "Now what would Nadine say if she heard you say that?"

"She wouldn't say anything. She'd kick my ass."

He laughed. "So don't be messing with your sister's man. You got to love your sister, girl. You're just a kid."

"Nadine was just a kid, too, when you married her."

"Go to school, little girl, before you get in trouble with your fresh mouth."

"Johnny."

He turned away from me, wrenched the cover off his mower, and oiled the clutch and the blades.

The birds sang their morning song as I slunk from the shed in time to catch the bus. I spent lunch on the nurse's cot. I was sick—sick with all the delicious things Nadine had told me about him over and over, and now sick too with his rejection. In Johnny's eyes, I was not as good as Nadine.

But he was wrong.

I was the good one. She was the bad.

After Johnny drove away, I went up to my apartment and shed my uniform, which smelled of grilled cheese and cigarettes. My bra and panties were next to go. I released my toes from the clumsy work shoes that had cramped them all day. In the bathroom, I stood before the full-length mirror and thought, not bad, really. My eyes had a catlike mystery to them, aided by the natural pencil-thinness of my eyebrows. My hair was a mess of healthy fullness. I was thinking of going dread. I could stand to lose a few pounds. But why should I? Too many men had told me I look good. Not good—the word they used was "juicy." They said I was honey-filled. They said I was a tall glass of sweetness. I was tall, somewhat, at 5'9". I was juicy, too, maybe. I wouldn't call myself a size twelve exactly because I could still slip into some of Nadine's size nines, and then I really looked juicy with my cinnamon-colored breasts oozing over the tops and my wide hips and healthy booty stretching the fabric in the back.

Not that it mattered to Johnny.

All Johnny wanted was Nadine and her pixie-like cuteness.

We were the same cinnamon complexion. I was the tall one.

She made up for it with heels, which she wore even at work. She always got the biggest tips. My breasts were much larger than hers were. In fact, now that I saw things from an adult perspective, she was rather on the flat side. Boyish, but cute. Around her small, angular face, she wore her hair cut short like a helmet. Her eyes were small and intense. She always looked you straight in the eye, even when she was lying. Each ear had three piercings. She wore a gold stud in her nose. Over the years, she had shown me all of her pierced parts, including her vagina. Recently, she had challenged me to do the same.

I said to her, "Does Johnny approve?"

She snorted. "It's not for Johnny to like. It's my body."

So, of course, I passed on it.

I stretched out in the tub and urged hot water from the tap with my foot. It burned good. I refused to kick the cold tap, refused to feel anything but the pleasurable tingle between my legs, that and the heat from the steaming water. I was determined not to use my hands. Not yet.

The water rose until it covered my face except my mouth and nose. Only then did I stop the flow with a deft movement of my big toe. If I didn't move, the water wouldn't spill from the tub, and I would fall asleep like that and maybe dream of Johnny. Or perhaps I would inhale too deeply and drown.

Speaking of water, Nadine was sleeping with big, water head Christopher, the night manager, who was twice divorced and spent an hour longer than necessary tallying the day's receipts with a pencil because he didn't trust the computer. Nadine said Christopher made her feel like Johnny no longer did. I couldn't see how; I mean, he had that big water head and wore a played-out flat top and droopy-crotch Sansabelt pants like he was some old man when he was only about the same age as the rest of us. I'm not even going to talk about how he waddled when he walked, because the man couldn't help being born with feet that point out at right angles. Just like his ears. But I'm not going there, because it ain't right.

Now Johnny's walk was a psalm of praise, going or coming. Hallelujah, the man could move. He led with his chest, followed

by his impossibly narrow waist and brawny legs. Going or coming, take your pick. Do you want the face so beautiful it could
heal? Do you want the chiseled flesh packed into faded blue
jeans? Curly-headed, smoky-eyed, slate-gray brother, Johnny was
sculpted to make a tired woman remember that she could bend
at the knees to do more than scrub floors.

And here was Nadine tripping with old water head.

Johnny deserved a woman who had trouble breathing when
he entered the room. Johnny deserved a woman who had loved
him from that first day her big sister had brought him home and
presented him as both her husband of two hours and the cause
of the three-month swelling in her abdomen. Johnny deserved a
woman who had picked all of her lovers based on how closely
they resembled him and dumped them at the first sign they were
becoming less Johnny.

"Johnny deserves me!" I told the walls.

Now it was time to use my hands. I found my clit beneath the
bubbles. I massaged one nipple with the other hand, Johnny's
hand. And the water became Johnny's body engulfing me. I
squeezed my thighs together and pressed down with two fingers,
Johnny's mouth, and Johnny's dick. Water spilled out onto the
tiles as I came.

My hot bath turned into a warm one, the warm one into cool,
then cold. I was shivering, my lust unabated. I gripped the chain
between my toes and pulled. The water seemed eager to leave my
body. Soon I lay naked in the empty tub, looking between my
breasts, which leaned to either side like melting sundaes.

I thought about masturbating again. I thought about attack-
ing the tub with Ajax. I thought about my calico, Cassiopeia,
who watched me from atop the wicker clothes hamper. Cassiopeia purred and licked a paw. Somewhere beyond the bathroom,
from outside in the street, there came the faint but familiar rattle
of a car whose muffler needed fixing. Could it be? I strained to
listen.

A few minutes later, someone knocked at the door, and Cassiopeia leapt from the clothes hamper and darted out of the
bathroom.

It could only be one person. I jumped out of the tub. "Wait a minute," I said, reaching for a towel, a comb, and the first tube of lipstick, burnt cedar, I found in the shoebox of makeup under the sink. I wiped on the lipstick in two quick passes, dropped the tube with a clatter onto the counter, then patted my breasts, my underarms, my stomach, and between my legs with the towel.

The knock came again, insistently. Cassiopeia purred.

"Coming!" I shouted.

I floated through the living room picking up my discarded work clothes. I raked my hair back with a comb. In the bedroom, I shoved my uniform, underwear, and shoes under the bed. I tied my hair with a scarf I found on my night table. There was no time to decide between good and better panties so I hauled on my silk housecoat over skin still damp from the bath. I knew I should wipe on some lotion, but the knock came again.

I opened the door, wondering how I looked, my hair in a silly scarf, one hand holding my housecoat closed. "Johnny," I breathed.

"Pam," he said, falling into my arms.

"Nadine's screwing around on me." His chin rested in my hair. He was soaking with sweat. He was wonderful to touch, wet or dry. He smelled delicious, the mint, the cut grass, the man musk. "She's fucking Christopher."

We held each other in the doorway, and he told me about finding them together.

"After I dropped you off, instead of going back to the restaurant to finish my shift, I went home. Christopher was just leaving. I saw her lean into his car and kiss him on the lips." A shiver passed through his sculpted body into mine. "He took off when he saw me. She ran into the house."

Johnny's deep voice boomed down the hallway. A neighbor's door opened, a head wearing rollers was stuck out, then disappeared, the door slamming.

"She was flushing them down the toilet," Johnny said. "Poems he had written her on napkins from the restaurant. She fought me when I tried to take them away."

Reluctantly, I let him pull away, and he showed me the red imprint of Nadine's nails under his chin. He opened his shirt. There were more scratches, just above the nipple, so small I could hardly see them on that great expanse of chest until I stopped focusing on the chest. Little things they were, like birthmarks. Then I went back to that chest.

He began to button his shirt. I took his big hand. "Let's go inside."

I was aware of touching his arms, his knees, his thighs, his hands, as we sat on the couch and he poured out his heart. The air seemed parched. The water on my flesh had completely evaporated.

"I never hit Nadine before, but I had to have those poems. I needed proof. I had to see with my own eyes . . ." He couldn't finish.

I put my hand on his knee to give him strength. It would serve Nadine right if I slept with him.

"You hit her," I said with a dry throat. "You hit my sister?"

"I just pushed her," he corrected. "But she collapsed right there on the bathroom floor, bawling. She said I had hit her for nothing, for accepting a few poems from a harmless geek. She loved me, she said. Couldn't I see that?"

"She said that?"

"That's what she said," he said. "And I believed her."

"You *believed* her?"

"I believed her," said Johnny, who had a bachelor's degree in African Studies. When he was not waiting tables at the restaurant or cutting yards, he was working on his Master's. He was as studious and hard working as he was gullible. He actually thought Nadine was a good girl.

I was her sister, so I could tell him about her wild days before he arrived. I could tell him about her drug dealer boyfriend, J.H. I could tell him about the threesomes with J.H. and his homeboy. I could tell him what "BUTT F LOVER" tattooed on her ass really meant and why J.H. put it there. It was their primary means of birth control. I could tell him about the year she dated only women—the same year that she got the fake ID and worked as a stripper to raise money for a lawyer to appeal J.H.'s conviction. Mom and Dad were glad to get her off their hands when Johnny came along. Nadine was a wild child. I could tell him that during their first year together, the year I kissed him in the toolshed, Nadine was still visiting J.H. in prison once a month. But Johnny already knew that part. He had caught her in the act and forgiven her. He believed she had changed. Now she was screwing big-headed poets. Poor, blind Johnny.

But gullible had its advantages. He actually thought my hand was on his knee for support.

"Christopher's poems weren't much, really. I guess I should be flattered. Who wouldn't be attracted to Nadine? She looked so helpless crying like that on the floor. So innocent. I have to admit it turned me on. She said that she and Christopher had done nothing."

"She said that?"

"That's what she said," he said. "And I believed her. It was crazy to imagine. Nadine and Christopher fucking. Think about it."

I was thinking about it. It was getting me as hot as it must have gotten him earlier that night. I moved my hand higher up on his thigh and put my face against his neck.

"I tore up the poems and flushed them down the toilet." He looked at me with those smoky, gray eyes. "I was sure they had done nothing, just like she said."

She was my sister, but I was not going to let her get off that easy. "Didn't you see them kiss in the driveway?"

He shrugged. "I love Nadine so much. It took something else to shock me to my senses." He clasped his hands together. "When I went to make love to her, I discovered a passion mark in a private place."

"Her breasts?"

"Her pussy."

"Poor Johnny."

He got up, went over to the window, and leaned his head against it. I followed him.

He wailed, "It's killing me just thinking about them in our bed. Nadine rolling on our sheets, looking all nasty and coy at the same time. That damned Christopher with his big head on my pillow and his mouth between her legs and she's making that sound she makes when she comes! I can't take it, Pam. I can't take it."

I put my arms around his big body. "It's all right, Johnny."

"I saw the mark, Pam. What did he think—I wouldn't see it? This is worse than what she did with J.H. I can't take it."

"Poor, poor Johnny."

He turned around. I reached up to throw my arm around his neck and bring his head down to my chest. My housecoat, which had many years ago lost its sash and each of the four buttons that fastened it, fell open. In a characteristic show of decency, Johnny turned his head.

I sighed, and covered myself.

"I'm sorry. I better put something else on."

"It's kind of like in the toolshed," he said, "when I had my shirt off."

Stung by rejection and embarrassment, I whispered cautiously, "You remember that?"

"I remember your lips were soft."

"You do remember."

"And your breasts were about the size of grapes."

"What! Now you're hurting my feelings."

"They were still so small, and you were so proud of them. Typical teenager."

"You can just get the hell out of my house right now, Johnny," I joked.

The lines in his face relaxed. "This is hard for me, but I'm starting to feel better, Pam."

"Well just keep right on picking at me if it helps. With Nadine as a sister, I'm used to it."

"Nadine used to pick at you?"

"I've always been chunky."

"Chunky? You crazy women have no idea what men like. We like . . . chunky." He appraised my body with his eyes. "Is that why you're always trying to take your sister's man?"

"I guess they taught you something in college after all." I pulled the housecoat around me tight. "I better go change."

"Did you have a crush on J.H., too?"

"All his teeth were gold. Yuck."

Johnny gave a piercing look he must have learned from Nadine. "Well?"

"No. I did not have a crush on J.H. I'm not like that," I said to Johnny. But I was *like that*, at least with him. "I'm sorry, I better go put on something decent." I turned to leave.

"No." Johnny pulled me to him. He was strong. "Stay here and talk to me some more. I'm really learning a lot."

"You're picking at me, is what you're doing." My body was pressed to his.

"Then let's change the subject," he said against my face. "Tell me about Nadine. Tell me everything you know about her."

I was holding him. He was holding me. It was an effort just to speak. I said, "Nadine's my sister."

"Good observation," he said into my neck.

"Nadine's the pretty one."

"You're the pretty one."

"Johnny," I breathed, warming to the touch of his inquisitive hand, "this is not like you."

"This is the new me."

I pressed against him hungrily, my housecoat falling open, and somewhere between kiss and shame, I said, "Nadine is going to be pissed."

"Nadine has Christopher," he said, his lips thick with burnt cedar. "Water head Christopher." I sucked on his tongue like sweet candy.

One hand massaged the back of my head as the other snaked around my waist. I undid the last remaining buttons on his shirt, shoved my hands inside. I felt the forest on his chest, reached down, and pressed my palms against the knotted stomach. The knots were soft, giving. I went behind, took the dare, plunged my fingers under the elastic of his underwear. I cupped a cheek in each hand and drove his hips against me, controlling the motion of our grind. I rode him down to the carpet like that.

When our lips separated so that we might breathe what was
left of the air, he said, "Wow," and then lowered his head to my
big breasts. He was a wet licker, not a nibbler. My nipples stiffened under his tongue, became sensitive as salted nerve ends under those licks. I chewed his neck and then his earlobe when it
presented itself. His mouth was driving me crazy.

He was on all fours over me with my hands still in his shirt,
around his torso, gripping his cheeks. I wrapped my legs around
his buttocks too and pulled myself up into him like a possum clinging to her mother's underside. I pressed my breasts up against his
chest to escape the licking, which was driving me crazy. I cried,
"Hallelujah."

"You're so juicy."

"So I've been told."

Finding my mouth, the one-woman man lowered me to the
carpet and traced my leg with a finger until it reached my open
wetness. The finger raised tiny bumps where it passed. My flesh
tingled. Johnny bucked my clit with his thumb. I parted my legs.
He inserted a finger and stirred. I released his tongue and said,
"Love me, Johnny. I'm so hot."

Johnny kissed his way down to the finger in my pussy. His lips
kissed the mound of Venus in small, respectful dabs. Then with
more fervor, like the way Cassiopeia drinks from her bowl, with a
twick-twicking sound. Another finger was up to the second
knuckle in my anus. Then I felt his teeth.

"Oh, Johnny. What are you doing to me?"

"I'm leaving a passion mark."

"Watch out. I'm all gushy when I come."

"You taste good."

My arms flailing, I thrust my hips against his tongue and the
bootie finger in wild orgasm. Johnny kissed his way back to my
mouth. I tasted my joy on his lips.

I kissed my way down his chest.

I unzipped Johnny's jeans and dragged the crisp, white drawers down to his ankles and stared at his stately dick, which
curved slightly like an on-ramp. The topside was smooth, but
the bottom was gently wrinkle-veined. How, I wondered, could
Nadine seek pleasure in napkin poetry when she had this great,

mahogany epic at home? I held it with both hands. I kissed the length of it. It was warm under my tongue, pulsing. I placed it between my breasts to feel its size. I brushed the underside of my chin with the head. Johnny put his hands on my head and hummed. I took him into my mouth.

Johnny was juicy, too.

He stopped just short of coming and said, "I want to be in you."

That was fine by me. I lay on my back.

Looking up beyond the curls of Johnny's chest, beyond his magnificent head, I made out the outline of a turbaned man smoking a pipe in the stucco ceiling. I heard the squeak of a properly stretched rubber sliding against wet flesh.

"You're so big. Don't hurt me."

Johnny entered me. I pressed my knees to my chest. My hips danced on his sturdy dick. Waves of pleasure washed over me.

"Turn over," he said a few minutes later.

"I like it like this."

It was our first fight. Johnny easily flipped me over, winning the fight.

On all fours now, staring at my silent television and the ash-tray on it that held the remains of my last cigarette—eleven months since, I'm proud to say—I felt his tongue, his finger, and then he entered me again. He filled me like no man ever had before. He did not fuck me in the usual way of big men, all clumsy power and push. He fucked with a plan. He fucked my flesh in the direction he wanted it to go. I had no idea where I was going to get off. And just before I got to there, he would take me somewhere else. If I resisted, he inserted the bootie finger.

"So big."

Water head Christopher must be a really special poet, I thought, because when it came to fucking, no man compared to Johnny.

"Johnny!"

"You like it, baby?"

"Yes."

"You are so juicy."

His rhythm changed. Two sudden deep thrusts robbed me of a breath.

"You coming?"

"No," he said. "I want to see your beautiful face."

He sat me on his lap, facing him, with my legs around his impossibly slender waist.

He bit my neck. "I'm ready to come, baby. I can't hold it back no more," he growled. He bounced me on his lap with redoubled vigor.

"Can't hold it back."

My pussy was slick and full as it rose and fell on Johnny's dick.

"Come, baby, come."

"Can't hold it."

I closed my eyes. Johnny pounded up into me in a frenzy. I lost it all. Control of my limbs. Track of time. My silly scarf. I screamed and exploded into Johnny's pounding rhythm.

We slept together that night, without sleeping much. All night, some part of him was in me. I thought we would break the bed.

In the morning, before he left to go cut yards, I gave him a good dose of my big legs and behind so that he would return. I served him breakfast in a pair of Nadine's shorts. He liked chunky. He fucked me standing up at the sink with the water running over the broken breakfast dishes. When he left, I prayed he wouldn't go home. I prayed he wouldn't go see her.

She called me around two.

"Johnny didn't come home last night."

"What happened?" I said with mock surprise.

"I don't know where he is. I don't know where he slept last night."

I removed all guilt from my tone. "You guys had a fight?"

"I fucked up real bad, sis." Then between sobs and brief pauses to tell the cook to leave her alone because she was on break, she divulged what I already knew about Johnny, the water head, and her. She ended with, "If you see him, tell him to at least call me."

"I will," I said, and hung up. But I would not. And it served her right. Treating a good man so bad.

Around three, I took a cab and picked up my car from the mechanic's. Then I went grocery shopping, came home, and cooked. Cassiopeia scratched to be let out, so I opened the sliding doors to the porch. I went out there, too, and sat down, watching over the parking lot, listening for the rattle of mufflers. I was relieved when he returned that night. I had prepared a special meal for him, but he went straight for the dessert.

"This time," he said, "I'm going to try something new."

"Something new?" I squealed.

"Put your panties back on."

We had been going at it for about a half-hour already. "I'm soaking wet," I complained.

"Wait till I get through with you," he said slyly.

I found my panties in the heap of tangled sheets on the floor. I tugged them on and hopped back on the bed. "Turn over," he said. "Bootie up. Close your eyes."

"This isn't going to hurt?"

"Worm love," he said. "I have no arms. No hands. No penis. Only this tongue. Close your eyes, I told you."

He began with my feet, his tongue, patiently loving the heel, the sole, then the stiffened toes digging into the mattress. I could feel no part of him, except for the wet, darting muscle. It was not kissing the skin, exactly. It felt light against the fine hairs, like an insect descending. The worm. It was frustrating. It was stimulating. I wanted to push him away. I wanted to pull him nearer.

With my eyes closed tight, I followed the worm's languid journey from my ankle to the backs of my knees. I became aware of the warmth of his mouth. I imagined I could smell his sweet breath through the pores in my skin. I became my skin. He moved up my thigh, over the rise of my butt. I could sense his weight hovering just above me but not touching, only the tongue. The worm. It made contact with the panties, tracing the contours of each buttock through it. He lingered in the cleft. I could feel it lifting the material of the panties from the cleft as a finger would. I could feel it anxiously probing, but not really touching because of the thin barrier of silk. I was gushing into the crotch of my good Victoria's Secret.

"Jesus. Let me take them off."

"I have no arms. No hands. No penis. Just this tongue to love you with."

I arched my butt to help him. He probed and probed and cheated. To unsheathe one cheek, he used his teeth. Cheating again, he nudged the material aside with his chin. He sucked the exposed half of my pussy, chewed the hairs. His face pressed into me from behind. The burrowing worm found my sweet spot. I was gushing onto the bed now. I juiced around his tongue. The worm passed in and out of me. He was emitting sounds of hunger. I was breathing in short gasps. He was slurping. I was grinding against his face. The worm ran over the perimeter of my pussy. I wanted to come in his face. He was cheating again, controlling my backward thrusts with his hands on my thighs. I would come in his face. I was too far gone to stop.

"Stop using your hands if you're a worm. Cut me loose so I can come. Stop cheating!"

He said, "I have no arms. No hands. No penis—"

I was too far gone. I would make his tongue my penis.

I would come.

I would come.

I came.

There was no time for rest. He lay atop me, our tongues intertwined—the worm in my mouth. The other worm, the big one below the waist, throbbed against my opening like a heavy club. It slipped in through the slick entrance with electric friction. I slammed upward to meet his thrusts. A loud slap was heard each time our bodies met. I wanted to cry out, I will love you forever Johnny, like Nadine never could.

"Johnny," I said afterwards as I lay in his arms with the radio playing Kevon Edmond's "Love Will Be Waiting," "I'm not a kid to you anymore, am I?"

"You're all grown up." He snuggled against my neck, his big arms encircling my hips.

I covered his hands with mine. "I've always loved you, Johnny. I always will."

"Now I know how it feels to be loved back. Nobody's ever loved me like this."

"Not even Nadine?"

He stiffened. I pressed my hands into his until our fingers interlaced. "She's your sister."

"You saying I should tell her?"

"No. That's my job. I'm her husband." He was quiet then. There was only the movement of his chest against my back and Kevon's velvet voice pulling at our heartstrings. Finally, he said, "There'll be trouble for everybody."

"It's not wrong what we did, Johnny, is it?"

"She did it with Christopher."

"It's not the same. We love each other. We found each other."

"We found each other," he said. "At last."

We went to sleep around midnight, exhausted and pleasantly, happily sore.

I rose early for the breakfast shift at the restaurant. I felt relaxed, confident, pretty. Nadine was there, looking disheveled and short, in clunky, flat-soled shoes. She kept asking, Did he call you? Did he come by? You think he'll come to work tonight? I kept my mouth shut.

Johnny was scheduled to work the night shift. He had not seen her in two days. The plan was for him to stay out of trouble with Christopher, work his shift, pick up his check on Friday, and then make a clean break. Nadine had to be told, the sooner the better.

Johnny did not follow the plan.

That afternoon, after I got off work, Johnny made love to me furiously, from behind, then hauled on his uniform and headed out to his rattling truck. About an hour after the sun set, Nadine called to ask if I had any money. There had been trouble at the restaurant.

"Christopher's hurt bad. They took Johnny away in handcuffs," she shrieked.

On the way to the ATM machine, Nadine kept saying it was all her fault, she should never have slept with Christopher. I kept my mouth shut about Johnny and me, but I was angry. Why hadn't he told her? He should have told her about the woman who had trouble breathing when he entered a room. He should have told her where he had slept the last two nights. He should have told her about the passion mark he put on my pussy.

"When I get him back, I'll be good to him. I'll never treat him bad again. I love him so much." She wrung her hands. She cried. She looked out the window as we rolled through neglected neighborhoods to get to the part of town where the jail was. "I never knew it would hurt so much to lose him."

I said, "You need to prepare yourself for whatever happens."

"I'm never going to lose him. What we got is special." She turned on me. "What the hell do you mean prepare for whatever happens? Ain't shit gonna happen. I'm getting my man back."

"You just can't go and do things and not expect . . . reactions. You messed up, now you've got to accept whatever happens."

"What the hell are you talking about, Pam? He fought for me today. He kicked Christopher's ass."

"He may kick your ass too."

She considered this, then spoke in a quieter voice. "When Christopher wrote me those poems, I was at a weak point. I'm not wild anymore. J.H. was killed in prison last week."

"That's no excuse!"

"Johnny and me have been together almost ten years. We have a child. If he looks like he's going crazy on me, Pam, you got to back me up." She said, "You tell him about J.H. He'll believe it coming from you."

"I don't know if I can do that."

"You have to," she said. "You're my sister."

"I don't know if I can."

At the jail, I gave the bail bondsman the $500.

We sat in a filthy, cramped reception area with a half dozen broken, depressed-looking people waiting to see their wayward loved ones. Nadine cried on my shoulder so much she had to take out her nose ring. She said it was itching.

Finally, Johnny appeared, looking a little shaken after his first time in jail. Nadine held my hand as he walked toward us. I tried to catch his eye, but it was no use. He went straight to Nadine

and kissed her. She let go of my hand, and they really started going at it: I'm sorry, baby, me too, I love you baby, me too,
there's a reason I did what I did, baby, I hope you'll listen to my
reason, I'll listen, baby, I'll listen.

My heart sank in my chest. I wanted to shout, don't listen,
Johnny. I'm the one who loves you. She's hurt you for ten years.
I've loved you for ten. Even longer. Forever.

Then he asked her, "Where'd you get the money to bail me
out?"

She said, "Pam."

He turned to me then. I looked up into his eyes. He put his big
arms around me in a dramatic hug, I breathed in his sweet man
musk, I relived in a moment our passion of the last two nights,
and he said, "Thanks, sis. Thank you so much for everything."

I held him. I locked his eyes with mine.

If he didn't tell her, then I would tell her, then we would go
away, and live happy together forever.

But there was nothing in his eyes. And that stung most of all.

REGINALD HARRIS

The Dream

I FALL asleep with the TV on, in the middle of watching some old mystery on the "classic movie" channel. All the men wear gray suits and sharp, snap-brimmed hats, and speak in what they used to call "snappy patter." I dream I'm an old-school gangster, striding into clubs in a tailored tuxedo, shooting out words faster than a machine gun spits bullets. I'm the only black man in the room who's not somebody's flunky, the only one not fawning over the movie's other stars. I'm being tailed on the way to yet another speakeasy and my chauffeur guns it, running two red lights to try to lose them. We get pulled over by the cops at a busy intersection. *"Don't you know who I am?"* I complain. It doesn't matter. We still get tossed in jail.

The chauffeur and I share a cell. We're naked, except for our hats. A pulled-down driving cap hides the chauffeur's face. My eyes wash down his body from his sculpted mahogany chest to the dark rope of dick between his legs. We lay on the cell floor and twist into a sixty-nine. We suck each other hungrily, slurping loudly until the tart aroma of the driver's asshole draws me in. I lap at his tiny pucker, tapping it lightly with my tongue. The chauffeur moans. A finger follows my mouth and tongue, quickly slipping in and then withdrawing. An electric shudder runs through his body as I probe and play with the chauffeur's man cunt. He cannot stop squirming as I finger-fuck his plump brown ass. There's a buzzing in my ears, the sound of bees, a sudden hail of bullets flying past me. I wake up with a start to the screaming of the alarm clock going off, my hands wrapped around a piss-filled morning hard-on.

Another boring night in the parking lot at the community college, keeping an eye on people's cars, making sure they don't drive off all by themselves. I feel like I'm on display in this god-damned little booth. There's nothing in here but a low shelf and the incident book, a heating/cooling unit, the emergency tele-phone (calls to the security office only), and a hard wood chair. The other security officers making rounds stop by in their Cush-mans every hour to see how I'm doing. "The new guy always gets the shit job," they say. "Everybody had to go through it." They laugh and wave as they ride away. Thanks a lot. As if that made sitting out here any better.

I'm supposed to "be vigilant at all times" but fuck it. I can read the paper or finish *Mama Black Widow* and *still* make sure no one breaks into somebody's ride. I could probably even sneak a pocket TV out here, catch a game or two, just so long as I don't get caught. Every now and then one of the students comes up and asks a question, or a visitor needs directions. Sometimes folks just want to talk. We're not supposed to "fraternize" either . . . what do they expect us to do, just sit and stare?

This one young brotha has started to hang out with me a couple of times a week after his classes, waiting for his ride to show. Very friendly, always smiling, cute as shit. A slim, light-brown-skinned guy, just turned twenty maybe. We talk and, well . . . okay, maybe I give him a little play, but it's nothing serious. I know a lot of guys can't keep their hands off youngsters. Me, I think it's best to just leave 'em alone. They may look phyne, but what do I have in common with some kid more than ten years younger than me? The way this guy keeps sniffing all around up under me and shit, I *know* what we have in common. . . . I guess I could sex him up, what the hell. It might be fun. I can't say I've ever turned down a piece of tail in my life.

I dream I'm climbing a long flight of stairs. People are sitting on them, waiting, one on the left side five flights from the bottom, the next on the right five above that; mainly guys, sitting like this all the way up to the top. I pass the first guy. He's beautiful, with amazingly full lips and heavy eyebrows above sparkling dark eyes, wearing baggy clothes and a black nylon head rag. I keep walking. The next guy is in a three-piece suit slightly too small for him. His muscles bulge the sleeves, the pants strain at his massive thighs. He looks like a model, his smile made even more intriguing by the slight gap between his front teeth. It's like this all the way up the stairs—a multihued spectrum of black and Latino men sitting on the steps, watching me as I pass. Cooks and police officers, maintenance men and judges in their robes, mechanics, football players, office and transit workers: all beautiful, sitting there, watching me.

A few women are there, too, jazz singers shimmering in sequined dresses, sprinters in tight-fitting track uniforms, the sista who won that big tennis tournament last year . . . I'm seeing all my fantasies stretched out before me. Soon the faces become familiar. I'm surrounded by my exes—Eric, Don, Marshall, Kenny, guys I've had relationships with, homeboys I did for trade, the one-night stands I thought I had forgotten, girls I experimented with in high school; my whole history flows up and down the stairs. As I near the top I turn and sit, surrounded by my dreams and fantasies of the present and the future. I sit and wait with them, not sure what it is I'm waiting for. I wake up confused, more tired than I was when I went to sleep.

"Javon," he'd said the first night. "Javon Webster."

He's from Michigan. Like a lot of kids at Glenridge, his family's army, stationed down the road at Fort Powell. He's been practically all around the world while I've been stuck in this damned town. He seems smart enough to have gone pretty much anywhere for college. Why he chose GCC is beyond me. He says he

wanted to stick close to his parents, needed some kind of stability in his life. But now he's feeling restless. "I have to move
out," he says. "Can't live with my parents forever. Need to get a
car, too, so I can stop borrowing theirs or wait on rides from
people. I want to have a life of my own, youknowwhatimsayin?"
He smiles at me. Wish he would stop doing that . . .

I tell him a little about myself, the various jobs I'd had before this one, which I'd just started with the school year. The
other security job I have on the weekends at a senior citizens'
building to help to make ends meet. I tell him what it was like
growing up here in this overgrown small town with people always up in your business. Having to keep everything on the
Down Low. He nods.

I don't really say much of anything to be honest. I let Javon
do the talking so I can stare at his full, plump lips. Then his ride
pulls in at the far end of the parking lot. Javon says, "See ya!" I
try not to be too obvious rearranging the hard-on in my pants.
Shit! I think, watching Javon's butt jiggle slightly as he trots off.
Screwing him would be like fucking a flower.

I'm wandering through a humid maze, naked men in the shadows along the walls: a bathhouse I used to frequent years ago. A
walnut brown guy with a short thick 'fro catches my eye. Slightly
taller than me, he's wearing boots and leather pants, a leather
vest over his bare chest. I reach under the leatherdaddy's vest to
flick and pinch his nipples, then dive in to kiss them. I close my
eyes. When I open them, he's gone. I'm in a classroom. No one
there but me and Javon. No sound comes out as he begins to
speak. Instead, sunlight spills from Javon's mouth. He reaches
out to touch me. His fingers brush against my arm, leaving dark
marks on my skin. I wake up with a start—half an hour before
the alarm is set to go off—to a flash of lightning, the sound of a
distant rumble, a morning thunderstorm rattling the windows.

Hot as hell tonight. Indian summer. I don't want to leave the
booth, where I've got the AC on so high it's almost chilly. Since
the air in my apartment is shot too, I wouldn't mind working all
night right here, just to be cool.

A lot of instructors let their students out early since most of the classrooms feel like they're on fire. Javon wears a Knicks tank top and shorts. I have to call him on that and pump up my Lakers. We talk hoop for a while, our favorite players, who we think is going to take it all this year. I want to invite him into the booth to catch some of my air, but there's barely enough room for me up in here. Javon just leans in at the door. It's hard to concentrate with his dark quarter-size nipples winking at me from behind the tank top. I can't even look down. Dark hairs twist up and down his bare legs like fine writing. My mouth fills with water. I want to trace those letters up and down his calves and thighs with my tongue, reading what it says.

"You all right, main man?" Javon asks. "You in there with all that AC but you're still sweating."

Yeah, dude, fine. Just fine.

So hot in the apartment I can barely sleep. The bed is like a swamp. Bare-assed and spread-eagled on top of it, begging for a breeze, my hand casually falls to my exposed dick. Might as well do something. I begin to stroke. I close my eyes. Guys I've been with, guys I'd love to do flicker across my eyelids like flash cards. My head fills with faces, reaching hands, offered necks, wet nipples, hard cocks, and friendly asses. Pulling on myself faster, I focus on a favorite scene from a porno, four Latino guys linked together in an oral daisy chain. Every Hispanic homeboy's mouth is filled with someone's *bicho* and I'm all up in it. On the downstroke that finally pops my nut, the guy sucking on my dick looks up. I wake up with a start. It's Javon. Our mingled sperm glistens across my stomach in the morning light.

I try to think of ways to get Javon to stay longer. I step out of the booth now, walk with him around the parking lot. He touches me on the arm as we talk, casually, as if it didn't mean anything. To be honest, maybe it doesn't mean anything. He always has to hurry off with the other riders in his car pool, and says he's too busy with school and two jobs at the mall to get together any time just to hang. Even his weekends are booked up.

I want to believe I get Javon as hot as he gets me. I know he's interested because of the way he continues to hang around. I'm not that great a talker. I've seen the way he looks at me, too, his eyes traveling up and down my uniform, checking me out. I'm sure he knows what he's doing to me, even though I haven't said anything. The truth is, he's probably seeing somebody. The truth is he probably thinks I'm too dark for him; I know how these light-skinned folks can get. The truth is he probably doesn't even want to think about messing around with a guy fifteen years older than he is. He gives me this "I'm busy" bullshit to spare my feelings. Hunger must be pouring from my eyes every time I look at him. To him it probably seems like an old man's desperation.

I stare at him tonight longer than usual, not saying anything. He stares right back, not telling me to stop. His eyes are like the openings to dark caverns I want to explore. Then he nods. "Okay," he says quietly. "Okay." We both look away.

He clears his throat. "I'm doing my midterm paper on Walt Whitman for American Lit class. You know *Leaves of Grass?*"

I shake my head.

"You should read it sometime. It's very good."

"He's some old white guy, right?"

"Yeah, so? You don't know what you're missing. Here, take this. I can get another one . . ." He gives me a thick paperback book. I flip through it. Nothing but poetry. Damn . . .

"All a this? I'll try, man, but I don't know . . . I'm really not a poetry kind of guy, you know what I'm saying?" I point to the worn copy of a James Earl Hardy novel I've been rereading in the booth.

"You don't have to read the whole thing. I'm sure there's got to be at least one poem in there you'd like. It's not that bad. Then after that, I can give you something else . . . I gotta go." Javon's car pool turned into the parking lot. "Show me love, man, show me love." We quickly hug and pat each other on the back.

I have no idea why I'm being so . . . *polite*. What's wrong with me? Back in the day I would've gotten into Javon's pants long before this. I'd've been banging that shit out for weeks by now. But I keep hesitating. I want to ask him out on *a date*, for god's sake!

I don't really want to have a relationship with this boy—*do I?*

After every other time I've tried to hook up with a guy has ended in a train wreck? I don't think so. Stick your neck out for somebody, share your life, give them your heart and you think they give you theirs as well—only to get used, cheated on, dumped for someone younger, phyner. Someone new. I don't want to go through that again. Better to go out and just fuck somebody when I need to get off than to go through all that again.

Still, as much as I'm attracted to Javon, this doesn't seem like it's entirely a physical thing . . . Wait, wait, wait, I mean, yes, of course, it IS a physical thing. The boy's phyne as hell and I'd love to tear that pale ass up. But it's more than that . . . It almost feels like . . . It's almost as if I was . . . Oh, fuck it, never mind . . .

I'm wandering through the woods surrounding the parking lot at school with some other security officer whose face I can't quite see. His uniform is plastered against his body. He turns around and leans against a tree, opening his shirt, unzipping his pants. The sight of his hairy body, his nipples plump as figs, and long uncut mansex curving like a boomerang to the left makes my mouth water. We kiss then reach into each other's pants. His pulsing hard-on singes my fingers. Our lips press tightly together as we stroke each other, two bulls huffing and flaring, each willing the other to climax. I inhale deeply. The guy's extremely musty, at the height of his funk, as if he'd just run a marathon. He wants me to lick him clean from head to toe. I gladly stick out my tongue to begin, but when I close my eyes I feel a gentle rocking. I'm in my car driving Javon back to my place. My dick is harder than the stick shift the whole way there. I open the door for him and want to grab him the moment he walks in. Instead we talk and laugh, staring into each other's eyes. Anticipation gnaws at my insides like a hunger. I wake up just as we move in close to each other as if we were about to kiss.

I've never felt this young in my life. Being with Javon has made time move backward. I feel as though we were back in high school, passing notes and shit. I see parts of him everywhere, guys who have his eyes, his hands, his shoulders, the same walk. Some of the people at the senior citizens building even give me an idea of what Javon would look like when he gets to be their age. Every week I imagine myself showing up in his dreams. I see our shadows on the asphalt in the parking lot making crazy love to each other while our bodies go on talking and smiling, acting like nothing's going on.

Javon's still booked up. He seems genuinely sorry but still keeps blowing me off. "You must be seeing somebody," I say.

"Nah. I don't have time for a relationship right now. Besides, I don't think I've found The One yet, ya know?" He glances at me, waiting.

"Really? As good-looking as you are, I would've thought . . ." He shakes his head. "But then, I'm not seeing anybody either, so . . ."

"No? Big good-looking guy like you, and with a j-o-b too?" He punches me lightly on the chest. "I would've thought . . ."

I shake my head. "You got no time at all? Not even for just one drink? A soda? Coffee? Come on . . ."

Javon sighs and slowly walks off to his ride.

Every night when I try to think of someone else, Javon cockblocks me. Tonight I try remembering the last young guy I used to know. Also in his twenties and darker than a moonless night, I used to suck his sweet hard cock, turn him around and tongue him clean, then slide my fat condomed dick far up his ass. He was the only guy I've ever met who'd suck his thumb as he was getting fucked. Weird, but it turned me on, and I would pound him harder. Just as I'm about to cum thinking about Cecil, I find myself back at work, in the booth in the parking lot, talking to Javon. My erection fades. I glance at Javon's lips. He mumbles something I can't quite make out as his face draws close to mine. Suddenly we're kissing. The first one is brief, to test the waters. The next is firmer, more certain this is what we both want. I dive in again. His lips are sweet like honey, with the slightly nutty undertone of almonds. I thought I was ready for this, expected it even, but realize I am not. I wake up and my head is spinning. I can't breathe. I feel as though I'm falling off the roof of the world.

* * *

Javon reads part of his Walt Whitman paper to me after his class. "Good job, man," I say with my head down. He nods. It seems like he's done, then suddenly he closes his eyes. Javon begins to recite from memory:

"Behold this swarthy face, these gray eyes
This beard, this white wool unclipped upon my neck . . ."

When he gets to the section of the poem where Whitman talks about kissing a "Manhattanese," he opens his eyes. At the last line, *"We are those two natural and nonchalant persons,"* he stares right at me. He's talking about my gray eyes, my dark beard with the two gray hairs on each side of my swarthy face. He means me.

I clear my throat. "You know that one, 'To a Stranger'? That one's pretty good too."

"Oh yeah? So you *have* been reading the book, then! How does it go?"

"Aww, I can't recite poetry. Here." I hand him the book, hoping my hand doesn't tremble. "You read it."

"You always this shy, bro? Shit, it's no wonder you can't get a date!" *I'm only shy with you,* I think. Javon moves closer to a streetlight to read:

"Passing stranger! You do not know how longingly I look upon you,
You must be he I was seeking, or she I was seeking, (it comes to me as of a dream,)"

"You don't have to read the goddamned thing aloud, you know!"

"Why not? There's no one here but us." I sigh and mumble "Fuck" under my breath.

"Okay," Javon says, "okay . . . I'll keep it to myself." He finishes the poem.

"Nice," he says softly. "Didn't know we were still strangers, though . . ."

I open my mouth to say something, but see Javon's ride turn into the far end of the parking lot.

"Since you liked Whitman, next I'll turn you on to something else. Somebody modern, somebody black. Essex Hemphill, Audre Lorde. Give you the Real Deal." He hands me the book back and presses a slip of paper into my hand. Holding our good-bye hug longer and tighter than usual, he kisses me on the cheek, almost on the lips, before grinning, and running off to catch his ride. "Call me!" sings out across the darkened parking lot. "I mean it, motherfucker, call me. I got a break from classes coming and we really have to talk!"

The memory of his kiss glows on my face all night, lighting my way home.

I'm wandering through the bathhouse again. A husky bald-headed guy stops me. He leans in to my ear. *"East Saint Louis,"* he whispers. I slide my tongue into his slowly parting mouth, squeezing both our fingers around his manhood. Heat radiates up between our fingers. He moans and grabs my swollen meat. Soon we are kissing feverishly, stroking each other. His lips are tasty, burning, as if he'd just eaten something spicy. The air blooms with our musk. I am mesmerized by the thick brown tower in my hand and go down, swallowing it in one gulp. The guy sucks in air and leans back, his chest heaving as I slurp and stroke his maleness. I move up, suck the flat brown coins of his nipples tasting sweat and metal. My mouth and tongue move across his broad hairy chest, then on to lick his neck. He sucks the taste of his body from my tongue.

He turns me around so I face the wall and presses against me. The blunt ridge of his cock in the crack of my ass feels good. It's been a long time since I've been fucked and I look forward to having him inside me. Instead the guy slips to the floor, spreads my cheeks and begins to lick. I moan softly as he eats my ass. Another hand reaches out and pulls me to an eager pair of lips as my salad gets tossed. Javon's face is in my neck. He is kissing me. He nibbles at my earlobe, then bites it. I wince in pain. He holds me tightly to him and chomps into my neck. I feel the blood rushing from me as he sucks my blood. I try to push him from me but grow weaker. I wake up with a start as Javon begins to devour me, moving in to take an enormous bite out of my face.

"So how come you didn't call me, man?" Javon asks the following week. I mumble, fumble, look away. Say something about thinking he might have had to study, not wanting to disturb him when he was with his family. Some other bull.

He nods. "Yeah, yeah, that's what I thought. That's okay, G. It's cool." I feel like shit.

I'm a typical man, okay? I didn't call. Instead I went out to a bar. The place was packed, everyone a little hyped up and horny as hell. Everyone could've gotten lucky if they gave it half a chance, even me.

I picked up this guy from out of town just looking for a good time, which was fine by me. We went back to his hotel room, and flew into each other. It was like we hadn't had sex in years. I don't even remember taking my clothes off. I think they just *burned* off from our heat. The guy, Rick, was the color of milk chocolate and hairless, sleek as a panther. We both made the same small sharp grunts of pleasure when he fucked me. Rick moaned, sighed, and damned near spoke in tongues when we flipped and I started to give him some dick. I was sure he woke his neighbors with his yelling when he came. It was a great night. I woke up the next day drained and exhausted, bedclothes on the floor, the room still funky from our fuck. He promised to call me when he comes back through town around Christmas. He wants me to wear my uniform this time, and make sure I bring my handcuffs and a nightstick.

I'm no fool. I don't tell Javon any of this. "Maybe you should call me," I say, ripping a strip of paper from the incident book to give him my number.

"Yeah, yeah, okay." Javon shrugs his shoulders. "That'll be good. I'll think about it." He folds my number in half, slips it into his pocket. I can tell he doesn't believe me, that he no longer really cares.

I also don't tell Javon that when I woke up next to Rick, for a moment in my morning haze I'd imagined I had been sleeping next to *him*, next to Javon, all through the night. I'm a fool.

Javon and I are in my apartment, watching a basketball game. We're both sweaty and tired as if we'd just played one-on-one ourselves. Our shoes and socks are off. Javon's long toes move back and forth as if waving in a breeze only they can feel. I bend down to touch them, then kiss them. I lovingly suck each one of his toes into my mouth. Moving slowly, we begin to explore each other's bodies. We memorize each other's faces with our fingers, explore our bodies with slow-moving hands. Suddenly, we stop. What was that noise? Our words trip over each other as we try to speak at the same time. We laugh. My dick has sprung to attention, making a thick lump in my pants, and I drop my hands to hide it. I glance into Javon's crotch and see he has done the same. His eyes follow mine. Javon shrugs. *"You can't control it, you know!"* We try to play off what has happened, is happening, will happen, as a joke, "just one of those things" . . . *"I think maybe I should go,"* he says. I nod. Neither of us moves.

The next week I'm the one who's saying, "So how come you didn't call *me*?"

"We had our finals this week. Too busy studying, I guess." He looks at me coldly. Guess he thinks he's put me in my place.

"What are you doing during the semester break? Going anyplace?

"Nah, I think I'll be here. Just hang out, you know?"

"Well, think about giving me a call. In case you want some company."

"Yeah, okay."

I start to say something then stop. Javon's carpool will turn into the parking lot at any moment. "Fuck it," I think . . .

"Look, Javon, I understand if you don't want to be bothered with me. I don't mind. I probably seem like just a desperate old man to you, all dried up and shit—"

"You're not old!" Javon lays a hand on my shoulder. "And you're certainly not dried up." His fingers slide down my arm, squeezing my biceps. "You still got lots of juice left in you." He suddenly reaches out and grabs my crotch. "One *hell* of a lot of juice, if you ask me."

I stare at him as calmly as I can with his hand wrapped around my dick and glance over his shoulder. "Your ride's here, boy."

"Uh huh . . . it's right here, Daddy." He gives my awakening jimmy a tug.

"Stop it, man, get out of here. Your ride . . ." The car is getting closer to us, its headlights becoming brighter. Javon drops his hand and we go into our good-bye hug. Again I hesitate, then pull Javon in tight and kiss him on the lips. I don't care who sees. "Call me," I whisper. "Please, Javon. Just call me. You don't know, baby, you just don't know . . ." Javon stares at me and slowly walks away.

"Please," he whispers. *"Please."* My body glows like polished bronze. Staring into my eyes, he carefully positions himself and eases down. His ass inhales me like a starving mouth. His head rolls from side to side as I fill him with my maleness. He puts two fingers in my mouth. I suck them greedily as he rides my rippling hips, a cowboy trying to break a bucking stallion. I piston into him as if I were on fire. He shudders. Thick seed bursts from his bouncing cock. His asshole clamps down on me and I'm ready to explode as well. I call out his name. Twin fountains spurt up, reaching toward the ceiling. His whole body vibrates, and I pull him to me, falling yet again into the plush cavern of his mouth. I hold him close, feel his racing heart against my skin. Our breathing returns to normal, and he is older, we both are older. We've lived together as a couple for years and years. It's our anniversary and we've been remembering our first time. Slowly I open my eyes and find myself alone in bed, tightly holding a pillow, my body cold and wet, the sheets stained with sweat, saliva, cum and tears.

The next morning the phone rings. It's Javon. He apologizes for waking me, says he's had trouble sleeping the night before. Seems he keeps having this recurring dream . . .

"You want to talk about it? Maybe we could meet somewhere. I could come over there . . ."

"No, I'll come to you." A pause. "Guess who bought a car yesterday with the money he's been making working two jobs?"

I give Javon directions and hang up the phone.

I feel like I'm falling. The entire world is silent, except for the pounding of my heart.

NATASHA TARPLEY

All of Me

All of me, why not take all of me . . .

hunger comes on morning
sails. where twilight passes me
wide is the river.

—Sonia Sanchez

FLOATING *somewhere between dreaming and awake . . .*
Ever felt Kai shift in his sleep beside her. A cascade
of his dreadlocks fell across her cheek and tickled her
nose, nudging her from sleep. Kai draped his heavy muscular
arm around her waist and pulled her to him. Ever's body fit perfectly in the shallow curve of his fetal position; knees rounding
over knees, her back pressed to his chest, the rhythm of her
breathing falling into sync with his. The heat of their bare skin
touching sent a tremor through her body that made her heart
race. Kai swore left and right that he was completely unaware
that he did this, but Ever loved the way he reached for her in his
sleep. Made her feel totally connected to him; like she'd seeped
into his subconscious; like he needed her.

She lay still, inhaling the air heavy with his scent, all of the major pieces of his life melded together: turpentine, from the paints
and materials he used to make his sculpture and paintings; orange, from the juice bar where he worked part-time; and frankin-
cense oil, the scent of the gods, as he called it, which he rubbed
over his body every day—one of the rituals of the eclectic spiritu-
ality he had devised for himself, borrowing something from all
the major religions and faiths he'd studied over the years.

Ever let her eyes flutter open reluctantly, not wanting to move forward from this moment. She looked around her room through the prism of his hair, her eyes resting briefly on each object, touch-stones to orient herself as the rest of her slowly came awake. At the foot of the bed was her great-aunt's cedar chest, covered with a piece of African cloth she bought on her trip to Senegal two years ago and family photos. There was Ever as a baby; her mom, Hope; old sepia-toned pictures from the 1920s of her great-grandparents on their farm in Louisiana; a black-and-white photo of her grandmother when she was Ever's age, her eyes bright, a slight smile on her lips as she stared directly into the camera, probably flirting with Ever's grandfather as he took the picture. There was the bookcase, with books jutting out from every cor-ner, spilling over into piles on the floor.

On the other side of the room was the tower, Ever's favorite part of the apartment. She lived on the top floor of a four-story brownstone and the tower, like a little sun porch set apart from the rest of the room, was its highest point. Three stairs led up to the space in the shape of a semicircle with three floor-to-ceiling windows. The first inklings of sunlight were just beginning to push through the pale blue curtain of early morning sky, landing in puddles like saucers on the dull hardwood floor. Soon the small arc of a room would be flooded with light. The sunlight was one of the reasons Ever decided to put her desk here. That and the view. From the tower, Ever could look out the windows as she worked, at the pretty tree-lined block of Harlem row houses, families putzing in their yards, and the colorful charac-ters who used the street as a stage to perform their own personal dramas. She was invisible here, so high up. But she liked it that way; liked to watch the world moving beneath her, and the dis-tance the tower gave her from its stickiness, its loudness, its heat, and its ice.

Her friend, Aviva, said it was like living on the set of *The Cosby Show*, Ever in her tower on her bourgeois Harlem block. All that was missing was the theme music. "You oughta con-sider having jazz piped over the intercom system, you know, kind of like a cue to let people know when to make their entrance and exit, what they should say or do next . . ." Aviva always teased.

Whatever, Aviva. As if Fort Greene, Brooklyn, is any different, Ever smiled, remembering their running joke. But the smile quickly faded as she stared at the computer collecting dust, and the mounds of paper and books piled on top of her desk: false starts and notes for a novel she was trying to get off the ground; ideas for articles; drafts of poems; two book reviews, one for *Emerge* magazine, the other for the *Washington Post*, that were already late, one of the books still unread. She was in that place again where her brain turned into a kaleidoscope, with words and thoughts swirling around in fragments, pieces she couldn't seem to fit together. It was like trying to scream in the middle of a bad dream, but the sound got stuck somewhere, and in the end there was only silence.

She was still recovering, that was part of it. Ever's eyes fell on two boxes stacked beside her desk. Inside were copies of her first book, an anthology of writings by women of all backgrounds from ages twelve to thirty on life and transitions. It had been published a year and a half ago by a small independent press, and had recently gone out of print. Ever hadn't made a dime off the book and she doubted that the people she wanted to reach even knew it existed. She had rescued the last copies from the remainder bins, intending to donate them to schools and organizations for girls. Everyone offered a reason why the book hadn't succeeded the way she'd hoped: anthologies were a hard sell; the press didn't publicize the book; she herself didn't have the time or money to really publicize it on her own. All these reasons, logical and true, but none explanation enough to heal the disappointment in her heart, or quiet the voice that told her she'd failed.

But over the past few months, Ever had begun to think about writing again. She had even pulled out her journal to write on the subway to and from work a few times, something she hadn't done since the book came out. There was also the possibility of a new project. The anthology had attracted the interest of a photographer who wanted Ever to write the text for a book of photographs she was doing on black women and love. She was still waiting for it to be sold, but Ever had a good feeling about it. *God, let me keep moving,* she uttered a quick prayer as she snuggled closer to Kai.

With his arms around her, she could forget for a moment the work that needed to be done; chaos was kept at bay. She brushed his hair from her face and turned to face him, stifling the urge to touch his smooth mahogany skin; to trace the outline of his well-defined cheek bones, his full lips, and then his finely cut, muscular shoulders and arms, the tight stomach and behind. Kai was a beautiful man. But his was a beauty to which Ever had no claim. There was nothing in him or on him that reflected her; no jewelry, no marks of her passion. Her scent did not linger on his skin; their bodies didn't tell stories of each other, no inherited movements or mannerisms. His beauty was hers to enjoy for the time he was in her company and after that he was gone. No promises, no obligation to return.

"Stop it, Ever. Stop it," she admonished herself before her thoughts ran wild, before she could give in to the yearning welling up just beneath the surface of her skin. That was the agreement, remember? A relationship of mutual convenience, good conversation, good company, sex when they wanted it, but no strings, no attachments. Initially, at least, this is what she thought she wanted. When they met six months ago, she was getting over the breakup of her last relationship, had just started her job at the magazine, and was using any leftover energy and time to promote the book. Kai was focused on building his own career as a sculptor and visual artist.

"Any woman I'm with has to understand that my art comes first. That's the way it is," he told her that first day, sitting across from her in a booth at the Uptown Juice Bar and Café on 125th Street where he worked. Ever had gone into the café for a strawberry-banana smoothie after an afternoon of pampering at a day spa downtown. She and Aviva had recently gotten deep into the spiritual thing, resolving to honor themselves every day, to live healthier in body and mind. To celebrate, Aviva had given her a gift certificate to the spa, and Ever had treated her to a concert at the Blue Note. Both of them had probably overdosed on Iyanla Vanzant books, but whatever this spiritual stuff was, it was working.

She felt beautiful, totally relaxed that day. Her favorite Bob Marley CD blaring above the conversation and clatter, and the spicy smell of vegetarian food blending with the sweet aroma of fruit from the juice bar and incense, lifted her spirits even higher. She bobbed her head and sang along with the music softly, as she joined the line to place her order, pressing her back against the wall opposite the long counter.

Ever noticed him as soon as she walked in. He was dressed in a white T-shirt that showed off his broad shoulders and narrow waist, and black jeans that hung on his hips perfectly. His shoulder-length dreadlocks were tucked into a red, yellow, and green knit beret. Rasta hats, Aviva called them. After that day, inspired by the hat, she and Aviva took to calling him "the Rasta," placing him among the ranks of men they encountered to whom they referred by descriptive title, based on some distinct characteristic: the Rasta, the Banker, the Poet, the Beautiful Boy.

As she waited, Ever watched him work behind the counter and began to fantasize about how his body would feel pressed against hers, how he would look hovering over her, the warmth of his lips . . . everywhere. Stop right there. Remember peace. Serenity. She was loving the space she had begun to create in her life for herself, by herself, without someone else's energy and needs to contend with. Peace. Serenity. Peace, serenity. Peace-serenitypeaceserenitypea—

"What can I get for you?" the Rasta asked, interrupting her mantra.

"Um . . . a strawberry-banana smoothie?" Startled, her order sounded more like a question as she quickly scanned the chalkboard menu.

"I don't know, you tell me," he teased.

"Sorry about that," Ever said still looking at the menu, slightly embarrassed. "I'll stick with the strawberry-banana smoothie and ah . . . a spinach pie."

"What about mix-ins for your smoothie?" He pointed to the list of natural ingredients, expounding on the health benefits of each.

"Trust me, you take one of these wheat grass shots and you'll be bouncing off the walls. You won't believe how much energy you'll have. Man, your boyfriend'll thank me tomorrow." He grinned, looking directly into her eyes, waiting to see what her reaction would be to this last statement. Ever smirked and rolled her eyes.

"Well, maybe he would, if he existed." She took the bait. "But I think I'll pass on the wheat grass."

"So that's one strawberry-banana smoothie, minus wheat grass, and a spinach pie. Are you sure this is what you want?" He leaned over the counter so that his face was close to hers. "Have you looked deep into your heart and searched for the right answer?"

"Yes," Ever replied solemnly, playing along. "I have consulted the ancestors and they have agreed that it is right and good." They both cracked up and Ever felt as though they had always laughed this way together, an immediate familiarity, intimacy, almost. A recognition, maybe, that they were from the same place.

"Kindred spirit," the Rasta remarked slicing bananas for her drink. "Nice to meet you." Ever smiled, glad that he had felt it, too, and went to find a seat to wait for her order. She chose a small table near the window and took out the Sunday *Times Book Review* section of the paper that she had stuffed into her bag before leaving the house.

"Here you are." He appeared with her lunch before she could start to read, and slid into the empty seat opposite her. The table was so tiny their knees touched.

He told her that his name was Kai, and that he was thirty years old, two years older than Ever. She listened as he spoke passionately about his sculpture and his painting, and watched the graceful motion of his long fingers as he grabbed and pointed in the air toward his dream. A man with a passion, her weakness. She could feel her gaze soften. She didn't pull away when he let his hand rest casually on top of hers. He didn't ask very many questions of her, but that was okay. She didn't feel much like talking about herself anyway. Too many jumbled thoughts and questions. It would take too much energy to even begin to construct a cohesive statement about her life. She liked to write. She had a new job as a reporter that didn't inspire her. She loved New York. This is what she told him and he didn't push for more.

"How come you're not with anyone?" he asked.

"I don't know." Ever looked out of the window. "Just trying to give myself some space, get my career off the ground."

"Me, too." Kai looked relieved. "My art is my life right now. I can't get serious about another person. I'm just not feeling that. That's not where my energy is. It's all about the work, you know?" He was trying to sound deep. Ever nodded, resisting the temptation to tease him about his corniness.

"That's cool. I admire your focus." She stifled a smile. He started stroking her hand. *Peace serenity peace serenity peace serenity lips peace serenity arms tongue peace serenity peace serenity him inside me peace peace . . .*

"I think part of honoring ourselves also has to be about honoring our need for sexual pleasure," Ever said later on the phone with Aviva, trying to justify why she had given Kai, aka the Rasta, her number.

"I'm not throwing stones." Aviva, who had been involved in an off-and-on relationship with a married man for three years. "But just know that you're going into this with both eyes open. He's told you where he stands. Believe him. That's all I can say. And if you do sleep with him, I need every detail. He sounds delicious!"

"Don't get involved," her mother, Hope, had urged, a thread of panic weaving through her voice. "This kind of thing only leads to disappointment. I know you, Ever. You don't do well with these kinds of relationships. You always end up wanting more."

In truth, she never really "got" the casual sex thing. She just never understood how two people could be so close, share such an intimate act as entering and receiving another's body, and yet not be "together," connected emotionally as well as physically. But with Kai it felt different. In her relationships before him, she had learned to live within the crevices of her desire; to take the crumbs, the glimpses of what could be and make-believe she was satisfied. This time, it felt more like choosing. Choosing to put her time and energy into herself as opposed to being consumed by a relationship. She and Kai had a mutual respect for each other's space. Yet they could still come together and talk about anything, share their work, enjoy each other's company. They could feel free together. But this was also what made it hard to maintain distance, perspective. The possibility of love dangled so close she could taste it, feel its warmth, but it was always just out of reach.

The shrill scream of the alarm jolted her. Ever quickly reached over Kai to turn it off. Kai turned onto his back and wrapped both arms around her, pulling her onto his chest. He gently grabbed a handful of her finger-length dreadlocks as he kissed her neck and worked his way up to her lips, planting a kiss there that made the sweet spot between her legs tighten. He caressed her back and then moved one hand lower to stroke her thigh, the other to her breast.

"I'm late," Ever whispered, but didn't move.

"Just a little bit," he begged into her ear, licking her earlobe and neck. She tilted her head to give him better access.

"Alright, then, mister." Ever straddled him, feeling his growing erection. "I'm going to keep you here forever."

"Ah, but my lady, you can't keep me. I'm a ship passing in the night. A leaf drifting on a gentle breeze," Kai teased, affecting a British accent. "But for the moment, a kiss if you please." He pulled her to him and kissed her, sucking her bottom lip. He moved his hand to the back of her neck and held her firmly, parting her lips insistently with his tongue. Ever teased him, making tiny circles around the tip of his tongue with her own before taking it between her lips. Tongues interlocked, Ever began to rock slightly, up and down, along the length of Kai's erection, loving the feel of his hardness between her legs.

"You're so wet," Kai groaned as he entered her with three fingers. She gasped and lay still for a moment, enjoying the slow thrusts of his fingers, then picked up the rhythm with her hips. "Come inside," she whispered in his ear. Kai shook his head, no, and rolled her onto her back. Without pausing to kiss her breasts or her belly button like he usually did, Kai parted her legs and slid down between her thighs. He entered her again with his fingers as he wrapped his lips around her clit. He had memorized the terrain of her body, knew exactly when to suck, where to lick. Ever came almost instantly. She lifted his face to hers and kissed him, her mouth flooded with her own salty taste. Kai reached for her hands and held them above her head as he entered her, then wrapped his arms around her as he moved urgently inside of her. Ever licked her lips and closed her eyes, wanting this feeling, the fullness of him, to last forever. Kai began to make the sound he always made when he was close, something between a moan and a growl that came from some deep place inside of him. He climaxed silently, as usual, his body heaving against hers as he rested his head in the curve between her shoulder and neck.

"Where do you go when you're not with me?" Ever heard the words and her voice just as their lips were about to meet, but for a split second, she couldn't be sure that she had spoken. Kai's embrace slackened.

"I'm sorry." She sat up abruptly. "I didn't mean to say that."

"I'm working," he answered as she climbed out of bed.

"It's not a big deal," Ever said, heading toward the bathroom, still surprised by her own question. Where had it come from? She looked back at him. He was already slipping on his pants.

In the bathroom, Ever stood in front of the mirror staring at her reflection. "Who are you? What do you want?" she asked, looking into her eyes, the same almond shape as her mother's, the same deep brown of settled clay beneath clear water. She stroked her face, the rich caramel skin Kai said reminded him of autumn, the way its tone seemed to deepen or become lighter depending on the season, the weather, her mood; her nose, with its high bridge and slightly flared nostrils; her lips, the bottom one pouty and a little fuller than the top, a gift from her grandmother on her father's side. With both hands, she ruffled her amber-colored locks, almost a year old now. Stretching her eyes wide open with her fingertips, then rubbing her temples, she asked again, "Who are you? What do you want?" No answer. Ever stuck her tongue out at her reflection and turned on the faucet in the shower.

She pressed play on the compact CD player. The sound of John Coltrane's "Dear Lord," her morning prayer, flooded the room as she drew the curtain back and stepped into the shower.

The warm water and Coltrane's saxophone felt good rolling off her skin. Ever touched the places on her body where Kai's hands had been, ignoring the sinking feeling where the weight of her questions—the one that had just escaped and those still unasked—settled like a rock in the pit of her stomach. *Wondering about love is just the same as begging for it,* her grandmother's voice came to her. Ignoring it as well, Ever turned her thoughts again to this morning. With the utterance of a few words, she had found herself in another place. She had, unintentionally, crossed a line with Kai and within herself. She knew this. But would it be possible, she wondered, for her to get back to the other side?

She pushed her way into the crowded subway car . . .

Almost a year in New York and she still wasn't used to the constant battle, the way even the slightest action, like walking down the street or riding the subway, could feel like waging war. And how, after the brief moment of confrontation, you became invisible. You could disappear, even in the midst of all these bodies pressed together.

She missed Kai. He usually rode downtown with her on the days he didn't have to work, but this morning he had popped his head into the bathroom to let her know he was leaving while she was still in the shower. She missed the private realm they created around themselves, fingers intertwined, leaning into one another, cushioning the jolts of the bumpy ride. Often he'd map out an idea for his next painting, drawing shapes and lines with his finger on a canvas of her arm or thigh. He'd tell her about the day he had planned—what supplies he needed, where he'd shoot the photographs he always took before starting any project, bringing the concrete elements of the piece together before he recreated them on canvas. She loved the way he could transform the world like that.

Occasionally, she'd tell him about the images she'd seen floating through her mind while she was asleep. Last time, it was the dream she'd had about a woman with wings staring up at the sky. The woman just kept walking and looking up, looking at her feet, touching her wings, trying to figure out the connection.

"You're grounded," he said matter-of-factly. "You've forgotten how to use your wings."

"Well, yeah. It's a pretty straightforward metaphor." Ever felt defensive.

"No, I'm serious. You've forgotten how to use your wings." Kai stared straight at her, straight into her. "What are you willing to sacrifice for your dreams, for happiness?" he asked. Ever squirmed in her seat, feeling crowded all of a sudden, boxed in by the conversation and his assessment of her, unable to defend herself, unable to pull back, close up the part of her that lay open to his probing.

Kai was about to launch into one of his sermons. He had dropped out of business school to paint, he preached, floating further and further away from her, until Ever imagined she looked like a small brown speck from the place where he simply became an inspiration to himself. "You've got to be focused on what you want; you've got to view everything in your life through that lens. Either it's feeding your goal or it's not. And if it's not, then to hell with it. Let it go. Walk away."

She was too much of a coward for that. She had gone from one safe thing to the next; from college to journalism school, and then the job at the magazine—one that hadn't thrilled her but had given her what she needed most, stability. She kept building her portfolio along the way, writing articles and reviews, taking notes for the novel she had been planning to write for years now. But somehow, she couldn't get all the way there, couldn't get immersed in her own work. Many of her friends had applied for fellowships and spent time at writers' colonies and retreats, did temp work to make money to support their art. Ever often thought about looking into some of these things for herself, but actually doing it was like walking to the edge of a diving board and staring down into the cool blue water, knowing how good it would feel covering her body, how the water would reach up and catch her, pull her into its fluid embrace. She was still trying, for once and for all, to work up the nerve to jump.

"What are you afraid of?" Kai would ask.

"That I have nothing inside; that the words won't come."

"But the words do come. Why don't you trust them?"

"I'm afraid that if I let everything else go, the words won't hold me up. I'm afraid they'll leave me if I need them too much."

"You've got to nourish your soul, so the words will never leave you. They can carry you, if you let them, if you believe that you have something of value to offer the world." Only Kai could say something that trite, and she would swallow it whole, believe him without question. His discipline, his passion filled her; lit a spark of inspiration within her that she would try to keep burning throughout the day.

Ever opened her eyes, her stop was next. If Kai were here, he'd rub her back quickly or squeeze her hand; he never kissed her in public. That wasn't his thing. But even those small gestures, an affirmation of their connection, gave her a surge of energy, made her feel more powerful in a world where her soul meant nothing. So why the question this morning? Ever felt her chest tighten as she went back over what had happened. Had she lost him? Had she caused another breach that she didn't know how to repair? Peace. Serenity. The words were paper-thin. Not enough to soothe her rising anxiety, as she confronted the possibility of her life without him.

Ever unlocked the door to her office at *Converse* magazine and flipped on the overhead fluorescent light, calmed for a moment as she looked around the room at the pictures and posters covering the walls, her one nod toward self-expression. She and Aviva had spent an entire afternoon covering the walls with prints and black-and-white photographs by African American artists and photographers. As one of three African Americans at the magazine, it was important for her to be able to see faces that looked like hers. One of the other black people in the office once asked her if she was afraid that having all that "black stuff" on the walls would isolate her from everybody else in the company. But sometimes, those pictures were what got her through the day. They brought her solace, made her feel at home.

"This came for you."

Before she had even taken off her coat, Kim, the office receptionist, knocked on her door and handed Ever a thick brown envelope.

"Oh, okay. Thanks." She took the package without even looking at it.

"The messenger said it was pretty important," Kim told her, fishing for information. Ever waved her acknowledgment as she turned her attention to her computer.

Seconds later, the phone started to ring. "Ever Morgan," she answered.

"Did you get it?" Ever recognized Irene's heavy Mississippi drawl right away.

"Get what?"

"The package. Did you get it?"

"That must be what the receptionist just handed to me. Did you have it messengered?"

"Yes, yes," Irene said impatiently.

"Well, I have it, what is it?"

"Oh hell, I'ma explode by the time you get 'round to op'nin' the damn thing. It's the first batch of photos for the book."

"You mean . . ."

"It's a go! We got us a book deal!!" Irene squealed. Ever joined her, jumping up and down around her office.

"This is such wonderful news! I can't believe it!"

"Well believe it, it's been a long time coming." Irene sighed. "Thank you, God."

"Yes, thank you, thank you, thank you!"

Irene and Ever met at one of Ever's book signings in Chicago, one of the few the publisher had set up. Irene introduced herself as a photographer and filmmaker and told Ever that she was working on a book of photographs about black women and love. "I want you to write the text," she'd said. Ever studied her smooth face, skin the color of dried tobacco leaves, her coal-black eyes, hair cornrolled into a bun on top of her head, trying to figure out her angle, to uncover the ulterior motive that always seemed to be lurking beneath the surface of conversations with other artists at book signings. Nothing on Irene flinched. "We'd be coauthors. I'll do the pictures, you do the words. Fifty-fifty. I've got an agent who's going to shop the proposal to a few publishers, but I need a writer."

"Why me? I mean, you haven't even seen my work."

"I read your introduction." She held the book up. "Your words are like, like music. And I really admire your vision for the book. You pulled something beautiful out of each of the women's stories in this anthology. That's what I'm looking for with these photographs." Irene handed her a postcard. "I live in New York, but a gallery down here is showing some of my work. Check it out. If you like it and want to work on the book then call me. I'll be in town for a few more days."

The next afternoon Ever went to see her show, a series of black-and-white photos titled *Life*, depicting the day-to-day lives of African Americans. She really captured the spirit of a people; the daily pain and joy. She captured the struggles with racism and violence, but also the ways African Americans held each other up, how they had lives beyond the "issues."

Her favorite was a shot of a mother and her young daughter in a dilapidated city park, sitting on a bench reading to each other. It reminded Ever of how she and Hope used to read together before she went to sleep; curled up in her and Daddy's huge bed, their favorite books spread all around them. During the summer, Ever's father would take her to the library and let her wander among the shelves for hours. But it was during her special reading time with Hope that the books took on their real meaning. Hope would look at each one. "You always pick the best books," she'd say, praising Ever's choices as though she had discovered a talent that she alone possessed.

"Yes," she told Irene when she called her that evening. "Yes."

Now, a year later, the project was finally getting off the ground. Irene gave her the details of the offer and told her that the deal would be finalized in another week or so. They'd have contracts soon after. Irene and Ever let out another round of squeals and tears.

"Maybe this is my blessing," Ever whispered. A month ago, a friend's sister, who had predicted all kinds of things for her family, gave her a psychic reading. Just for fun. "Are you planning a trip?" she asked. No. "Somehow I see you surrounded by green. Things are growing around you. There will be light and clarity. You're about to receive a tremendous blessing," she said. Ever had told Irene about it afterwards. Aviva would never let her live it down if she found out that she had visited a psychic, but Irene took these things very seriously. "Could be," Irene said, lowering her voice, too. "Could be."

Bolstered by her good mood, and against her better judgment, she decided to call Kai. Nothing he could say, or not say, would bring her down now. Kai picked up just as his machine was coming on. "What's up," he said when he heard her voice. Ever could tell right away that he didn't want to talk.

"Got some good news this afternoon," she said, looking for an opening, a way to reach him again.

"Oh yeah, what's that?" His voice was flat. She heard him shifting the phone around.

"We sold the book!" she announced, her enthusiasm dampened.

"What book?"

"You know, the one Irene, the photographer, wanted me to write the text for. On black women and love."

"Oh, right." She wasn't convinced that he remembered. "That's great. Congrats." Kai's voice was one straight monotonous line. Hang up, now, she told herself. Hang up while you still have an ounce of happiness left.

"Aviva and I are going to that Senegalese restaurant in Brooklyn tonight to celebrate. Wanna come?" Idiot!

"Uh, thanks, but I can't." There was an awkward pause. "I've been working on this piece all day, and I really don't want to leave it," Kai added.

"Okay . . . Well, I'll let you get back to work." Ever got off the phone quickly. She tried to ignore the hurt that began to blossom like a flower in the pit of her stomach, reaching for the envelope with Irene's photographs, still unopened, on her desk. She felt a little better holding it, its promise wrapping around her like a shield.

* * *

Home.

The scent of eucalyptus from the large bunch in the terra-cotta pot, like a sentinel standing guard at the door, greeted her as she stepped, exhausted, into her apartment. Without stopping to put down her things, Ever went straight to the kitchen to start the kettle for tea. In the living room, she dumped her stuff on the black papasan chair curved like an empty bowl, lit a stick of jasmine incense, and put on her favorite Cassandra Wilson CD.

With the sweet calming aroma of the incense swirling above her head, Ever sank down onto the sofa, deep into the plush cushions that seemed to rise up to meet her body, engulf her in softness. She leaned back against pillows covered in mud cloth, breathing in the earthy scent still embedded in the fabric. Earth that held the memory of long journeys.

The whistle from the kettle brought her back to the kitchen. She spooned honey into her cup from the jar, using her finger to swipe the little bit that spilled over the rim. "Honey is always better from your fingers, your lips, your everywhere," Kai once told her, licking each place he named. The taste flooded her mouth now, its sticky sweetness suspending for a moment the lingering pangs of disappointment she felt from her conversation with Kai this morning and afternoon. Ever returned to the living room, pausing at the threshold of the tiny room to survey the collection of her things, markers of her life: two built-in bookshelves lining one wall, overflowing with books, photographs, candles, odd things she'd saved over the years, old playbills. And she was once again on familiar ground.

The phone rang as she settled back on the couch. "Hey honey," Hope's voice sang on the other end.

"Hey, Mama-me," Ever said, calling Hope by the pet name she'd made up when she was little.

"How was your day, Daughter-me?" Hope asked.

"Wellll," Ever stretched the word out. "I have some good news." She got up and took the envelope with Irene's photographs, still unopened, out of her bag.

"Irene and I sold the book!" She clutched the envelope to her chest. Hope shrieked and then was silent. "Hope?"

"Oh Ever, Ever . . ." she sniffled. "This is so wonderful.

You've wanted this so badly." When she heard Hope crying, Ever started bawling herself.

"I'm happy, but I'm so scared," she said when she was finally able to speak. "I'm scared this book will be like the last one; that I'll fail all over again."

"No, don't you dare do that," Hope admonished her gently. "This is a new beginning," she said. "I want you to promise me that you won't look back. Will you promise me that?"

"I promise."

"We are going to make this a beautiful book." Hope and Ever always spoke in "we" terms. Hope had read and critiqued everything Ever had written. Yes, Ever thought to herself, reassured, it will be a beautiful book.

The phone beeped. "Hold on, Mom. I have another call." Ever clicked over. She was instantly relieved to hear Kai's voice. "Want some company?" he asked.

"I don't know. Look, I'm on the other line with my mother. Can you call me back?" Ever said sharply.

"Come on, Ev. I want to see you." His voice slipped into that sexy register.

"And I wanted to see you earlier, to celebrate my book." Silence.

"Please," he begged. Ever had to catch herself, remind herself what *this* was. This was sex and company. This was not love, not accountability or commitment . . . and she could use some company.

"Fine," she relinquished.

"See you soon."

She clicked back over to Hope. "Kai?" Hope asked. There was no keeping secrets with Hope.

"Yup," she answered, wishing for just a little bit of privacy, a little space between them.

"I'm surprised you two aren't out celebrating."

"Aviva and I went out to dinner."

"You know that's not the same."

"Well I asked Kai if he wanted to come, but he was working. Now, can we not talk about this?"

"We don't have to go into any long conversation, but, honestly, is that enough for you? I mean, Ever, the man can't even take you out to celebrate a major accomplishment. People don't sell books every day."

"It's not a big deal. That's not the kind of relationship we have." Ever felt five years old all over again.

"Don't you want someone who'll love and cherish you? Celebrate and share in your accomplishments?"

"Right now what I want is some company," she snapped.

"You can keep your own self company. I know you have work to do."

"I know I have work to do. But haven't you ever just wanted not to think about work? I just want to enjoy a little male companionship. That's all." Ever spoke in staccato.

"But if you keep settling for company, as you say, you'll never find a relationship that's truly fulfilling." Maybe company is all I can get, Ever thought but didn't say. "Okay, let's drop it," Hope said. "I'm the last person who should be giving relationship advice. I'm sorry."

"It's okay."

"Congratulations on selling the book. I'm so very proud of you. We'll do something special when I see you. A new beginning. Promise?"

"Promise."

"I love you so much, baby."

"Love you, too."

Ever hung up and rushed to her bedroom to change into something sexier before Kai got there, being very careful not to look over at the silent computer. She was supposed to FedEx the book reviews tomorrow afternoon, and she still hadn't even glanced at Irene's photos. She'd get it done, even if it meant getting up at the crack of dawn tomorrow. She'd get it done, she always did. But for now, there was company. She deserved that little bit of pleasure, didn't she?

Love is blindness, I don't want to see . . .

When he rang the bell, Ever opened the door to find Kai holding up two bottles of Starbucks Frappuccino. "Your idea of a peace offering?" Ever smirked, taking the drinks from his hands. As soon as she set them down, Kai wrapped his arms around her and kissed her. His mouth tasted of smoke. Ever noticed his heavy, droopy eyelids, the whites of his eyes clouded red in the corners, and she knew exactly what he'd been up to, could almost see the tip of the slim white joint, burning black between his fingers. On any other night, she would've told him how much she hated it when he smoked—which he already knew. "It helps me work," he'd claim. She would've refused to kiss him, at least momentarily. But tonight, she decided not to let it matter. She wanted to swim in the heat of his mouth, to be the burning between his fingers. Later, when he entered her, she'd cling to him, tight. Tonight, someone else would drown in her ocean, and he would be her steady thing. An anchor, a rope, that she could climb and keep on climbing until she reached the top.

JABARI ASIM

Rocket Love

I FELL in love with Emerald Turner on our very first date. She'd accompanied me to a party and left me at the bar almost as soon as we arrived. An old friend had important news to share, she explained apologetically, then disappeared. Finally I grew tired of waiting and went out to the porch for a breath of air.

Night, soft belly of a blues goddess, swelled evenly against the tops of trees. Moths circled the lampposts lining the curb. In the park across the street, moonlight twinkled on the surface of a pond. Close by, two young men shot hoops on a dimly lit court. The squeaks of their sneakers and the sound of the ball hitting the pavement were lost in the music from the party. I stared into the distance as Stevie Wonder's earnest pleadings filled the air.

I've longed for you since I was born . . .

Almost unconsciously, I began to sing too, in my own heart-felt off-key way, softly and sadly.

"May I have this dance?"

I jumped, embarrassed. Emerald came toward me and I

wrapped her hesitantly in my arms. She moved to the music and I followed her lead. "I'd almost given up on you," I said.

"Sh," she said. "Just dance."

Good idea. She pressed her warmth against me, melting all the frustration and impatience I'd felt just minutes before. Her hips moved surely and smoothly, her feet were quick and graceful.

I closed my eyes and inhaled Emerald's scent, filled my insides with her sweetness. I told myself if our relationship didn't go any further I'd still be grateful for this one magnificent dance.

The song ended all too soon. We separated and she leaned on the solid porch railing, turning her head one way then the other, as if bathing in the moonlight. I drank in her beauty without fear or shame, savoring her dark cheeks, full lips, her bottomless eyes. I wanted to seize the moment, to thrill and wow her somehow, to tell her things that would endear me to her, make clear all my dreams and aspirations. Damn if I knew where to begin.

I babbled, perhaps foolishly, taking her on a fumbling trek through my earliest memories to my awkward present; I opened up as I never had before, let her read everything scribbled in my feverish consciousness, even the rough drafts and half-finished ideas. I made myself vulnerable, risked her amusement—or contempt—by talking, boldly I hoped, of using my art to claim a place for myself in the world, by telling her I'd been shaping words to fit my soul. Somehow it worked.

She encouraged me to pursue her. For seven straight nights I called her and talked with her until we were both too sleepy to continue. I had to wait until midnight before phoning because she worked ridiculously long hours at a theater company. After putting in time behind the scenes, she'd run home to her computer to tap out her own ideas. I knew all about chaining yourself to the keyboard and cranking up the ol' imagination, so I tried to respect her discipline and dedication. But as soon as the clock struck twelve I was dialing and smiling.

I'd wonder what she was wearing. A nightgown? A camisole? Maybe nothing at all. Reclining on my bed, I'd grin in the dark while the two of us confided and giggled like two teenagers. And on each of those seven nights the same dream flickered behind my fluttering lids, a black-and-tan fantasy unfolding in the weirdly washed-out style of an Edison kinescope: Emerald, magnificently naked, stands under the skylight in her apartment, twirling slowly like a music-box dancer, poised on a single pointed foot, arms thrown out and head tilted back in radiant celebration, as a column of moonlight illuminates her. Stargazer blossoms levitate from the floor and hover magically around her.

I didn't tell Emerald or anyone else about my dream. It was a private pleasure best savored alone. Still, just thinking of it helped me through my many summer drudgeries, encouraging me to work hard and stay so busy that I hardly noticed the heavy drag of humid days. I got so I looked forward to falling asleep almost as much as I anticipated my late-night chats with Emerald.

A couple weeks later, she picked me up in a sleek luxury car. She drove us out to Larsen College, a small suburban school that sponsored an outstanding film series. We were eager to take in a double feature of Charles Burnett's *To Sleep with Anger* and *The Glass Shield. My Brother's Wedding* and *Killer of Sheep* had graced the screen the previous night.

We held hands during the double feature, then grabbed some dinner at the Lipogram, a hip new restaurant not far from the campus.

Emerald, looking luscious in a tie-dyed dress that flattered her fabulous form, asked me if I found it odd that we were the only black people at the screening.

"Not really," I answered. "Burnett is a challenging artist. When brothers have $7.50 to blow on a flick they usually want to spend it on something a little simpler, like the Wayans brothers or Eddie Murphy."

Emerald sighed. "I guess you're right. It's a shame, because Burnett's a genius."

"Yeah, our people are missing out on some fabulous stuff."

"Not only that," Emerald said. "Some of our best artists can barely make ends meet, while some of our worst are getting rich."

"Usually the case," I said.

"I want to be rich," Emerald said.

I was a little surprised. After all, she was working at Blackstage

Productions. I figured she barely made enough to pay the rent on that nice loft of hers. I asked her what she meant by rich.

"I call people rich when they're able to meet the requirements of their imagination," she said with a sly smile.

"Well you can be true to your art and still be fairly well off. Look at Toni Morrison, or Wynton Marsalis. Of course, when you've got an imagination like Morrison's I'm not sure it's even possible to meet its requirements."

My own imagination went into overdrive while we rode back into the city. Emerald smiled when I told her I'd brought along a couple of my stories. "Good," she said. "You can come back to my place and read them to me. I'll make us some tea."

It was a small leap from tea for two to a cottage by the sea, as far as I was concerned. So fierce was my fever that I envisioned connubial bliss—even though I'd yet to snare even a cuddle or a kiss. In my Walter Mitty world this woman was going to have my children; in reality, though, we'd only exchanged a brief hug. My fanciful musing had lost itself in her promising possibilities so often that I'd become convinced I already knew the taste of her succulent lips, the versatility of her tongue.

I sat on a stool and watched Emerald move around in her kitchen. She turned on some Stevie Wonder and put the teakettle on the stove. We were talking about acting on impulse. "My brother says I'm too patient," I said. "He said I analyze and think it over and reexamine things until the opportunity is lost. He says I should just obey my instincts."

"Jeff, can you get that box of tea for me? It's on a high shelf."

I joined Emerald near the stove. I reached up, grabbed the box and handed it to her.

In the background, Stevie read my mind.

Your body moves with grace in song

"Thanks. I'm all about instincts myself," she said, turning to face me. The space between us seemed to shrink. I imagined I could feel her breasts just barely brushing my chest. Or maybe I wasn't imagining it at all. "But you have to give them time," she continued, "make sure it's really your instincts and not your body forcing wishes on your brain."

Now I'd always been one of those guys who liked to make love with all the lights blazing. In college, my girlfriend LaMonica was always tossing a towel over the lampshade in her dorm room, leaving me half-distracted with thoughts of sudden, terrible fires sneaking up and frying us to a fare-thee-well while we thrashed on her narrow twin mattress. To her chagrin, I liked to see everything that was going on. For me that's always been half the pleasure, and that's why I delayed kissing Emerald when her lips were so tantalizingly near. I had to savor the moment, eat her up with my eyeballs for just a few more seconds. But her teakettle reached its boiling point, shrieking shrilly as vapor shot out its round spout.

Emerald turned away to make our tea. The moment was lost. Fuck!

"Hmm?" Emerald looked at me.

My god. Had I said that out loud? "What?"

"I said do you want honey or sugar?"

She'd asked me a question and I hadn't even heard her. Stay cool. You don't want this woman to think you're a weirdo. "Whatever you're having," I said.

Before I knew it I was across the room and pulling her close. "Actually," I said, "I want sugar. Sugar's what I wan—"

I knew her lips would be so warm and inviting. Her tongue tasted sweet as we hungrily explored each other's mouths. Our hands kept pace, pulling at the clothing between us, fingers rushing under elastic and fabric to get at the hot flesh beneath. We kissed and rubbed and finally came up for air.

"Still want that tea?" She flashed me a breathless smile.

"Nope," I gasped.

"Neither do I."

She led me to her bedroom. I walked behind her, admiring the mesmerizing wobble of that wondrous onion. When we got there, I put my arms around her neck and dived for her mouth. Her lips were even quicker than mine, and oh so eager. She sucked at my tongue and I gobbled at her ravenously. We both would have moaned if there had been room for sound to escape, but there was none. Finally I tore my mouth from hers and licked my way to the soft hollow of her throat. I gently bit her as she urgently rubbed the back of my head. I dipped my mouth lower, toward the ripe swell of her cleavag[...] away and stepped back. I sat on the bed, g[...] behind her and unhooked her bra. She w[...] pulled it through the top of her dress. Toss[...] advanced. I was ready for her. I slid my[...] haunches, bringing the edge of her dress u[...] forward and kissed her thigh. Emerald giggled and pulled me to my feet.

"Put your hands on me," she hissed, "through my dress." She raised her arms and folded her hands atop her head. The dress clung to her as if it were wet. Her nipples poked through the tie-dyed patterns. I couldn't resist reaching out to pinch them, but Emerald shook her head. "Uh-uh. Rub me," she instructed. "All up and down."

"Happy to," I think I said. Speech and thought were running together into one delirious haze as I stroked her from her breasts to her knees, feeling her warm, responsive flesh through the thin fabric. I let my hands linger in the lush place between her legs, summoning the moistness there. I ran my palms along the length of her smooth flanks, caressed the sensuous curves of her hips. Emerald sighed and turned around. She wiggled while I rubbed and squeezed her ass, slowly undulating to a tune only she could hear. Once again she turned, and I sat down. I licked my lips while she gracefully shucked the dress and stepped toward me like a vision from a dream, the dress a puddle of color at her feet.

We stretched out on the bed. This time when I went for her breasts she just smiled and held me close. She made encouraging noises while I licked one nipple then the other, before sucking each for a long time. They were tastier than tea and hotter too. My fingers slid slowly down Emerald's sweaty torso to her slick center, dipping, plunging, and rubbing until she shouted and lifted her ass off the bed, clamping my hand between her thighs. She yanked my head and kissed me hard, even harder than before. When she pulled back we were both panting. "Get naked," she said.

That's the kind of thing you only have to tell a brother once. Looking back, I'm amazed I had the presence of mind to remove my shoes and socks before taking off my jeans. I managed

all without taking my eyes off of her. I was afraid that
...ng away for a moment would somehow shatter the fantasy,
...at I'd turn again toward her and find myself back in my own
bed, cold and alone. But soon I was naked and she was still there:
nubile, perfect, and smiling slyly at me. My penis was swollen
and alert. She pointed at it and winked. "Hey," she said. "Bring
that here."

Every brother has a nickname for his thang, and yours truly is
no exception. I call him *Umkhonto we Sizwe*, which is a South
African expression meaning "spear of the nation." Sometimes I
just call him *Umkhonto*. Go on and laugh if you want to but it
sure beats the hell out of "Dick" or "Johnson." I obeyed Emerald's siren call, letting Umkhonto lead me like a divining rod
straight to the source of exquisite pleasure. When she wrapped
her fingers around me and used her tongue to tease my sensitive
tip I could only grunt with gratitude. Soon she was pulling me
on top of her. Mercy.

I'm superstitious about euphoria, have been all my life. I
avoid giving in to sheer, uninhibited happiness, thinking that
such bold release invites malice from the gods. Still, I felt ecstasy's sensitive fingers enveloping me in their seductive grip. I
suspected—hoped—that the same joyful sensations were stirring
Emerald's soul.

She expertly slid a condom onto me and guided me inside
her. It was my turn to tease. I slowed my entry, pulled back until
I was only about a third of the way in, then began to rotate my
hips. Emerald caught my rhythm and began to grind against me.
I pulled farther back, until I was barely inside her, still rotating
my hips. Emerald murmured soft protests but continued to
grind. I slammed my hips forward, shoving myself deep inside
her. Emerald grunted and smiled but I drew back once more,
torturing her with just the tip. Emerald was moaning loudly
now, the center of her a wild vibrating tunnel of tightness as I
slowly leaned forward, inch by mesmerizing inch. Umkhonto
felt like he was lowering himself into hot butter. As soon as I was
all the way inside her, Emerald clamped her legs around me and
dug into me with her heels.

"Just ride," she ordered. Her eyes were rolled back in her

head, and she was whipping her dreads from side to side. "Just ride. Ride. Ride. Ride ride rideride . . ."

And our motion became an oceanic thing, full of crests and ebbs, boiling currents and whirling suction. I was hot, wet, nearly drunk as we rolled together through wave after wave. Mercy. Double mercy, God. God. God. This is too good. I may die, I just may die. Yes, Lord, calling me home through this circle of heat. Mercy. Mercy . . .

Emerald yelled her pleasure, rising to match the urgency and volume of another voice, one that deep in my delirium I recognized as my own. Finally I could stand that sticky ecstasy no longer. I fell, through a net of fire into a pool of honey.

And returned to awareness on Emerald's damp sheets. We held each other. "You okay?" Her voice was soft.

"Yeah. Why do you ask?"

"You sounded so intense," she said. "Almost like you were praying."

I'd first seen Emerald at Right Mind Books. I stared at her while she watched the speaker, an ex-convict who'd written an unapologetic memoir about his days as a thug and rapist. She was stunning, I thought, but perhaps unapproachable. She looked so haughty as she glared her disapproval at the strutting author. I wondered if disdain was the only form of passion she knew. And now here she was, expertly rolling my penis between her skillful palms. Then she pumped me, moving her fist with just the right degree of pace and pressure, and I quickly stiffened in her grip. We began to kiss again, devouring each other until we were right back where we began.

She rolled over on her belly and tucked her knees under. I slid into her from behind and we rocked together slowly, feeling the warmth spread from our locked loins until the heat became too much to handle. The fever we felt urged us into overdrive and we pushed and panted until we both bubbled over.

I slept until morning. I awoke, threw on my boxers and wandered into the living room. Emerald was relaxing on her couch. She was still naked, and lovely enough to make me want to weep with joy. She was sitting with one leg tucked under her. The other was folded so that she could rest her chin on her knee.

When I finally tore my eyes from her smooth haunches, I saw that she was reading one of my stories.

I went to her kitchen and made us both some red zinger. I returned with two steaming mugs as she was turning the last page. She smiled when she saw me.

"You should think about adapting this for the stage," she said. "The dialogue's kicking."

"You liked it?" I tried not to sound too eager. I suddenly realized how important it was for Emerald to take my work seriously. I didn't want her to think I was like so many of those other brothers who haunted the scene, hanging out at open mikes and readings and pretending to be writers but really just scoping for pussy.

"It's appealing," she said. "In a peculiar sort of way. You're an intriguing writer, Jefferson Spann."

I tried to exhale as subtly as possible. My relief, however, was short-lived. What if she was jiving me? And "intriguing"? What did she mean by that?

"What do you mean by 'intriguing'?" I took another deep breath.

"I mean I liked it, Jeff." She smiled. "Now don't you think you should let a little air in before you pass out?"

"Very funny."

"It's a good story," Emerald said. "But to tell you the truth, I'm sort of in the mood for poetry." She leaned over and inserted her fingers into the fly front of my boxers.

"Poetry? Is that what they call it where you're from?"

"Maybe," Emerald replied.

There's this spot on my ear. A very sensitive centimeter of skin that causes instant insanity upon contact with a woman. I'm not sure of its exact location but I know it's there. LaMonica used to blow gently on that spot just to watch my nature rise. In desperate moments I'd try to find it myself, staring wild-eyed into a handheld mirror while nearly poking out my eardrum. It was never any use though.

Pulling me next to her and straddling my lap, Emerald extended a single, meaningful finger and found my spot. She stroked it and smiled.

"How's that feel," she cooed.

I swallowed. "Really hits the spot," I said.

"I want some poetry," Emerald purred.

"Okay. How about some Eugene Redmond?"

"That'll work." She licked my ear, right where her finger had lingered. Emboldened, I pressed my face into her breasts.

"My tongue paints a path of fire," I mumbled into her flesh.

"Across her body
My tongue trickles unseen
And indelible tracks
Through the center of her metropolis—
As a flameless torch,
I burn beyond the color
Of heat into infinite fire . . ."

Emerald moaned and locked her fingers behind my head. She pulled me against her skin.

"Oh yeah," she sighed.

". . . Where her passion
Is one long sigh of molten air
That my tongue
Banks to a burnsong:
Against the anvil of her geography:
That my tongue rings—
Where my tongue plunges plunges
Into the waters of her country—
Into the ravines,
The crops,
Of her forests."

I licked a slick trail down the center of Emerald's torso.

"Umm," she panted. "What's that from?"

"It's called 'My Tongue Paints a Path.' "

Emerald offered a nipple to my lips. "That was hot," she said. "And so am I."

"Um-hmm," I said. My mouth was full.

"My turn?"

"Um-hmm."

"I feel like a little Gwendolyn Brooks. Does that sound good?"

"Um-hmm."

Emerald found my hardness, placed it at the entrance to her moist center. Sliding down slowly, deliciously, she leaned forward and whispered warmly in my ear.

"You know that poem where she compares a woman's body to a honey bowl? I'm like that woman. My honey is deep . . . and hot . . ."

A few weeks between the sheets with an armful of warm woman can do amazing things to your confidence. Getting a story accepted by *Collard Greens*, a literary journal I'd been trying to get into for years, also put a bit of pride in my stride. I was learning to trust my instincts, so when they suggested I pay an unannounced visit to my beloved's lair I didn't hesitate for a minute. I tucked my acceptance letter into my coat pocket and hit the streets.

"It's Jefferson Spann, your lover man," I purred in my best Barry White bass as I pressed the intercom button in the lobby of her building. Emerald seemed genuinely delighted when I showed up at her door. It was the first time I had come by without calling or being invited.

"I've got something to show you," I said, trying to sound mysterious.

"That's cool," she said, bearing a strange expression. She looked like she'd suddenly seized a brilliant idea. "But I've got something to show you too. Mind if I go first?"

"Not at all." Now she was the mysterious one.

She directed me to a chair in her bedroom. It faced a four-panel room divider, which on this side was covered with four full-length mirrors. I sat while she fiddled around in her bathroom. "What do you have to show me?"

"Oh, some shoes. Jeff, can you turn on the stereo for me? Just push play."

I did as I was asked and returned to my chair as Percy Sledge began to sing.

"Shoes? What kind of shoes?"

"High heels."

"Really? And all this time I had you pegged for a Birkenstock woman."

Emerald giggled. "Silly man. It's going to take more than a couple of months to figure me out."

The buttery strains of Sledge's "Warm and Tender Love" rose up and floated around the room. Emerald's voice interrupted his Southern-flavored soul.

"Do you like?"

The shoes were see-through, like glass slippers. I suppose they were lovely enough but I hardly noticed them. Aside from those elegant pumps, Emerald was wearing a black pillbox hat, a thin strand of black beads, a pair of long black gloves and, aside from a light application of baby oil, nothing else. And she expected me to comment on her footwear?

"Excellent," I gasped.

"Not too simple?" She acted like she was fully clothed.

"No, no, just right," I assured her.

Emerald turned her back to me and swayed sensuously to the rhythm of Sledge's serenade, one hand atop her hat, the other spread out in the center of her belly. The mirror afforded me multiple perspectives: in front of me her buttocks flexed and swung hypnotically; in the luminous sheen of the looking glass her breasts shook like ripe mangoes in an island breeze. She turned and moved toward me, and though she was smiling right at me she seemed lost in a dream of her own. Afraid of ruining the spell, I said nothing.

I stayed silent even when she placed one foot solidly on my chair, between my spread thighs. I leaned forward and buried my face in her glistening crotch, inhaling deeply, as if I could absorb her completely just by drawing in her scent. Emerald dropped to her knees and unzipped my pants. The tight round ring of her confident lips made my toes curl. I moaned. Through half-closed eyes I spied quadruple images of my great good fortune, Emerald's bobbing dreads, the taper-tipped heels of her tucked-under pumps, the delectable spread of her glistening ass.

She looked up from her licking. "Ooh, you're getting wet," she observed. "Better put on your raincoat."

I struggled out of my pants and into a condom before joining her on the floor. Our sex was loud and uninhibited, an exhausting, exhilarating thrash of limbs, tongues, and lungs. Our bellowing drowned out both Percy Sledge and the numerous noises of the outside night. I stayed inside her long after my passion had subsided, clinging to her and soaking in her sweat-slicked softness. Finally I rolled over onto my back, sinking into the sweet comfort of a well-earned slumber. Or so I thought.

A series of short, sharp nips on my neck and shoulder blades jarred me into open-eyed awareness.

Emerald asked me what I thought I was doing.

I smiled at her. "Just trying to catch a few z's," I said.

"Not a chance," she replied as she climbed on top of me. "It ain't over yet. Your work's just begun."

I reached for her breasts. "I could get used to this," I said.

"And you will," she said, licking her lips. "If you know what's good for you."

LEONE ROSS

Drag

TODAY I feel like a drag queen. Walking down Soho way through the tourists and the catcalls. My crotch is aching under the good jeans and the bad underwear, watching the freaks go by, acres of eyeliner and jangly earrings and crap T-shirts that pass for fashion, walking and making sure my hips sway in calypso circles.

Today I feel like a drag queen. The top layer of me is a bouncin' an' behavin' woman; I'm all rounded tits and a belly button so deep you could play strip poker inside it. But underneath that I feel like a boy. Eighteen years old, slim hips, shoulders so strong I could carry the world, baby-soft face and mascara eyes. The boy in me lengthens my stride and gives me attitude. He looks out from under my eyelashes. I'm working it. I'm being seen. I'm shimmying.

"The only thing I want to drink more than beer tonight is you."

I look up. He's not my type. His head would bang into doorways. We couldn't dance; I'd be stuck just above his navel. I don't like licorice-flavored men. But today the boy inside me needs a fuck. From any body.

He's leaning against a porn shop; I can see those plastic ribbon thingies that they insist you pass through, like a time machine— no, like a seedy entrance to a boudoir. I think that his face is open, that it reminds me of a child's. He is even yummy, with a second glance.

I look at him. Grin.

"Going inside?" I say.

"No." He laughs.

"Come inside with me," I say.

We wander around the interior. It's dark and silly and small waves of embarrassed men part before us. They try to pretend that none of us are there. I pick up the worst of the porn, speak loudly, point out come shots and women dressed as little girls; I even find a puzzled, swollen donkey. We discuss measurements at the tops of our voices, pretending to be serious. Men begin to leave. The proprietor looks indignant. I turn more pages and laugh in my boy's face. Watch our arms, side by side, both bruise colored. His lips thrust through graceful stubble.

"What's your name?" he says.

"Jo," I reply.

He looks amused. As if he knows.

"Joanna? Josephine?"

"Just Jo, call me Jo," I say.

"I'm Jason," he says. I like the way he says his name. Like it fits him; like he's new. Like he's the only Jason in the world. The proprietor grimaces and rolls his eyes. We are nearly alone in the shop. The last man is trying not to look me in the face as he wriggles past us. He wants to fuck me, but he doesn't want me to see that. Jason moves to let him go by; I love that he does not try to protect me from the lust in the man. He stands next to me, trusting me in my own space, like I'm his equal. Like I'm strong.

Back at my flat he lays me across my bed, in between pages of my thesis. I am writing about black people in British ads. Like, how there are none. He doesn't care. The head of his dick is swollen and purple-red. He is watching me closely. I tighten the muscles in my stomach, flex my shoulders. I want my body to feel like concrete when he touches me. I run my hands along my thighs, pretending the hair there is pepper-grains. I'm holding the bunch of roses he bought me in Leicester Square. Tight. A thorn sticks through my flesh and I can feel a tiny bead of blood on my palm.

Jason crouches over me, pulls the roses away slowly. Then he is ripping them apart and scattering petals, stalks, thorns, across my breasts.

"Tell me how you want me to be," he pants.

"Fuck me like I'm a boy," I say.

He puts a thumb up my cunt, parting the folds. It is a small sword through honey. I twist away, annoyed. "No," I say. My voice is shaking, I want him to understand so bad, but I don't want to talk. "Like you're fucking yourself."

He's lying on top of me, his cock rubbing against my tummy. It's wet there. He rubs himself across me, hipbone to hipbone. He's running a bass line through me, I can feel it everywhere, in my wrists, making my mouth reverberate. He licks the blood off my palm, thoughtfully.

"That's hardly safe," I say.

"So?" he says, and flips me over. My clit's rubbing against the white duvet and I can feel it growing, swelling, tumescent, hard against my belly. He's spitting on his fingers, rubbing them up and down my asshole. His breath is lost in my hair. He pauses against the entrance, like there's a stop sign. Like he needs permission just one more time.

"Go on," I say. I've never done this before and it needs to be now. *"Go on."*

He pushes gently. The head slips in. Agony. I twist, trying to accommodate.

"Oh fuck," he groans against my ear.

I feel like a girl, about to be taken; I fight against the femininity. I don't want it, not today. I want the abandonment, the urgency of a boy, but it's no good. I'm afraid. Straining, anxious, I push myself onto my elbows. He's still being tentative, he's halfway in, but my body is groaning, rejecting it. He is sliding into a tube of sandpaper. My whole body is shaking, my head is shaking. I can't be a boy this way. A million pins dance the length of my ass. I hear myself calling for time-out.

"Jason, let's stop—"

He ignores me, thrusts a hand underneath us, begins to play with my clit, twisting, insistent, rubbing me in hard circles. I love the weight of him on top of me. I am pinned in a slow-moving dream.

"No . . ." I say, but it's working. I can feel my ass melting, widening, moisture seeping out of chocolate walls.

"Your name is Jason." He whispers it against my hair. "You're up against a wall. It's Carnival, and you're up against a brick wall, and I'm fucking you in the ass. Your cock is rubbing against the wall. You're so hard. We met five minutes ago, and I rubbed the muscles in your arms—"

He's all the way inside me, a metal bar against my ass cheeks, the heel of his hand grinding into my clit, and nothing hurts anymore. I can hear myself. I'm growling and I can hear the soca in the distance and when I look up I can see shocked grannies, amused revelers. I can see a policeman cocking his head to the side: *Are they really doing that?* He starts up the street, and I can see him, ready to arrest two queer niggers.

"—I rubbed the muscles in your arms and now I'm all the way up your ass. Your name is Jason—"

I have no breasts. My chest is flat. I shift, undulate; I've become a smooth runway that pours from the base of my arched neck, down my shoulder blades, spreads around my hips, pushes my ass up, into him. I'm an oiled machine, gleaming with afternoon sweat. Jason takes a breath, pulls halfway out, plunges into me, savage, uncompromising, his hand a blur.

I howl. Delicious.

Afterward, he knows how to be. I tell him my full, girl name.

Today I feel like an executive. My hair is scraped off my face and the makeup is effortless. Walking into a classy restaurant, the London sun streaming through the French windows, melting the clientele like individual ice cream cakes. I'm in a black suit and underneath the lingerie is apricot. My heels are sensible. Before I leave the office my boss tells me to use everything I've got. He winks. Everything. He thinks he's a feminist. But he is not above pimping me out.

Today I feel like an executive. Facts and figures flow from my fingertips. My voice is controlled and assertive. But underneath is so much more: an ambitious twenty-five-year-old who lies in the bath and dreams of power. Rubber duck in the bath tells me that I should have a flat on the Riviera, a penthouse in New York. Bubbles promise me a walk-in closet of designer clothes, three personal assistants, and gleaming, expensive technology. I am a multimillion-dollar deal.

"Josephine . . ." I love his voice. I look up. He's in a sharp suit, dark. Women's heads swivel. I think: blond bitches, and hold on to my glass of water tightly. He scoops condensation from the edge and rubs it between his fingers. Back and forth. I can't stop looking. I remember his hands on me and shiver in the heat.

"Long time no see," I say.

"So?" he says. Climbs right in next to me.

"You can't stay," I say. My thighs are humming. "I have an important client coming . . ."

He stays. He introduces himself as my colleague when the client arrives. The client orders tea and discusses cost-effectiveness, the implications of visual versus voice-over, whether we need a celebrity or normal actresses; tells me that there are other ad companies waiting in line. I nod and sound intelligent. Jason puts his hand up my skirt. My knees snap together instinctively. He is cupping me, like I'm a small, precious thing. I can smell myself across this sophisticated room: pussy mixed with golden marigolds at the windowsill.

He uses one, long, insistent finger. Rubs just above my clitoris. I try to edge him nearer the brink of me. Inside I'm an empty roll of wet muscles; I could play him like a flute, if only we were far from here. His finger is still stroking the hair, just the hair. I wonder if the teasing is on purpose. Suck in my breath as he hits the mark, just to show off. Back to the top. Then down again. Light circles. I try to slow my breathing.

"You see, we think that speaking to women in their own language will knock the socks off the competition," says the client. A single crumb sits on his neat moustache. I want to lick it off. I want to grab his head and push it between my breasts and scream. I want them both to fuck me across the table.

". . . perhaps animation . . ." says the client.

"Mmm-hmmm," I say.

Jason's finger eases inside me, taking all the daylight in the room with it. I am sitting in a pool of summer. He puts a thumb back on my clit and it jumps up like it's Christmas. I push my hips forward, they're doing circles. Tight, wide, urgent. Jason's skin is boiling.

"Could you, um, order some coffee?" I say to the client.

He turns and signals for the waitress. Jason pulls his hand out of me and licks his fingers. One. Two. Three. I hide a groan in my napkin. The client smiles at me, clueless. I smile back. Jason asks him a question. I can't hear him. I am literally deaf. The client leans forward. Jason leans towards him, his fingers back, twiddling me. I sip scalding coffee. Burn my tongue. Put my hand on top of Jason's hand. Press him into me. My eyes are begging.

"Harder . . ." I say.

"Pardon?" says the client.

"It must be hard to . . . deal with established competitors. It must get harder every day. Harder and *harder*."

"Ah," says the client.

I want to close my eyes. I can feel my orgasm tickling the base of my spine but I'm talking and talking and the words are scrabble squares on a board, meaningless, but full of potential. I want to lean back in my chair. Tell them both that one day I will be able to buy them with a flick of my well-manicured fingers. Jason puts his hand on my inner thigh, pushes my legs as wide as they can go. Grasps my panties and pushes them roughly aside. I can hear a rip. He pushes something small and cold up me. I bite my lip and my hand on the table goes into involuntary spasm. He makes me touch myself with the other one. He bites his bottom lip as our entwined fingers touch two tiny balls. They feel as if they should be silver. We stir them around, coaxing juice out of me. My hand is frothy. They tinkle, I am sure. The client is talking. Jason leans into my shoulder.

"Pussy music," he whispers.

My hips begin to buck. I'm beyond speech. All I can do is nod, and the waves are getting more intense. My breasts are spilling out of my bra, they're so swollen. I'm breathing through my nose and yes, he's giving me what I want, he's rubbing my clit the way I like it, hard and God, so dirty, and the balls are revolving, tinkling, pulling it all out of me. I surrender, lean forward into the tablecloth.

"Are you alright?" The men chorus it above me. The client is calling, "Waitress, waitress, she's having a fit"; everybody around me is looking afraid and concerned: *Is she choking, someone do the Heimlich on her ass* and Jason is all the way up in my face, one arm round my shoulder, "Jo, you okay, hush baby, hush," but there's a fierce twinkle in his eye and his whole body is saying, Be quick, Josephine, be cost-effective, exert your power, come for me, before the place erupts, I'm going to have to take my hand away COME FOR ME. And then I'm screaming; I can't believe that I'm letting my body jerk all over this posh restaurant, but there's something so powerful about it all. I'm coming *in their faces* and nobody knows, my nails are scraping the tablecloth and someone cries out as the coffee cup shatters on the floor and I'm trying not to laugh, my cute little ass still jerking, you know those slow-wave, post-come jerks that feel like aftershocks and I've put my fingernails through the flesh between Jason's neck and his shoulder and I can tell it really hurts him, but he's trying not to laugh too and even as the waitress rushes over Jason coaxes another little one, just a tiny, baby orgasm out of me, 'cause he's greedy like that, and then it's done and he's wiping his hand free of pussy juice, wiping it all over his face and his pretty-man cheekbones and I'm like fuck, fuck, I want to laugh, that's all I feel like doing: laughing.

So I do. Delicious.

Afterward the client calls to make sure I'm all right. We get the deal. Pussy power.

Today I feel like a bride. Walking through the special room set aside for me in the back of the church. All Vera Wang class; if I could blush I'd be blushing in the mirror. There is one hour to go. My bridesmaids, all ten of them, have floated away, leaving "me time." I do not know where they came from. None of them are my friends.

My dress has cost eight thousand pounds. Microscopic pearls are almost invisible at the hemline, the bodice. Diamonds snigger in my ear and make promises. The dress reminds me of Victoria Falls, in Zimbabwe at sunset, a huge flow of everything white in the world: roaring snowflakes, pools of chalk dust, bleached frost.

Today I feel like a bride. Fragrant. I am every love song ever played. I am pink confetti. I am the wedding march personified. I am God's best promise, an open sack, waiting to be filled with matrimonially blessed seed. I am Hope. But underneath I am a thirty-nine-year-old woman who is slipping, gratefully, off the shelf. A wedding cake, blind drunk with rum. I am the solemn, desperate hopes of my mother. I have lost my way. I have no choice.

"You're beautiful." I look up. I don't know how he got in. Gray hair fondles his temples.

"Thank you," I say.

"So . . ." Jason says. He sits down at my feet, cross-legged. I can barely see him over the lace.

"What?" I say. "What do you want?"

He shakes his head. Gets up without using his hands, so graceful. Then he is back, with a sky blue bowl. I can smell the lotion: my grandmother's kitchen.

"What is it?" I say.

"I made it," he says.

He takes one perfect shoe off my foot. His hands are warm in the autumn breeze dancing through the church cracks. His palms are tender, and my body is already sweeter than it was before, like someone dropped sugar cane into my heart, pumped it a thousand miles a minute through my bloodstream. He draws patterns on my soles, my ankles, my thighs, pushing up through miles of dress. I sit down, legs akimbo, my back against the wall. I am whimpering as he runs his soft tongue through the hair down there, plaiting me, dipping his mouth into me. Drinking me. His moistened hands have slipped under the dress's bodice, and my breasts feel young again. Perky, coffee-colored beginnings. My nipples are tiny silver balls.

He is rubbing his magic lotion into my crotch, pouring it across my thighs. It is slick and drips off my soft belly, puddles and sinks into eight thousand pounds' worth of promises. He parts the lips of my pussy, as if in prayer. I watch him rubbing warm lotion over his cock, one hand on my hip. Then there are careful inches, pushing inside me.

I groan.

Oh, I groan.

We have never made love before. I wonder why as I gather him into me. I wonder why, because this is a symphony of scent and breath, high notes of lemon and the pure sob of cinnamon and the darkness of cloves. I wonder why as I say his name, over and over, like I'm hushing a baby. It is almost too good.

He watches me writhe as he fucks me. His hand dives between our bodies. I listen to the old, familiar sound of him rubbing me. His eyes are kind as I gasp and drum my fists against his back.

"So this is what you feel like . . ." he says. He is trying to be cool, but his voice is too shaky. I smile, my eyes closed.

"Does it feel good?" I want him to feel good.

"Oh yes," he says, and pushes his hips forward once more. His penis is kissing me, tiny wet kisses along the length of me, so certain. He looks into my face. One finger, delicate, gathers the tear on my cheek.

"Who am I?" I say.

Jason pushes into me and reminds me who I am. He tears off one pearl and fucks me juicy. He tears another and fucks me deep. I join him, fingernails sliding through cloth and lace. The dress disintegrates, baring me dark and sticky against the church floor. I am throwing pearls across the room. We sound like animals being loved, coughing primal sounds over our lips and down our thrashing bodies. My hands are digging into his ass, pushing him further in. I have a finger inside him where it's hot and secret, guiding him, showing him how to move, how to please me. He is whining, but through it all: Who are you, who are you, who are you he's saying and I'm a drag queen, eighteen years old, trying a little something-something with the new beat of my clit; I'm a twenty-five-year-old executive even though I never made a million; I'm years of expectations; I'm a cop-out, thinking I needed to be Cinderella 'cause God knows my mother needs grandchildren. I'm a fuck, I'm a friend, yeah I remember who they are. I'm enough, I'm enough, I'm just right.

Birds whistle at the window as we swirl into orgasm.

Afterward, I leave him in a pile. Run down the aisle, cupping what's left of Vera Wang to my tits, the wedding party's mouths all O's of shock, but I can see delight in the ones who are glad. Out into the shuddering light of an autumn afternoon. I hail a cab. Kick my bare feet up on the glass between me and the cab man. Delicious.

"Drive," I say.

TONY MEDINA

Random Acts of Violins

PREMISE

A COUPLE in a room furnished with two beds. She on one bed, he on the other, as if on separate islands. They are both naked, passing a blunt to each other, pretending to be other people. They speak to each other occasionally by cell phone or written and verbal correspondence. She reads him entries from her diary, as he composes dreams to her in his sleep.

She was tall.
He was short.
When they went to kiss his lips smacked into her breasts.
She smacked the shit out of him.
That's how they fell in love.

That night they rode the F train into a cliché. She said, I always fantasized about doing it on a train. With a lot of people packed in like sardines. Uhm, yeah, she said, licking her lips. They tried to do some midnight maneuvers, but the futon was like a brick wall with lumps. Woke up like the Elephant Man, all twisted and gnarled, hungover-like.

She loved waking up to his body slouched over the side of the bed. The morning sun lighting up the room, his presence filling it, making her feel somewhat secure.

She watched him as he slept. His body rising and falling with each violent wheeze. He breathed through his nose, and every so often would inhale long and wide enough to suck back the entire room, nightstand, dresser, closet, TV, antennae and all.

A tape recorder sat on a stand near the bed, taking it all in.

He took full advantage of his asthma. He used what he recorded during his sleep at night to lay under the beats he mixed by day. Between his wheezes he would make his music.

That's what she likes about him.
His ingenuity.

He made a rap song of monosyllabic stutters. Blew up overnight. Thought his shit was the shit. Eventually, as the cliché goes, he ended up behind bars; something ridiculous and petty. Was hounded by the paparazzi. Dogged by the press. "Player haters," he said.

AT THE TIMBALE NATIONAL CEMETERY

He lived on a rough block too. His block was an endless parade of despair. He lived above an alley where winos and junkies and the homeless met with relative hostility rats and roaches and back alley cats joining together to turn old garbage can lids into new timbals. And they banged them up pretty regularly, fucking up somebody's high. With that kind of racket you could barely keep an erection, let alone hold up a thigh. Nothing ever came of those first few fast furious dry humps. When they rolled through like George Clinton and Earth, Wind & Fire wrestling and breaking and battling the Commodores and Kool and the Gang, it was like a New Orleans cemetery above sea level and out in the open where timbals buried despair. He called it the

Timbal National Cemetery. At the Timbal National Cemetery shit came to life. In the alley beneath his window, garbage cans made a silly music of their own, as stray cats fought and fucked on a wino's face.

He lived somewhere up in there,
                                    trying to turn her bed into a stage.
Enter Gludiola Maximola

Gludiola Maximola was thin but thick at specific ends of her spectrum.

She had too much ham for two eggs. Thick rumbidy rumbidy ass the way it rattles along the avenue up the stairs imprisoned suffocating in tight strangulation jeans wishin' your face was them panties that clearly need a rest, two bongos where the pockets used to be, rise and fall rise and fall, smooth palm music for my heart paralyzed and gulp make my eyes do the dizzy dance and my mind back flips as my pants and my zipper yodel with each violent arrogant shake.

The stage couldn't help itself. It couldn't hold her up holding up all that ass.

Her gyrations were a cottage industry. I wanted to ride the freight train to the anthills of her savannah.

She not only stripped for a living, she catered, had a go-for and messenger service, worked out of her crib, using her car, had a computer, E-mail, Web site, cell phone, fax, and beeper. And sold weed on the side, every chance she got.

What did she look like, you might ask?
Let's just say:
                Well . . .

She had big ghetto stompers on, a roach's worst nightmare, and hair that looked like a flare with epilepsy, frozen in the sky. The brick-laid space between the second floor window and the entranceway door had to be plowed away to let her big hair through. It took twelve hours to set her hair in place; the Christmas lights alone took up half the afternoon. After the haircut it took a team of engineers to push the broom. At night on the street the sparkles in her hair directed traffic. Her butt stopped it as her kicks clopped through the streets holding ant farms in the heels. The next day the hairdressers called in sick because they didn't get paid overtime. While the hospitals were full with the accidents she made with her stockings rubbing together, setting off sparks and attracting flies. Her hair brought down telephone poles; her heels cracked open like eggshells when she tried to tap-dance down the avenue and a double-decker tourist bus going through the safari of Harlem mowed her down, letting out an army of ants carrying her off to Bellevue.

***

It was a nice spring day in November. You know the kind only New York could have. Daylight slanting off buildings and cars. Fast and melancholy like jazz. You be in some dimly lit café, flirting. Rain outside. Not knowing what time it is. Not giving a fuck. Wanting to fuck instantaneous. Thinking about should you have a one-night stand, or something steady for the winter.

She was so good-looking she was a threat to humanity. She had "fuck me" on her face, in her attitude and dress. She was an around-the-way girl, or some middle-class chick pretending to be from the 'hood, stylin' out off what she saw in some rap video or some magazine. She could have easily been in some. But she hadn't. She was the real deal. The kind that makes your nuts crack, gettin' hard just thinking about her. Scared to call out her name, you get a dick stroke and die. She get to cursin' your ass out, head rollin' back and forth with attitude make your pores open up to sweat, thinking of her giving head with such ferocity. May bite your shit off, the light hit her ass just right.

We were at an art show where other artists made cameo appearances—commercial breaks—in the middle of the feature's show by holding up their paintings and pacing the room like Vegas showgirls in a boxing ring.

That's where I met her.

She wore a skirt so short that if she inhaled it'd be a bra.
If she took another breath, it'd be a bandanna.

Soon as the wine ran out, we jumped into a cab and got off at the first café we saw. Played some pool. Watched her put chalk on my stick. Crack my balls. Sink them in her pocket. On top of the pool table, her tender knees pressing against the velvet green tarp, she played with his balls as his stick kept driving to her hole.

BACK AT THE RANCH BLUNTED ON HOSTILITY . . .

—Don't feel guilty about killing me in my sleep.

—I could never do anything to hurt you.

—I know you've stood over me with a pillow in your hand wanting to smother me in my sleep.

—Don't say that.

—I know the feds paid you to take me out.

—When I was young I used to want someone who would dress me.

—Like a mortician?

She came over while the bubbly was cooling. My bed was nice and warm. So was my body as she brushed her goose pimples against my flat skin. The fine pimples along her ass raised up slight, pale red-brown hairs that swirled back into a thick black velvet forest. It was there he made his way through, whistling in her cave. Before he knew it he was swimming inside her, grabbing for a life raft.

BY NOW HE SENT THE FIRST MISSIVE . . .

In the dream we're fucking on a raft. I was on my back, at first, with her on top of me. The sun spanked my face as I squinted up to look at her. She had on my shirt, which was unbuttoned and draped across her pretty nipples. I remember how spectacular her smooth skin looked as my shirt opened up on her with the rhythm of the raft and wind against her humping. I held on to her shirttails for dear life, the water surrounding, as she twisted onto me slowly, methodically. There was a melody in her eyes, the way they rolled up inside her head as her lips swallowed me whole.

SHE ANSWERED BACK WITH . . .

Dear Diary,

I took a bubble bath for the first time in what seems like a really long while.

Maybe it was something I heard on *Oprah*, where someone was talking about taking time out for yourself. I never was one for pampering myself, but I do consider myself to be somewhat high maintenance, even though my current means of employment may make some people think I don't. I was always into girlie things like hair and nails, and clothes, of course. But spending an hour in a hot tub, uh-uh.

But this time I had to; I couldn't front. I was about to have a nervous breakdown. I mean, there I was workin' and all, and in walks the man of my dreams. I felt like such a fool, trying to hide my face and all, and here he comes like Billy Dee Williams or something with a bill in his hand and his phone number on it. I turned a few times, tried to play it off by moving back past the pole, but then he said it, just like in the movie, "Do you want my hand to fall off." To which I responded with a slow James Brown split along the bar. He took the bill and gently placed it in my garter. Then nodded and slightly smiled as he walked out the door past the bouncer.

When I got off the stage and into the dressing room, I noticed that he had slipped me a fifty-dollar bill wrapped tight around a business card. The card stated that he was a photographer. On the back he wrote: I'd really love to shoot you.

Shoot, I been meaning to have my portfolio done. So, with slight hesitation, and some coaxing from my girlfriends, I called a few days later.

HIM (after the sentence)

I want to lead the kind of life that you don't see any people for a hundred years, and you only communicate with cobwebs and dust.

HER (after the sin tense)

—Isn't it a nice spring day?

—I think it's a great day. I wish I would've stayed inside longer.

HIM

In the dream, you appear in my prison cell like an apparition. At first, I am startled by your presence, thinking you're a guard coming to fuck me up. But from the shadows you emerge, not carrying the usual cake with the file inside.

HER

Dear Diary,

It turned out that the photographer was a bust. I mean he had a camera and all, but that was his way of getting females to come by his crib. He couldn't get them naked any other way, without having to pay. I said, hell, we could've made an arrangement. You didn't have to go and get my hopes up and all. We could've worked something out.

*   *   *

LOOSE CANONS

He was on the toilet calling out to her to pass him the blunt. She grimaced as she approached the door. Ooh, she whined, wash your hands first, reluctantly passing him the blunt. He stood on the other side, wiping his ass with one hand, while sticking the other out, waiting for her handoff.

HE SAID:

I really don't appreciate you not worshiping me more.

She smiled and kept playing with her pussy.

He watched her stroking her hair. Two pretty lips opened slightly each time her fingertips stroked up toward her belly. He licked his lips in unison till he noticed his own breathing, his heart's racing pace, pounding inside his head.

She was a single mother who at times could be single-minded. A simple animal who just wanted her food and sex and fun whenever she wanted it. Most times he wasn't displeased with this arrangement or attitude. To him the pussy was delicious—and pretty. He couldn't get enough of it. If it was up to him he'd spend the rest of his life in there, bring a cot and a blanket, his reading glasses, some books and papers. He could spend the rest of his life dicking her down good, she was that nasty. But he had other shit on his mind. Impatient, he had a short attention span and wandering eyes. On top of that he was always horny.

You gotta take it to the mat, he said, passing her the roach.

Nah, I'm done, she said, lying back with her legs open.

The news from the TV was that the Knicks beat the Heat by one. She said, they're going to be smacked by Indiana. Reggie Miller is my man. He's gonna whip y'alls ass. He said, don't make me have to fuck you up in here. She said, that's a promise?

She loved double entendres and had a couple of innuendos up her sleeves as well, but she spared him the petty banter and started to give him head, right then and there.

Afterward she said she needed money. For what, he said. Pamprin, she said. Pamprin? Yes, I'm in pain.

HE SAID:

I don't particularly care about your pain.

LATER

I can't take all this violins, she said.
Violins? Fuck you talkin 'bout, violins?

She was a Black Russian wiff a lisp who came out West once the Wall came tumbling down. What I luff about this city is that I always feel like a refugee, she said.

But I can't take all this violins.

Before he could interrupt, his cell phone rang. Hello, he asked, as if he didn't know who it was.

What are you wearing? the voice on the other end asked.

An electric wave ran through his body, making his dick heave up out of his drawers like a shark onto shore.

Why don't you bring that over to my boat, she said. He couldn't take her accent and began to get even harder. He heard what sounded like swallowing and gurgling on the other end, and realized that she had begun to stick the cell phone slowly inside her. Her clit kept dialing 911, but the persistent punching sound made it hard for him to respond to her emergency, until she could no longer take it. Suddenly the phone went dead. She could no longer feel her antenna. He tried calling a few times to locate the phone but eventually had to go in and manually retrieve it with his forefingers and tongue.

This is the part I live for, he said.
Now, if we could just do this with a ball peen hammer . . .
***
When they left the café it was sprinkling out. He stuck out his tongue to catch some drops, and thought how lovely her clit tasted, her smell still on his face. They walked the street arm in arm, without an umbrella. When it began to pour they ran into a corner, and he took her standing up, a foot in each pocket, her lips and hands fumbling inside his jacket. He was feeling fierce and cocksure, her pussy juice having energized him. New pussy always made him ferociously horny; and she studied his smile to see how much he liked it. It was good, wasn't it, she said, keeping a close watch for his wandering eyes. Her eyes keeping vigil, as his skirted along the avenue at other shapes and sizes wrapped in jeans, skirts, and tights. He loved ass. Worshiped it. Couldn't live without it if his life depended on it. Ass was the first thing he saw. Then feet and hands, in that order. Didn't care too much for tits, though he'd rather have bite-size rather than those serious Kilimanjaros some sisters be luggin' around like furniture or weapons. One time he rode the train and two teenagers playing hooky walked through the car doors, grabbing their dicks, fiendin' for some pussy. One blurted out, I want some slim pussy. That phrase stayed with him, as he sat on the stationary train, contemplating the nature of his own lust.

—What are you thinking about?

—How tight you are.

—Not anymore. Not since that long-distance call.

—Ma Bell should've never charged you for that one.

—Luckily I had you to bail me out.
                    *   *   *

Let me sing you a song, he said.
Sing to me, she said.
He said:
    Okay, I'm gonna sing you
       a song:

Cho-cha	Than I	I really love
You mean more	can see	you so
to me	*Cho-cha*	Cho-cha

This time she was on her bed fully dressed. She lay on her stomach, one leg raised, dangling an open-toed white pump from her foot, a rock quarry of Prince CDs piled up around her, speaking on the phone to him in song titles.

I wanna be your lover do me baby like you've never done before rock hard in a funky place grind dead on it cindy c like 2 nigs united 4 west compton 'cause when 2 in love bob . . . ain't that a bitch superfunkycalifragisexy let annie christian jack u off around the world in a day irresistible bitch the most beautiful girl in the world hate u billy jack bitch do u lie under the cherry moon life can be so fine girls & boys new position I wonder you kiss mountains lemon crush scandalous trust sexuality controversy private joy purple rain erotic city let's go crazy darling nikki when doves cry take me with u baby I'm a star I would die 4 u beautiful one in the purple rain let's pretend we're married lady cab driver little red corvette free dance music sex romance automatic delirious international lover something in the water does not compute computer blue diamonds & pearls sex in the summer when the lights go down there is lonely curious child in this bed scream new world slave the human body face down sleep around style the love we make jam of the year soul sanctuary somebody's somebody courtin' time we gets up friend, lover, sister, mother/wife damned if I do I can't make u love me one kiss at a time get yo groove on right back here in my arms dreamin about u curious child the love we make the holy river emancipation sleep around joint 2 joint arranged, composed and performed by . . . old friends 4 sale old friends raspberry beret she's always in my hair why you wanna treat me so bad when we're dancing close and slow a love bizarre 4 the tears in your eyes the dance electric uptown sister party up it's gonna be lonely with you bambi . . . dirty mind all the critics love u in new york www.emale.cum it's on it's on it's on . . . if i was your girlfriend head starfish and coffee play in the sunshine dance on . . . beautiful ones . . . i wish u heaven future the electric chair the arms of orion . . . always smash the picture always every time

From her bed she faxed and E-mailed him her dreams. He no longer cared for her snatches. What he wanted was wet dreams. But she grew bored with his remote-control orgasms. She wanted more than just panting on the other end of the pillow, on the other end of the phone. She wanted serious touchtone service. She wanted him to direct-dial her.

THE TV BLURTED OUT:
                    Tonight on Investigative Reports
                    federal police track homicidal hobos

You think I'm a homicidal hobo, he asked her.
She laughed.
You think that's my goal in life? To be a homicidal hobo?
I have the capacity to be a homicidal hobo . . .

This time she stretched out with her ass sticking out from having one leg swung up over the other. A patch of hair springing out of the slight crack caught his attention. He tried to inhale her from where he was sitting, Indian-style, sucking on what was left of the blunt. "Don't you rock, don't you rock, my boat," came off the stereo. She batted her New Orleans eyes and said, with a slight girlie-girlie lilt, "You're so silly." Oh yeah, he said, his eyes looking up at her, his tongue on her thigh, making its way toward her ass. His fingers spread her open. Each palm pressed against her ass. His tongue darting around like a gun. He couldn't stop the trigger, she smelled and tasted so good. He loved the way her wet hairs felt on his tongue. She made his mouth water, wanting more and more. He lapped her up so heavy and deep, trying to swallow her butt-cheeks. He loved burying his face in her ass, rolling around in her juice. He wanted to carry her scent all over his skin. Smell her at any occasion, wherever he felt the urge, to think about her, his dick in his hand, eyes closed shut on a memory—real or imagined. Yeah, ride that shit, he said, digging his way through her tight hole, trying to stick her wet and open, so he could long-dick and stroke. Yeah, this is workin' out just right. See those legs up in the air. Two ankles in one palm. Those pretty feet. Her toes. Put the big one in your mouth. Watchin' your dick disappear in her red-hot bush. Yea-uh.

Pretending to be other people is exhausting, she said to herself, hugging a pillow. But it's not so bad, I guess, when that's all there is. I mean, the pay is low, but the beatings are worth it.

She rolled a small joint with the remnants of a dime bag. He noticed that she held it for a long time after lighting it. She caught him browbeating her and laughed, finally passing him the joint. Shit, I have to keep vigil on your ass, he said. Keep a close watch, for you smoke up all my shit.

They were listening to a top ten R&B song, "My Sweaty Balls," when the doorbell rang. It was the pizza delivery man. He was accosted at the door with "My sweaty balls, my sweaty balls, Girl, you make my balls sweat . . . why don't you sweat my balls" wrapped in a thick cloud of ganja smoke.

Why did he put her through that torture, he asked, talking about what was on the TV. A girl who hadn't seen her father in eighteen years has just developed cancer and wishes to see her father before she dies. She's on *Montel* wearing a wig and pleading to the cameras to bring her her father. Everyone is moved to tears, including Montel, and us, well us, I mean we, just kind of went along for the ride, and she's like tapping into our buzz.

Cut to a commercial and the bitch is talking about lotion—and she's white!

Do you believe what she's saying, he said. About their lotion having more Alpha . . .

No, I don't believe that bitch, she said. There are a lot other lotions out there that smell a whole lot better than that shit. That ho' is lyin'.

She curled up beside him, and he caressed her hesitantly, unconsciously keeping her at a distance. His dick is hard from the buzz. Kill that light, mamí, he said. I need to feel sequestered. But see, now you're writing, she said. Baby, I can see with the light off, he said. I'm an alley cat.

Montel went on in the background. The next woman was a former junkie and prostitute. She reached for his pants. She took a year unzipping his zipper. By the time she got it out he was on vacation. His shit flew south for the winter.

It was like he was wrestling an iguana. He had to throw her off him, make up an excuse. Whoa, what's up with that big corn on the cob on your toe. She stopped dead in her tracks and feverishly checked her foot. It's not a corn, it's a scar from a blister. Yeah? Must've been a big-ass blister—it's the size of a Buick!

See, and you still didn't take a shower, she said. I'm rebelling against water, he said. Since it rained all weekend.

They walked down the street as if they were in a movie or a painting; people looked like characters out of a book, surreal. She began with the manipulation process.

—You didn't get your sunflower seeds today.

—You mean: Let's go to the bodega so I can get a loosey because I reminded you of the sunflower seeds, and didn't suck my teeth, reminding you of the salt.

Across the street a guy walked by whose Afro was so huge it was parted by the wind. A pretty young woman with her little daughter walked by. A dude walked past her. What the fuck are you looking at, she said, sucking her teeth under her breath. My face ain't no movie screen.

See, lookit, she says, sticking her toe in my face. This after having greeted me with legs open wide and a lit joint up to her white cotton panties. Pass me the joint, he says. No, hit it from here, she says. Don't make me have to burn your ass with it. You think it'll come off with cocoa butter, she says, now picking at her little toe. Huh? Cocoa butter? You mean a chainsaw, he says.

—All you like to do is complain. You probably get off at the customer service lines of department stores.

—I have never heard you concede. I heard you conceit, but not concede.
—Conceive?

See, I wish that I could meet the other women in your life. We could have a seminar on you, so I could know more about you, she says. I bet you their story is right.

—Somewhere along the line you didn't get something in childhood. Maybe it was that big green lollipop in the window display case at the Woolworth's on Main Street.

—No, you're the one that acts like you didn't get what you wanted when you was a kid, and now you're making everyone else pay for it.

—All I ever wanted was an air of deathly silence.

We should be like pals, he says, pulling her toward him, his arm around her shoulder, her face finding refuge in his chest.

—I don't know what's going on. I'd say 90 percent of the time I like hanging out with you.

(Pause)

She says: You should be saying thank-you right now—that was a compliment.

He says: I know, but you're going to have to hold up the cue cards a little higher; the light from the halogen lamp is blinding me.

Go to sleep now, he says, pushing her head down.

—You treat me like you would treat a kid.

—What do you mean?

—Always telling me what to do. Then pushing me away. Telling me to go away.

She crumbled into a corner. Collapsed in pain. This was on the TV, of course, breaking the silence.

I'm sorry for snapping at you, he said. I appreciate you saying that, she said. And if you need me to snap at you again, let me know, he said. I'm always available.

He was doing his old-man routine, acting like someone in an old-folks home, with slight memory loss and nostalgia. He leaned back on her to lead him to the bedroom. Let's go back to the house so we could sparky sparky, he said, flicking his thumb like a lighter. She giggled at his antics as she led him to the back room so they could smoke the remainder of the blunt that put them out the night before. What time is it? he asked. Put it on *Soul Train* so I can jerk off.

I had a dream last night, she said. Did it involve a large amount of penises dangling before your face threatening to bang into your forehead incessantly? he asked. No, she said, nodding her head slightly, staring at the screen of her laptop. Good, he said. You're still the good old Catholic schoolgirl I raised.

She said the word cock a thousand times. Somebody said, What's that clucking sound. Finally, she said, did you see that stuff that was in your pocket? What are you doing rifling through my pockets? Is there any cereal left? she asked, patting him on the nuts as he sat on the couch in boxers; and went to the back room to spark up.

Boy, it's cold outside, he said, looking out through the mini-blinds. The weather's crazy, he said. One day it's summer, the next day it's winter.

Do you want your cereal to be mixed with bran with some fruit and fiber? she asked, coming from the kitchen. Is it to my benefit? he shouted. Yes, she said. Okay, he quipped, as she walked away.

Those biscuits are too good, she said. That's what you said about the ranch dip, he said. She sucked her teeth clean. Everything is too good to you, he complained. You have the appetite of a mule. Everything you see, you graze at. Tell me, she said, when you were a kid was it taught to you to be cruel to girls? No, he said, not paying her much mind.

That afternoon they went to a wedding in the park. The scenario was warm, beautiful, and spiritual: the stuff of real romance. But any old kook from around the city would wander on the set, in the middle of the proceedings. This pissed off many a squirrel. Fortunately, the reverend was a diplomat. He kept everything calm, until some acorns came with the rice, knocking him upside the head a few times, leaving a trail of knots to the pork chop lips of his mouth.

The marriage ceremony lasted a few seconds.

THE REV

    You two know each other?

(Bride&Groom nod in agreement)

THE REV

    You already did the nasty?

(Bride&Groom nod in agreement)

THE REV

    Alright . . . let's get the hell out of here.

Before they left the park they watched two squirrels fucking in
the tree.

—That's pornographic.
                    —You mean acrobatic.
  —No, pornographic.
                  —Acrobatic?
—Pornographic!
                  —Acrobatic!

This went on for quite some time like Abbott and Costello's
"Who's on first?" routine, until he said, You know, it's hard not
to get into pornography. Who're you tellin', she said. But then
you have the cum shots fuckin' shit up, he said. Then, there's
always that close-up shot that never really tries to purposely expose that one flaw you were waiting for—always that sad scar—
to give your guilt some substance. This is how you rationalize.
Make sense of the world. That some people actually fuck on film
for money—the whole cast—and swallow cum, and take it up
the ass by complete strangers you need to get high in order to
fuck. She tried changing the subject. You know I started seeing
someone . . . He gave me this to play with, she said, stretching
out her zoom lens.

He's a photographer too? Where did you meet him—in a dark-
room? he said, bursting out laughing at his own pun. He said,

that's more dangerous than a cell phone any day, with or without the radiation . . .

***

Lunch followed breakfast in rapid succession.

—I like these noodles better than real spaghetti.

—Ain't that the truth, though. They're big and fluffy like house slippers.

***

—Was my hair shorter when you met me?

—Why do you ask?

—I'm just wondering when it started to grow out.

—You let it grow out when you started singing backup for the Bee Gees.

—Funny, funny. You're a funny man. A regular riot, as Ralph Kramden would say. Bang Zoom.

***

Somebody's child is not too happy right now, she said. Why do you say that? he asked. Because, look, she said, pointing to the ground. That pacifier. Believe me, he said, they have backup contingency pacifiers. In the hood babies do not go without their pacifiers.

***

—I have to take a picture of where you live.

—Why? So you could give it to the feds?

—Yep, she said, squatting and giggling, trying to keep the camera steady.

What's wrong? Are you depressed? I'm just thinking about having everything ready for the fall. How long do you have till school starts up again? Almost a month. That's enough time to get your shit together. It's called reentry. Yeah, I call sex reentry. It's to bring you down from your culture shock. He got up and handed her the blunt to relight it. I feel like an isosceles trapezoid trying to take a shit that's a triangle. Where's the light? I thought you had it.

***

—Here you go (passing him a steaming plate of pasta and tomato sauce with spinach and onions).

—Thank you for your niceties.

—What are you gonna do when I leave? she asks.

—Lay around like Howard Hughes without money.
***
—What is a cock for? he asked her.

—I keep asking myself that too, she said, looking at herself in the mirror.

But that was yesterday. And I'm merely carving memory.

They ended up sitting up in bed, she listening to him talk about some rapper, talkin' 'bout, yeah, you know Frisco is gay. He's into thongs, alright . . . the other way!

In the dream she went from doing hothouse porn to full-fledged commercials.

Dear Diary,

I don't think I could roll with this thong thing no more. I mean it's all about hands and grabs, I feel so divided. Plus, I gotta use the radiator for a pole, damn near put my back out. I like it better when I was back on my island, seeing my man every now and then for our conjugal visits. Just me, him, and my cell phone . . . call waiting, of course.

The city is noisy, dirty, and hostile. The roaches don't get along with the rats, the winos can't stand the junkies, and somebody keeps stealing the garbage-can tops. The stench is unbearable. Plus, I can't take all this violins!

Violins? 'Fuck you talkin' 'bout violins, he said, waking from his dream.

People who need people . . .

played on in the background.

They floated to each other on a cloud of sunlight and smoke.

are the luckiest people . . .

They danced with each other close and slow. Naked, and warm with a buzz.

MARCI BLACKMAN

Hail Mary Full of Grace

C AN you do it?" Mary asked.
Our bodies were wrapped around each other, naked, in my bed. We hadn't had sex; neither of us was into it. We had both endured equally trying weeks at work and it felt more urgent to just lie there and cuddle. To strip down out of our armor and curl up inside the warmth of another's arms. Someone we each wanted desperately to believe understood the ravages of the independent wars we were fighting outside the walls of my studio.

"I mean, do you think that person might live inside you somewhere?" she asked.

"Sure," I said, matter-of-fact-like, even though I wasn't.

Mary wanted me to dress up like a homeboy, a gang-banger, she said, and kidnap her at knifepoint from a dark and deserted alley. It had been a lifelong fantasy. Well . . . maybe not lifelong, she admitted, but at least since 1979. When the Mother Superior of her Catholic prep school called a "What if . . ." seminar after receiving the shocking news that Sister Betril—one of the school's nuns—had been car-jacked out in Los Angeles.

Citing financial distress and declining enrollment, the Church held an emergency meeting to discuss the closure of a number of its prep academies. Mother Theresa's—Mary's academy—was one of the schools in question, and Sister Betril had been chosen by the diocese to present the argument against its closing. But on the way to the meeting (never having been to Los Angeles), Sister Betril took the wrong exit off the freeway. Instead of arriving at the Bonaventure Hotel, which was downtown, she became lost and confused in a maze of disgruntled, forgotten streets in South Central Los Angeles.

Although the sister was unharmed, and would later come to view the terrifying ordeal—like Christ in the wilderness—as a test of her faith and endurance, the Mother Superior at Mother Theresa's was shaken and disturbed enough to pose the question. What if, she asked the assembly of wide-eyed, pink-faced girls, those poor unfortunate creatures in South Central had decided to break the chains of their mental bondage? What if they'd gotten it in their heads to stop killing each other and attack those responsible for their condition? Or worse yet, she cautioned, what if they unleashed their pent-up rage on neighboring innocent communities like the one surrounding Mother Theresa's? What can you do, she told each of the fresh-faced girls to ask herself, to quell the violence before it reaches catastrophic proportions? How can we convince these people that God has not abandoned them? The Mother Superior then called for a moment of silence to allow the girls to reflect on all they had learned during their years at the academy. How—once their stay there concluded—they would go forth into the world and set about the task of ministering Christ's love to the likes of those lost souls in South Central.

But instead of deep reflection, all Mary could think about was Sister Betril. What thoughts ran through her mind when that boy—barely fifteen, the officer said—jumped in the passenger seat of her rental car, brandishing a gun? Did her body tremble with fear when he placed the barrel against the side of her head? Did she plead for the Father to remove this cup from her lips when the boy told her to pull into that alley? Pray that she could fly away like her TV counterpart? Did her heart sink when he then instructed her to get the fuck outta the car? Or did she secretly become wet with panic, red with excitement, like Mary as she imagined herself in the sister's place?

After the moment of silence, the Mother Superior ended the assembly by having the girls bow their heads with her in the Lord's Prayer. But even a powerful pubescent chorus of *Our Father who art in heaven* failed to dissuade Mary's mind from fixating on the image of Sister Betril, stranded in a dangerous alley in South Central Los Angeles. In fact, not only did the syncopated rhythm of the mantra fuel Mary's newfound desire to learn all she could about opposing gang sets and their varying hierarchies, but its continued recitation soon took on the tone of background music to her obsession with reliving the nun's experience.

When she snuck out of her dormitory in the middle of the night to take the late bus to the "off-limits" side of town, *Hallowed be thy name* repeatedly crept from her lips. When she donned a pair of dark sunglasses that covered most of her face and slipped into the back row of the Cinedome to watch *Boyz N the Hood*, *Thy kingdom come, Thy will be done* resonated throughout her head. And even now, when she sifts through the bins of recycled vinyl like a rabid dog down at Tiny's Records, hoping to unearth the first release by N.W.A. or Easy E, if Tiny—who is anything but—paid close attention, he could hear her quietly singing *Forgive us our trespasses* as she slides her trust fund cash across the counter to pay for her secret sin.

"Will you be a Crip or a Blood?" Mary asked excited, once I had agreed. "Or how about a *Norteño?*"

"I'm not Latina," I answered, quietly. I was growing increasingly uneasy with the role I had just consented to play. I didn't share Mary's enchantment with inner-city violence. Unlike Mary, I had grown up with it. And it's hard to find fascination in something as prevalent and ordinary as the blades of grass fighting for life among the weeds in your backyard.

But Mary was right about one thing; as hesitant as I was about continuing on this road we'd just turned down, there was a place, hidden deep inside, not warmed by the blood pumping through my heart, that shivered with delight at the prospect of making her beg for her life. Of forcing her at knifepoint to understand that what she was playing at, had been fanaticizing about all these years, was no game. That we were mimicking real lives here. My life. My brother's life. My father's. His father before him. Perhaps that's really what made me uneasy. I was afraid of how far I would go. That once I'd tasted even the smallest morsel of revenge, its nectar would be too sweet to deny. That safe word or no, I knew I wouldn't be able to stop.

We set the date for the following Friday at midnight, the mirrored noon of the dead. Sycamore Alley, a desolate one-block strip of dirt and gravel in Old Downtown, buried in the middle of two solid blocks of burned-out storefronts and abandoned warehouses. Her safe word would be blue, the color the body turns postmortem. We would have no contact until then. Mary felt—and I agreed—it would lend the scene the semblance of realism it would need to work.

I spent the next week making comp tapes to blast in the car—old P.E., Ice Cube, Dr. Dre. And after much internal debate, I opted to front yellow and black—the colors of the Saints. They were the crew that controlled my block. Mostly because I already had a black and gold flannel and a pair of black Dickies hanging up in my closet. All I needed was a black bandanna to tie around my shaved head, which I could pick up at Kmart for ninety-nine cents. Out of respect for the Saints (and probably a healthy sense of fear of my own), I planned to leave the house dressed in my usual attire (Levi's, combat boots, white T-shirt), then change in the car, after arriving in Old Downtown.

I was surprised to discover how much I looked forward to it. Once I settled on my outfit, Friday at midnight was all I could think about. Even work couldn't distract me. Finally, on Friday, after getting paid, I went down to Teewan's Pawn and Loan on my lunch break to buy a switchblade.

"Now what's a sweet young thing like yourself want with a knife like this?" the gruff old man—I assumed to be Teewan—asked as he unlocked the case and removed the blade.

"Protection," I said, flatly, trying to mask my excitement when he handed it to me.

"Protection, huh?" He laughed. "From what?"

"That's just it," I answered, shifting the cold steel back and forth between my hands to test its weight. It was heavier than I expected. "No telling what might be crouched around a corner, hidden in a shadow these days."

"Crouched around a corner, huh? If they's somethin waitin for you out there young lady, little knife like that ain't gonna stop it. 'Less you know what to do with it. You know how to use that thing?"

"Doesn't look all that complicated," I said as I traced the edge of the blade with my finger, admiring its sharpness and gleam in the light.

"Your boyfriend don't protect you?"

"Don't have a boyfriend."

"No boyfriend!" Teewan squealed. "Right there's your answer!" He laughed. "You know I gotta son 'bout your age. Handsome too; looks just like me. And in a few years," he added, spreading his arms as wide as his smile, "this'll all be his. Soon's I cross to the other side."

"That's all right," I laughed back, returning the knife to its case. "I think I'm doing fine on my own. How much?"

Teewan charged me twenty dollars for the knife, then shook his head as I shoved it in my pocket and walked out the door.

Walking back to work, with the means to take a life stuffed deep in the bottom of my pocket, I wasn't sure what to feel. When I entered the pawn shop I was brimming with excitement and anticipation. But now, the weight of my new switchblade banging against my thigh with every step was making me angry. Angry at every face I saw that wasn't black, even some of those that were. Angry at Mary for being ignorant enough to believe that this was only a charade. Angry at myself for agreeing to do it.

The rest of the afternoon crawled by without incident. Still, with each slow tick of the clock, my anger quickened. Time is funny that way. Like the tortoise, it marches on at the same unhurried pace no matter the ceaseless flurry around it. Even the constant hovering of death fails to break its rhythm. By six o'clock, when at last I returned to my apartment, my whole body shook with a quiet rage—fury minus the sound. Midnight seemed a lifetime away.

I passed the hours checking, then rechecking my supplies. Comp tapes, Saint's clothes, knife, pillowcase, flashlight, candles, duct tape, rope, latex gloves, condoms, lube. I chose to strap on my harness and pack at home. It was one thing to get caught changing your clothes in the backseat of your car while parked in a deserted alley, quite another to try to explain to a police officer what that rubber thing was in your hand and why you were trying to stuff it down your pants.

When the clock chimed eleven, I decided I couldn't wait any longer and headed for the car. Grand Master Flash rattled the windows of my Falcon as I rolled through the forsaken streets of Old Downtown.

Don't push me, 'cause I'm close to the edge.

I pulled to a stop in a cluster of thick shadows, across the street and a few feet back from the rear entrance to the alley, where I was sure to be hidden from view. Once again, after I changed clothes, I checked my supplies. At five minutes to twelve a taxi eased to a halt at the other end and I could just make out the shadow of Mary, handing over her money before the driver pulled away. What had she told him, I wondered, that persuaded him to bring her down here at this time of night?

Rumor had it that Old Downtown was haunted. That the ghosts of the tenants who died in a rash of unexplained tenement fires some years back roamed its charred streets in search of new shelter. Some people believed it, some didn't. Haunted or not, everyone found a reason to steer clear. Even the homeless stayed away, it's said. I knew that's why Mary chose the location. She wanted to make sure we wouldn't be interrupted.

When she was halfway down the alley, I started to get out of the car, then hesitated. I decided to fuck with her head a bit. Make her think that I'd forgotten or had changed my mind. See, I was her ride out of there, and if she was serious about wanting to relive Sister Betril's experience, she would need to feel her fear. She would if she believed she was truly stranded.

For thirty minutes I watched her. She was calm enough at first. Lighting a cigarette and checking her watch at five minutes after, then again at ten past. At twelve-fifteen she lit another cigarette and started pacing. The frequency of the watch-checking increased. By twelve-twenty she was up to once every thirty seconds and the cigarettes started to burn faster. Every three minutes or so the whiteness of her face flashed in the dark as she lit one fag after the other. At twelve-thirty she walked back to the spot where the cab had dropped her off and began to pace some more.

Twelve-thirty-five: Mary lights her last cigarette and throws the empty pack on the ground. She's angry. The echo of her voice cascades down the vanquished walls of Sycamore Alley as she curses me. I slip on a pair of latex gloves, then tear off a piece of duct tape and place it—sticky side up—in the palm of my hand. Twelve-forty: she walks back to the middle of the alley, gets down on her hands and knees and combs the ground with the flame from her lighter for a half-smoked cigarette. Again she curses me. "This isn't fucking funny!" she yells as the fire sears her thumb. Twelve-forty-three: she slumps down against the wall and starts to cry.

It's time. I grab the rope and pillowcase and slip out of the car, leaving the door slightly ajar. I toy with the idea of not moving. Of teaching her a lesson. Hunkering down in the trench of my backseat and waiting. Watching her pace until the sun comes up, counting the hours—minutes—before she becomes completely unglued. But anger still guides me and I am determined to make her tremble with fear. Not the contrived fright that hovers over a safety net, waiting to be whisked away at the stammering of a word, but real fear. I want her to look upon its ugly pockmarked face and hear her own scream pierce the dead of night as though it were coming from someone else. Then I want her to find the beauty in it. To caress it, kiss it, come to rely on it when she realizes it will never leave.

Twelve-forty-five: she picks herself up, dries her eyes and walks toward my end of the alley. I cross the street and crouch in the shadow of the singed and half-standing building on the corner. Twelve-forty-seven: she reaches the end of the alley, then stops and sighs with relief when she sees my Falcon—illuminated in the moonless night by the interior light triggered by the open door. The knife is anxious in my pocket. "Where the fuck are you!?" she yells again, twirling and squinting back down the alley. I remain still, crouched in my shadow. "Not funny!" she screams. "I've changed my mind, all right? I don't want to do this anymore." Still, I don't move. Slowly, she turns back around.

"I'm cold," she whispers as she inches toward my car. "I just want to go home."

Twelve-fifty: she reaches the open car door and peers inside. I'm on her in seconds. Cupping the duct tape over her mouth with one hand, pressing the switchblade against her neck with the other.

"Don't move," I whisper as she struggles to break free. "No, really," I laugh. "Or you'll slit your own throat."

At once, her shoulders become still.

Quickly, I remove the knife from her neck and tie her hands behind her back with a short length of rope.

Again she begins to struggle; again I sink the blade into her throat, just deep enough to draw a thin line of blood.

"What'd I say?" I growl as I scoop the blood from her neck with my finger, yank back her head and smear it under her nose. "Smell that? Move again and you'll drown in it."

When she stops squirming, I glance around to make sure we're alone, then reach in the car and grab the flashlight before pushing her—knife resting eager against her throat—toward a burned-out building on the corner.

We enter through one of the large, gaping holes the city never bothered to board up. Three or four rats scurry into the dark when the beam from my flashlight hits their eyes. Mary lets out a muffled scream that ricochets off the duct tape and slides back down her throat.

"What's the matter?" I taunt as I fan my flashlight to see where we are. "Scared of a little rat?"

We are in a small entryway at the top of a flight of stairs that leads underground. Mary struggles as I force her down the steps. We descend into the remains of a basement that has been converted into a crude apartment. There are no windows. Cobwebs lace the walls. Five shredded and water-stained mattresses, speckled with rat droppings, cover the floor. The air is dank and rancid. Thick with the stench of feces and piss. Mary jerks her head back in an effort to escape the smell.

"Welcome to hell, Sister Betril," I whisper, laughing at my own joke as I search for a place to tie her up.

I didn't expect to enjoy this. I thought I'd be so disgusted by now that I'd have to fight to keep my rage in check; wrestle it to the floor to keep it from causing irreversible harm. I don't know why, but for some reason, I'm not angry anymore. In fact, I feel good, excited again. My skin is starting to tingle. It's like I'm high. No, not high, but that moment just before. The second after you hit the joint, or put down the pipe. Depress the pump on the rig. The slow lazy blink before your eyes glaze over. That brief suspension in time before you let yourself come, or squeeze the trigger. You feel a little something begin to stir, then BOOM! your entire being is swallowed whole in the rush. Of adrenaline. Of dope. Ecstasy. Power. Control.

In the corner about a foot above one of the mattresses is an old drainpipe. Mary writhes and kicks, shrieks something inaudible through the duct tape as I drag her toward it. She's still screaming as I pull her arms over her head, thread the rope through the pipe and bind her wrists tight against it.

"Speak clearly!" I bark as I rip the tape from her mouth.

"I'm not lying on this filthy thing!" she wheezes, digging the heels of her pumps into the mattress and arching her back in the air to keep her butt from touching it. Her hair is wet with sweat and sticks to her face. "What!?" she yells, coughing, when I laugh out loud.

Mary's right. This is a game. One of thousands we'll play before we die. And suddenly I realize the game itself, the nature of it, has no importance. It's all about who makes up the rules.

"It's funny," I snort, uncontrollably.

"What's funny?" she spits out, annoyed. A wad of hair is stuck to the corner of her mouth. She keeps darting her tongue in and out, hissing like a cornered snake trying to push it out, but she can't reach it.

"You," I answer, still laughing. "Thinking you have any say in what goes on here tonight. Look at you! You're a fucking mess! You can't even get your own hair out of your mouth. You're just like a little baby, you know that? Crying, wheezing, screaming a bunch of gibberish nobody can understand. I bet you're even about to shit your panties, huh? That is, if you have any on. That's it isn't it? You didn't wear any. Bad girl, sister. Walking these dark and deserted streets with no underwear. What if some stranger happened along and kidnapped you?"

"You can't make me lie on this thing!"

"Don't have to," I laugh as I slip the pillowcase over her head. "Holding yourself all contorted like that . . . you're bound to get tired sooner or later. And when you do . . . the mattress'll be there to catch your fall. All I gotta do is wait. See ya later, Sister Betril."

"Wait!" she yells through the pillowcase as I walk toward the stairs. "Where are you going?"

"To find you a diaper to catch all that shit you're about to let loose."

"You can't leave me here!" She's beginning to panic.

"Oh I'll be back. You just concentrate on keeping that sweet little ass from touching that mattress."

"I have to pee," she yells in desperation.

"So pee," I answer as I start up the stairs. "Won't be the first time somebody did on that mattress."

Back at the car, as I retrieve the duffel bag of supplies from the backseat, my whole body buzzes with realization. I take out one of the condoms while I contemplate games, rules, and past events. Like the time that cop buried my brother's face into the concrete with the heel of his boot. *Be still nigger! Be still nigger!* Or that day back in eighth grade, when my history teacher had to separate me from the girls threatening to kick my ass. *Your people don't like you very much do they?* Or the time my mother tried to move us to a safer neighborhood, when *I'm sorry, the apartment has already been rented* greeted us at every door— even though we had been the first to call. Whose rules do I live by? 'Course, Mary grew up playing a different game, a Catholic game, with Catholic rules. Then she got wise, started making up her own. Well, tonight, we'd play by mine.

When I return, she is shivering in the corner, hands rubbed raw by the rope and twisted around the drainpipe. Although her butt has dropped significantly lower, she is still holding herself above the mattress. Her arms twitch with exhaustion. Her legs and pumps are soaking wet. The dank now smells of fresh urine.

She jerks her hooded head toward the sound of my feet on the bottom step as I reenter the room.

"Wh-who's there?" she calls out, frightened, when I drop the duffel bag on the mattress beside her. "That you baby?"

I don't answer. Just unzip the duffel bag and place a few candles on the floor.

"B-b-baby?" Mary yells again. "T-talk to me. Is that you?"

"No, it's the boogeyman," I answer, striking a match and lighting the candles.

As the faint glow from the candles begins to reveal the rest of the barren room, I brace myself for more rats. The unmistakable clamor of a dozen pairs of fingertip-size claws, scampering across the concrete floor, trying to survive their own game. Luckily, the sound never comes.

I remove the pillowcase from Mary's head and use it to dry off her legs. Her eyes are calm and sad when she looks at me. Puffy from crying. And it occurs to me that she's never looked more beautiful—vulnerable—than she does right now. Face streaked with makeup, fear, and embarrassment. Neither of us speak. I pull off her pumps and wipe the piss from her feet. Then lift up her skirt and clean her crotch before untying her hands and easing her onto the mattress. She doesn't fight. Her will is gone.

I take off my gloves before kissing her. First on her eyelids, then her nose, her lips, the thin scratch on her neck. Reluctantly, her body begins to move below me. I pull her into my chest as I unclasp her skirt, slide it down over her feet and place it on the mattress beneath her before lying her back down. After unzipping my pants and letting them fall to my ankles, I lower myself on top of her. She closes her eyes and begins to cry. Again, I kiss her on the mouth, soft at first, tasting the salt from her tears, then hard and deep as the burned-out building creaks and groans above us. Slowly, our bodies writhe against each other. Awkward, initially. Separate and seeking. But soon, we agree on a rhythm. I pull my dick through my boxers and ease into her. Watch her as our rhythm builds into one single deliberate motion. Her eyes are still closed, but the tears start falling faster. Pouring down her cheeks as our thrusts turn violent.

We thrash and flail against each other like snakes, trying to shed our skin. The noose of knowledge that has governed our existence. The building creaks and moans louder. Mary is sobbing now, lifting us both off the mattress as she drives her body into mine. My head is reeling from the stench. I feel like I'm going to pass out. A voice whispers in my head, "Whose game are we playing now?" Mary's mouth is moving soundlessly as though she is speaking. In my head I hear more voices, but I can't make out what they're saying. Mary thrusts against me one last time, then falls limp on the mattress. I pull out of her, then shake my head to clear it. The voices are gone. All but one. It's Mary. She's curled up in a ball in the corner by the drainpipe, whispering over and over:

"Hail Mary full of grace, the Lord is with thee. Blessed art thou among women, and Blessed is the fruit of thy womb, Jesus. Holy Mary, mother of God, pray for this sinner now. And at the hour of my death. Hail Mary full of grace, the Lord is with thee . . ."

CHRIS BENSON

Click

WHAT the fuck was I doing? Prowling the bridal salon at an upscale downtown department store. Stalking make-believe virgins in white dresses and happily-ever-after fantasies. Was this what it had come to for me? Creeping the women's departments like some fetish freak, searching for trace evidence. One of those foot fuckers, the kind who pick up shoes on the sly. Not the brand-new ones on display, but the ones that have already been tried on. What drives men to do that sort of thing? I thought about that as I found myself fantasizing about the wedding gowns in the back rooms of that place; the ones that had already been tried on. Were they cleaned after the fittings? What was left behind? Some fragrance? Could some part of a woman live on in a dress?

Wait a minute, what the fuck was I doing, thinking about bullshit like that? Was it obsession? Was it? I don't think so. It was more like the natural order of things. I mean, I was like an animal, barely out of sight, hidden in a jungle of Escada racks and displays across from the bridal salon, scoping my prey. I was a panther, black as midnight, or a lion with a mane of dreads. Lean, muscles taut, fixed on my target, waiting for that moment when she might stray a little too far from the pack. And just like that, the moment arrived. Other customers, fittings finished, scattered. The receptionist took a break. The seamstress stood up and walked off, leaving her there in the middle of the open area, alone and vulnerable. On instinct, without hesitation, I pounced, swift and powerful. She had only a second to glimpse me over her shoulder before I was on her. She must have been wearing five-inch heels. I mean, I'm six-three and she practically looked me straight in the eye before I forced her off balance. She sucked in a shriek as I grabbed her arm, yanked her toward the dressing room area in the back, past the tea service and champagne.

Once back there, hidden from view, I quickly looked down the row of louvered doors. She was pulling against me, grunting, but not screaming. I picked door number one. Good choice. On hooks next to a trifold mirror were the clothes she had been wearing earlier when she got there. I shoved her in, followed in hot pursuit, closing the door behind us. Right away, she began swinging, pounding at my chest. I moved around to avoid her, lost my footing in the tiny space and fell down on the bench. Without missing a beat, she raised a leg and rammed a satin shoe dead into my chest. She pressed her back to the closed door, bracing herself, locking her leg, pinning me against the opposite wall. Face flushed, she was breathing hard, searing me with a laser gaze. I sighed, rested my head back against the wall. Her stiletto heel was cutting deep into my chest. I might have been bleeding. It must have hurt like hell, but I couldn't tell. At that moment, the only thing I knew for sure was that I felt the most intense throbbing. My dick was as hard as it had ever been, and it was pointing like a compass needle true north—straight up at her, beneath the skirt of that wedding gown draped across me. I felt the pull of gravity under there, the heat of the center of the earth. There was no turning back now. I had her just where she wanted me.

"What the fuck are you doing here?" She was talking in breathless spurts, somewhere above a whisper, somewhere below full voice.

Why did she even have to ask me that? She knew damned well what I was doing there. She had driven me to it. More than anybody I had ever met, she knew how to work that shit. In only two years, she had done a number on me. Hadn't just touched a nerve. She had rewired my circuits. So of course she knew where the buttons were, knew which ones to push, too, when she left that message on my service: too busy with this fitting today to pick up the rest of her things. Wanted me to ship them to her. Just the thought of her things made my temperature rise.

"What the fuck are you smiling about?" She was nothing if not demanding, and tough. I have to admit I liked that about her. What can I say? Strong women are my weakness.

I was smiling at the sight of her. That vision of purity looming over me in a white dress. The same woman who would fuck me raw three or four times in a single night. What was it that kept me coming back—obsession? Was it? I don't know. More like a natural reaction. The way you're just drawn to great challenges, the way you automatically go after the thing that's just beyond reach. Was it love? Not sure. It had never been the pretty music, hearts-and-flowers kind of love, more of a storm-cloud-and-lightning-bolt kind of thing. Glass-shattering eruptions. Seismic rumbles way, *way* off the Richter scale. Like the world just opened up and swallowed us whole. And it all came together when we fucked. It wasn't like the earth moved, more like the planets were realigned. We had fucked with the forces of nature. Did she really expect me to give all that up?

"Are you going to say something, or just sit there smirking?" She might have been tapping her foot, if she hadn't been walking across my heart with it.

I checked her for a beat, then spoke. "I just wanted a chance to—"

"No!" She did that "Stop-in-the-Name-of-Love" thing with her hand, dug her heel deeper into my chest, and clenched her jaws. "You *had* your chance, okay?"

I sighed. "You still don't get it, do you?"

She blinked in disbelief, as if wondering how I could possibly try to turn this shit around. "So, help me out here," she said.

Okay, so she was right. I'd *had* my chance. Had it. Blew it. Couldn't commit. But, it wasn't my fault, really. I mean, what was I supposed to do? Not what she asked me to do. I couldn't do that. After all, I wasn't just a photographer. I was an *artist*.

Didn't she understand that? I was building a reputation, a body of work. And it was about more than money, much more. I couldn't possibly stoop to do *commercial* work, sell my soul, even if she had thrown some of her ad agency clients my way. No, I had too much integrity for that.

As I spoke, I looked deep into her eyes and had a playback moment of Randi as my model. Damn, she and my camera adored each other. She wasn't exactly pretty, but she had a way of making you think she was. Altogether she was a work of art. Fluid in her movement, she had the grace of a thousand dance rehearsals and a sturdy body forged by hours of martial arts training. And she had the spirit of five thousand generations of black womanhood. She was what her ancestors had lived to become, the evolution of their power, the sum total of their consciousness, the accumulation of their passion. She had the look of that ancient fire, too. Working a monochromatic thing. A reddish complexion, eyes like flaming chestnuts. Tightly wound frizzy brown curls shooting up and out from her head like a Roman candle. Then there was that mouth, the full, heart-shaped lips. She branded you, burned her mark with every kiss. Damn. Made me sweat just being close to her. And the smell of her. That hot, intoxicating elixir that oozed from her pores and always made it seem like she had just stepped in from the sunshine. No doubt about it, the fire burned bright in her. But fire needs tending.

"You abandoned me," she said, leaning into her heel.

"I've never left you," I said, wondering how you could ever go so deep within yourself that you lose sight of such an important part of yourself. "And I never will leave." It went on like that, back and forth for a short while. I could tell I was making some points when she paused for a minute, gave me that look.

"How do you keep doing this to me, Jason?" It must have hit her, like it was hitting me close up and in that little space, the memories, the connection. We couldn't be that close together without reacting to each other. It was just the natural order of things. She softened but only a little bit. I had learned something about pushing buttons, too. And I kept pushing. At least I thought I was getting over. Finally, she eased back on the foot, then stepped to me, taking my face into her hands. "You know I would have waited for you forever," she said, looking down at me on the bench. "But you didn't give me any hope."

I put my hands on her waist, gazed up at her, thought about what that lost hope had led her to; some nigger just an elevator ride up from a street hustler. Okay, so it was Wall Street, so he was a new technology stock analyst, so he had bank. But he was still just a hustler. Getting off on other people's money. And she had gone for it. This, this Brooks Brother from New York. This high stakes, high tech, high roller. This digital dick. How could she give me up for him? Trading the Big Bang for the dot-com.

I pulled her close to me. She didn't resist as I kissed her in the center of her gown, at the navel. I knew the map of her body. I had explored every part of her.

She gave in to me for a moment, but then tensed up and pulled back. "No, Jason, really . . ."

I tightened my grasp at her hips, pulled her back, kissed her, lower this time.

She moaned softly. "Jason, don't . . . please."

"Do you know how much I've missed you, Randi?" I began slowly pulling the gown up. Then, she moved again. I thought she was trying to wriggle free, but this time she was moving toward me, pressing her body to my face, belly-dancing across my mouth. She raised her hands to my shoulders, massaged through the leather jacket. Finally, I raised the dress enough to feel her firm bare thigh. Automatically, she raised her leg, put her foot on the bench. I reached again for her thigh, pulled it close to me. She did the rest, lunging, rubbing her leg against my arm, her torso against my face. I moved my mouth up the middle of her body, kissing, biting at the silky smooth fabric of her dress.

Then I backed off, pushed her thigh away from me, opening her wide, moving my hand up until I could feel the moist heat coming through her panties. Suddenly, she bent down to kiss me, softly at first. But, as I worked my hand around the panties, touching her deeper, she started biting my lips. I pulled back again, and as she straightened her body, I leaned forward and kissed the inside of her thigh. She stepped back slowly off the bench, grabbed at the shoulders of my jacket, pulled me back with her. I eased to the floor on my knees, then pushed her by the hips, back to the door that rattled on impact.

I wondered if somebody out front might have heard the noise. But I only held the thought a moment as I kept moving, lifting the skirt of her gown, kissing each knee and working my way up her thighs, nibbling as her dress draped over me. I pushed aside the crotch of her panties, and kissed her, first side to side, then straight up the middle of her pussy. She trembled and I could have sworn she was kissing me back. She was that good. I reached up from under her dress and took both her arms by the wrists, pinned them back against the door. I could feel her tendons tense as she gripped the doorknob with her right hand. I pressed my tongue hard up against her and, with one broad swipe, moved across the wettest part of her. I lapped at her clit as she writhed, backing against the door, then jerking forward right up against my mouth. I started sucking her as she trembled again, violently.

"Oh, God," she heaved.

"Miss Sheridan, is everything all right?" It was the seamstress, on the other side of the door.

I felt Randi's arm tense, as if she was holding the doorknob tighter, keeping the woman from twisting it.

"Say yes," I commanded, pulling at her with my mouth. "Say yes," I repeated a little louder.

"Excuse me?" the woman asked.

"Yes," Randi said. "Oh, yes! Everything's . . . fine."

"Well, I just wanted to make sure, because—"

"It's good," I said. "So *fucking* good."

"Beg your pardon, Miss Sheridan? What did you—"

"The job," Randi said. "The work, it's, it's really . . . good." She raised her leg over my shoulder, pulled me hard against her. "Perfect. Just . . . perfect."

"All right," the seamstress said. "Well, call me if, you know, if you need anything."

As I heard the woman walk away, I made one more broad pass with my tongue, then pulled Randi's clit deep into my mouth. She erupted, tried to free her arms, but I wouldn't let go until I was finished with her. When I released her, she rushed down to me.

She was excited by the smell of herself on my lips and couldn't get enough of it. She was ferocious as a cannibal, licking, biting. And sounding that deep resonant moan that was tuned to my pitch. It vibrated the very fibers of my being. How could it not? Randi had long ago strip-searched my soul for things she could use against me.

I worked her zipper from behind and pulled the dress down from her shoulders until I saw it, that explosion of a tattoo at the top of her left titty. "Click." I kissed it and wondered if Mr. Dot-Com could read between the lines. I wondered if she had translated it for him. What it meant to us, those late nights in my loft. She loved it. Flash dancing to the beat of my studio strobes, getting off on the hum of my motor drive as I kept hitting it. Every shot. Zoom. Flash. Click.

She nuzzled into my neck, kissing me on my ear and behind it and then down and then up again. She began pulling at the shoulders of my jacket, down around my arms. Binding them. Then she pushed me back against the bench. And that's where I stayed. Still on my knees, leaning back, arms locked in place, while she raised her dress, kicked off her shoes, spread her legs, straddled me on her knees and began rocking her body, savagely kissing my face. She worked my tee shirt out of the cargo pants and up to my chest. Then she bent forward to suck my nipples. She kissed her way down, gently across the mark of the stiletto, licking the wound, then moving lower still, tongue-surfing the ripples of my abs.

In a rush, she reached down, unfastened my pants, yanked at the zipper, and took me in hand. But then she stopped short of the mark, gripping the base of my dick, squeezing until the veins bulged and making it stretch and strain at the top. Her lips were hovering there. Tantalizing. Just beyond reach.

"Zoom," she said softly. "Zoom." She repeated the mantra with bursts of hot breath that ignited me. "Zoom." This was not foreplay. That had happened back when I yanked her by the arm, when she rammed her foot into my chest. For us, *that* was foreplay. This was just part of what we did. And she kept doing it for one long agonizing moment. Anguished, I threw my head back, found myself gazing up at a sprinkler on the ceiling. Who would have thought to put a sprinkler there? Someone who could see the future, the heat of our moment? Even *I* couldn't have seen this one coming. I had been with at least a half-dozen other women since we broke up, but Randi was making me feel like I had been saving it up for years. Ready to explode and set off that fucking sprinkler.

As she lifted her skirt again and began working the crotch of her panties, I knew what she wanted. What she wanted was for the seamstress to come back. Not to come in, but just to stand outside, *poised* to come in. Balancing on the razor's edge is what really got Randi juiced. That's what it was for her. The risk. Like sneaking little teenage boys into her house after school, just before her parents got home. I might have been one of those boys. If I had been in her crowd. I spotted the dangerlust in her early on. Though we were still in our early thirties, we had a lifetime of experience, tempting fate, dancing on the lip of the volcano. Without a doubt, I've done my own share of risky business with Randi. A lot of things in a lot of places. A thousand fantasies come to life. Like in her boss's office after hours. I was the boss. She took dictation. Took it good. All over his desk, while the late-night cleaning crew made a slow march down the hall toward us. Then there was the Fifty-Ninth Street Beach under that midnight moonlight, at the very edge of Lake Shore Drive. From-Here-to-Fucking-Eternity with a triple-X rating. Cops on the prowl in the park only a few hundred feet away. And, of course, there was that blanket trick in Grant Park on the Fourth of fucking July, rockets' red glare, a million people cheering.

Randi eased me inside. It was slow at first, as she stretched to fit around me perfectly. It wasn't like we were made for each other. More like we had been made together, as one, at the beginning of time, then ripped apart like ancient continents. Now we were reunited, two great bodies that belonged together. Rocking on red-hot tectonic plates, swaying to the familiar rhythm of the ages. Driven by a desperate desire to fuse. Was it obsession? Was it? Seemed natural to me, like when you see a world map and just want to push Africa and South America back together.

Randi pulled up, slow and tight, stretching me with her, then she drove down, taking me so deep I could feel her pelvic bone cutting into me. Again, and again, that slow rise, that deep plunge. I pushed up hard against her, with a slight turn, probing every part of her. Suddenly, as I pushed up, she arched her back, rested her palms on the floor behind her, forcing me in at a sharp angle, intensifying the pressure on her clit. I caught her looking into the trifold mirror, at all of us. After a while, she straightened up again, reached for my hair, yanked my head back, and pushed all the way down on me, furiously, then stopped. Just stopped, altogether, and muscle fucked me, contracting and relaxing while I grew inside her, harder, longer. Telescoping. Stretching, beyond my own natural limits. Even completely still like that, we fucked better than any two people on the planet.

I glanced up at the sprinkler again. Were we pumping enough heat to set it off? What would that be like, one big simultaneous eruption? Like a geyser. Randi. Me. The sprinkler. All at once.

I knew she felt it, too. She started moving again, back and forth, turning slightly as I pushed up into her. Faster now. She pushed down on my shoulders with both hands, pinning me back.

Maybe the sprinkler would hit it first, coming all over us.

She moved one leg forward, then the other, pressing her knees up near my chest, squeezing my sides with her thighs. She was sitting on me now, doing a hydraulic rock, forward and back. With my arms still tied up in my jacket, I could barely reach her ankles, but I did, gripping them, locking her feet there on the floor. Then, with one powerful surge, I pushed straight up into her, as deep as I had ever been.

I could almost see the sprinkler vibrating with our explosive pressure, opening, releasing a hot, steaming spray down on us, just as we crashed against each other once more, in sync, a perfectly timed combustion.

For just a minute in the afterglow of that dressing room cum sauna, nothing existed but the two of us. I was still on my knees, back against the bench. She had come to rest her head on my chest. After a pause, she sighed, began to lift herself. I felt her muscles twitch and throb as she pulled off me, like her body was telling her not to, like it wanted to hold on to me. She stood, stepped out of the gown. Silently, she held the dress in one hand while she adjusted the sticky panel of her panties. As she did, I watched my life trickle down her leg. Without a pause, she turned the skirt of the gown inside out, wiped her thigh clean.

Bemused, she looked down at the spot on the inside of the gown. "Something old? Something *new*." She smiled. "Something borrowed?"

"It sure the fuck ain't blue," I said.

She pursed her lips, that cute curl of a smile. "Now I know how Monica felt." She held a beat. "I think I'll keep it. Sure answers a big question for me."

"Question?"

"Whether you'd show up at the ceremony." She looked down at the skirt, shrugged. "You've already come."

"Wait a minute. You're going through with this?"

"Was there a question about that?"

Apparently not. The outcome was clear from the start. I had to admit this wasn't just about my career choice. This was about my failings, all the disappointments. Okay, all the women, too. Would I change? Not likely. She had a point. Funny, I had always thought I had this great controlling power in sex, but I had met my match in her. That had become amazingly clear in our little dressing room bout, competing as we had for the soul of our relationship. I had come to conquer and was vanquished before I ever charged onto the field. She had already set the rules of engagement. Now she would set the terms of surrender.

"You *know* it's better this way," she said, downshifting. She held a beat or two, eyeballed me. "I'm still getting married. But nothing will ever change between you and me."

Yeah. Right. Whatever. The very fact that she felt the need to say it meant things already *had* changed. They would never be the same.

"We'll still be able to get together," she said.

I raised myself up to the bench again. "What, you mean like this?"

She let go that wicked laugh of hers. "Well, I do plan to do a lot of shopping," she said, glancing around. "But, now we've done the dressing room thing. I think we can come up with something new."

She handed me the wedding dress. Vera Wang. Of course. I straightened myself out and watched as she dressed, pulling on her pants, raising the black sweater over her head. I got a fresh buzz seeing her titties jiggle as the sweater came down like a curtain on our little one-act play. Could have sworn that tattoo flashed me just before it disappeared from view. That's when it hit.

For some people, a revelation comes on like a lightbulb, in a rush of illumination. For me, it's always been like the click of my shutter. That's when I know I've got the picture. Clear, focused, perfectly exposed.

So, like that, I finally got it with Randi and the deal she put on the table. Great sex, no strings. What can I say? Life is filled with compromises. Between what you want and what you'll accept. For me, the line was blurring. What I was willing to accept seemed like the best of all possibilities. And wasn't that what I really wanted? Damn straight. I mean, that pussy was off the hook. So, was that obsession? Was it? Who really gives a fuck? As for Randi, well, for her, this new arrangement would pose the ultimate risk. The ultimate thrill.

She touched her belly and seemed to glow. "And here I thought I was saving myself for marriage," she said. "But, who knows what you've set in motion today?" She looked down on me, took the gown. "Maybe no one will even notice the difference. Then again, you're so much . . . *darker* . . . than he is." She said that word, "darker," as if it was the most delicious thing she had ever tasted. She had quite an appetite for dark things and feeding that hunger had exposed the darkest parts of me.

She smoothed her sweater, kissed the air between us, and prepared to leave me there alone with an offer I couldn't refuse. At the door, she turned, gave me a wink over her shoulder. "Last one out, hit the lights."

Click.

RM JOHNSON

Slipping and Falling

I LOVE you," Dabny breathed into Richard's ear. She hovered above him, her bare breast grazing the hair on his deeply rising and falling chest. She stared down at him, relishing the sweet look of satisfaction on his face. She saw the way his shiny black eyelashes rested on his cheeks, the way the corners of his mouth turned up in a smile, letting Dabny know that Richard was playing back in his mind the way she'd made love to him just moments ago. The way she'd gyrated atop him, hung above him, tempting him to grab her and feel her love for him coursing through her skin, through her breasts and into his palms, tunneling through every inch of him and into his heart, his soul.

While she was giving her love to him, he felt it. Oh, how he felt it, and she showed her love more to him, rolling her hips faster, sliding down further onto his stiff organ. She did all she could to let him know there was no question about her love for him, because it was an all-consuming love, and even though her attempts never seemed to fully display that love, she tried to show him as much of it as her body would allow.

Her passion must have found its way through to him, because just before Dabny felt Richard let go of himself inside her, his body tightened and went rigid. His eyes opened to look deeply into her face.

"I love you," he gasped through the pleasure his body was experiencing. "Marry me," he said. And before Dabny could acknowledge what he had said, his hands were grasping tightly onto her hips, his fingers digging deep into the flesh of her ass.

He was giving himself to her, his body tremulous under hers, and she went warm, his fluid erupting into her like hot, thick lava. Then it hit her. Out of nowhere, it hit her. And her body shook, the muscles tightening about her spine, her lower back, as she threw her head back, was almost trying to fight it, for she had no idea it was coming, had not felt it around the corner. She had been nowhere near orgasm, but there she was, crying out, whipping her head from side to side, babbling like a fucking atheist hit by the Holy Ghost. It was the marriage proposal: why it triggered her body to respond like that, she didn't know. But all the proposals she saw on *Oprah*, the skywriting, the billboards, the old ring in the bowl of soup trick, the proposals she thought were just the end all, be all, now were shit. And regardless how many tears of joy those women shed in the faces of their men, she knew they had no idea of what a real proposal was like. A proposal that, at the same time, made you shed tears from your eyes and spray cum from your pussy.

"Are you sure?" It was all Dabny asked, not wanting to question him further, not wanting him to confess to something if it was just said in the fit of passion.

A small smile widened across his face.

"Yes," he said, without opening his eyes, without moving a muscle.

Dabny looked cautiously at him, as if needing more proof before allowing herself to be truly taken away.

"But what about—"

But Richard reached up, placed a soft finger to Dabny's lips.

"Shhhhh," he whispered. "There's nothing we can do about that," he said sweetly, as his other hand went blindly searching for something under his pillow.

"And if you don't believe I'm serious, why don't you take a look at this."

Richard held his palm open, to reveal a little blue velvet box.

This couldn't be happening, Dabny told herself, as she felt her head start to spin, her body to weaken. This couldn't be happening because of all the times he said he would never marry her, because he could not give her what he knew, what they both knew, she'd wanted.

But Dabny had asked him, did he know for sure? Had he ever had tests run? He said no, that he just knew. And Dabny should have left it at that, because the day that they did return to the fertility specialist's office, she felt ashamed, like she had taken a part of his manhood away when the results that came back proved what he had already told her. He could not have children.

It was all he'd ever wanted, and that night, he crawled into her arms, his head resting on her breast, crying, telling her how sorry he was, and that someday he would have to leave her so she could be with a real man.

But now he was proposing, and as Dabny's trembling fingers raised the box from Richard's hands and slowly opened it, she still didn't believe it was happening. But when she opened the box, witnessing the brilliance of the small stone that seemed to hold a bit of sunlight within it, she knew that it had to be true.

Richard pulled the ring out of the box and gently grabbed Dabny's left hand, guiding it slowly onto her finger. It was a perfect fit.

"So will you marry me?" he said, smiling.

"Yes!" Dabny yelled, leaning forward, throwing her arms around her man, kissing him all over his face, his lips, his neck. This was what she had been waiting for all her life, to be able to settle down, with one man, share her life with him, grow as one, as her parents had. They had been loving each other for thirty-five years, still enjoying every moment, and all Dabny wanted was an opportunity to be as happy.

Five years ago she thought she had been heading in that direction when she was dating Tony. She loved him, and she knew he loved her too, because he had lowered himself to one knee one night and asked to marry her. She accepted and was prepared to spend the rest of her life with him—till the day she

came home early from a "girl's trip" out of town and walked in
on Tony as he was getting his brains fucked out by some stank-
ass bitch. Dabny couldn't believe her eyes as she stood there in
the doorway of her bedroom. She just stood there, her heart fail-
ing in her chest, her knees threatening to buckle under her, as
she watched this woman slide up and down the length of her fiancé's dick. But what was worse was that after a moment, Dabny
realized that the teddy the woman's breasts and ass were spilling
out of was hers.

"That bitch has my shit on!" Dabny yelled, racing over to
the bed, grabbing a fist full of the woman's hair, throwing her
to the floor before she could slide down Tony's pole yet another time.

A week later, Tony waited by Dabny's car till after work. "I
still love you," he said. "It was all a mistake. I still want us to get
married. All I ever wanted to do was love you, raise a family." As
Dabny stood there, fighting the tears, she wanted so much to
believe him. She wanted to forgive him, because that was what
she wanted too. But she couldn't allow herself to just forget the
terrible thing he'd done to her. And even when her mother told
her that men make mistakes, and one mistake shouldn't ruin the
potential for a wonderful life together, Dabny still couldn't find
it inside herself to forgive him.

Six months later, Tony married the woman. Three months
later, they had their first child, and till this day, Dabny could not
help but quiz herself as to whether or not that child was con-
ceived in her apartment.

That all happened five years ago, and they were still married,
happy, kids, minivan, dog named Sparky, everything she always
wanted, and for all those years she told herself that she let her life
walk away from her because of one mistake. But that was all behind her now, because she would soon be married, she would
have that life, and with a man she loved more than any other, a
man she could trust without question.

Dabny walked into the bathroom, stepped into the tub, and
leaned down to turn on the shower. But as she reached out with
her left hand, she stopped and looked down at her finger.

She pulled her hand closer, her eyes fixed on the ring, gazing at the diamond there, and then her mind filled with images of the future, of her life with Richard. She saw the wedding; Richard smiling as he slowly lifted the veil from her face. Dabny saw the honeymoon, saw her man standing naked over her. She saw herself kneeling before him, taking him in her mouth, pleasuring him like never before, like she would never pleasure another man again, because this was her husband now, and they would forever be together. And then she saw the bright lights overhead of the delivery room, felt the greatest, dearest pain ever known to a woman, that of her womb expanding to allow her child to enter the world. Dabny saw that, and it would happen, because she knew something Richard didn't. She knew something that she was going to tell him after they had made love, but he'd beaten her to the punch with his proposal, so she decided to wait, as not to lessen the importance of his news.

She would tell him later, over the dinner celebrating their engagement. And there she would tell him how her period hadn't come in two months. She would tell him how she was overcome with joy when she had stood over the toilet, squinting down at that wand, and saw those two little lines magically appear. She would tell him how just that morning she got the call from her doctor confirming that she was pregnant. She would tell him all this, and he would be the second-happiest person in the world.

Dabny turned on the water, adjusting the temperature and flow. She grabbed the washcloth and soap, then went about the task of washing herself. She lathered up the patch of dark hair just below her flat belly, and watched as the soapy lather crawled down her body, all the way down to her pink fluorescent painted toenails, and then spiraled down the drain.

During the whole time she was washing herself, she couldn't wipe the stupid grin off her face, couldn't help thinking about finishing so she could go back into the bedroom and lie down with her soon-to-be husband. Just lie there with him, share his space, feel his warmth, breathe his breath as he expelled it.

The constant thought of him made Dabny reach toward the faucet to turn off the water, but when she heard Richard pad into the bathroom on his bare feet, she continued her needless bathing, hoping he would join her.

Richard planted his naked body in front of the toilet bowl, reached down, lifted the seat, stood up, reached out both arms, and let his body fall forward till his palms halted his movement. He looked as though he was ready to do pushups against the wall while urinating.

A hard, strong stream of golden, warm piss raced from Richard's penis, and he let out a moan of appreciation, as if it was the next best thing to an orgasm. It was a long piss, like so many are after good sex, and he swayed his hips from side to side, back and forth, keeping the fluid off the rim of the bowl, or at least off the floor.

Dabny was trying to find something to say to him, which was ridiculous, because she'd never had this problem before, and she knew it was because of her joy and excitement.

"When is a good month?" She finally decided to ask, scrubbing her knees all over again, as if she really had no interest in the answer.

"Hunh?" Richard said, his voice groggy, his naked behind still swaying from side to side, piss still splashing into the toilet bowl.

Dabny pulled back the shower curtain halfway so she could hear him over the water, but still didn't look at him.

"When do you think is a good month to . . . you know . . . get married?" And she was smiling again, like a child, but she didn't give a damn. It felt good. So good.

Richard was done pissing now, and he was thrusting his hips forward in tiny jerking motions, coaxing the last remaining drops of urine out of his penis without the use of his hands, which were still propped up against the wall.

"Ummmm," he started.

Then Dabny said, "I was thinking, maybe, in the spring," and she pulled her eyes away from her knees for a moment to look at him. His back was still turned to her, so she went back to her washing. "Maybe March or April, or maybe as late as—" Then something happened. Something in her mind happened, and it told her to replay what she had just seen. Instead of just looking back at Richard, she did just what her mind told her to do. And she shook her head in disbelief.

Damn, I scratched the hell out of him while we were making love, Dabny thought as she reached to turn off the water. But then she stopped, just as she had before turning off the water. But instead of looking at just one finger, she looked at all of them. What she saw were nails as short, rounded, dull, and harmless as those plastic scissors given to children. But what was worse than that was the knowledge that even if there was a chance in hell that her stubs could do that damage to Richard's back, she didn't have the opportunity. The entire time they were making love, he had been on his back, and she was on top.

It couldn't be, her mind was lying to her, Dabny tried to convince herself. But she was so scared that it took a long time before she had the courage to look again at his body. So long that Richard said, "You were saying, maybe as late as when?"

Then Dabny looked up as Richard was bending over to flush the toilet. There on Richard's back were a number of deep pink, angry-looking scratches—more like slashes almost. And in the bright, hard, bare-bulbed light of the bathroom, the scratches appeared so violent, so ravenous, that the marks should've been something on the back of a mortally wounded victim lying on a slab in a morgue, rather than on the back of her living, brand new fiancé.

"Where did you get those scratches?" Dabny asked, trying hard to maintain her casual tone.

"What?" Richard said, turning.

"I said, where did you get those scratches? On your back."

"Oh," Richard said, then looked over his shoulder, as if he could actually catch sight of them. He turned, reached for the hand mirror off the basin, faced the wall-mounted mirror, then held the hand mirror behind him. He moved it this way and that, trying to see the marks on his back, bouncing the image from the small mirror, to the larger one. Once they appeared in the handheld mirror, he threw his free hand around his back, as if he were trying to reach the scratches. "I've been really itching lately," he said, continuing to try and reach them, but he couldn't. There was no way, because they lay sideways, and at an angle that she knew he couldn't get at even if he had an extra joint in the center of his forearm.

But he stood there, still reaching, as if trying to not only prove to her but to himself that he had not been sleeping around. But he had, and recently at that, for the scars looked fresh, so fucking fresh, that last night could not be ruled out of Dabny's head.

The water-heavy washcloth dropped out of Dabny's trembling hand and fell to the bathtub floor with a loud smack, which pulled Richard's attention into the wall mirror. His face floated there, looking at Dabny, and Dabny stood there in the bathtub, her wet body trembling against the cold air.

Why doesn't he turn around and face me, instead of looking at me through that mirror, his back turned to me so I can still see the scratches?

The look on his face was of pure guilt, whether he knew it or not. And by that expression, he was all but admitting to his crime as sure as if the other woman was sitting before him, her bare ass on the edge of the sink, her legs wrapped around him, locked around his ass, scratching his back right there for Dabny to see oh, how guilty he was.

He lowered his eyes, set the mirror down, then walked slowly toward the door without saying a word. Dabny kept her eyes on him, on those beastly scratches that did not belong on his back, and on the rest of his bare body that she once loved, that she still loved, as he walked out.

Dabny had to stop herself from fainting, crashing through the shower curtain, pulling it down atop of her, and banging her head against the floor.

He had done it! What Tony and all those other men had done, and just when she thought that she was done with the games, with the bullshit, with the "Where the fuck were you last night!"

But he had proposed marriage to her, hadn't he? Dabny knew he had. She heard it, felt it. She was wearing his ring on her fucking finger! But now it all felt untrue, surreal, as if it were a story told to her, an experience that happened to someone else that she had overheard.

Dabny was trembling violently now, her skin coated over with goose flesh, and there came a spinning, flipping of her stomach; if she didn't sit soon, she would fall—if not from grief then from illness.

She stepped slowly over the tub, onto the floor, puddles of water draining from her feet. She wanted so badly to cry. To scream out and let go all the hurt she had endured over the years, all the hurt she was suffering right now, but she wouldn't. She wouldn't let Richard see her fall to pieces, so she just put her hands to her face, covering what tears did come, as she instinctively moved across the bathroom floor to the toilet, turned and sat down. But when she sat, the seat was not there, and as she fell, she realized that Richard hadn't put the seat down. He never did.

So Dabny fell into the toilet. Her feet lifting off the floor, her knees bending over the rim, the small of her back banging hard against the cold hard mass of porcelain. The round cheeks of her warm behind hitting the frigid water, her entire body folded like a lawn chair, ready to be stuffed in the trunk of a small car. Pain shot through her back, racing to the tips of her toes and to the top of her skull. With the extreme emotional pain she was already feeling, Dabny could no longer hold back the tears.

They came. Hot tears that burned her face, and as they fell, she made no move to pull herself from the toilet. She just sat there, her hands to her face, weeping, her body shaking from the hopelessness she was feeling. She paused and turned, almost startled when she heard Richard's voice.

"What are you doing?" he asked, and he was standing in the doorway, completely dressed.

Dabny didn't say anything, just started smoothing the tears from her cheeks, trying to control her heavy breathing.

"Get up from there," Richard said, in a commanding voice, no sympathy for her.

Dabny struggled for a moment, then hoisted herself from the bowl. She stood nude before Richard, feeling out of control, feeling both love and hate in her narrowing eyes.

"I'm not sleeping around on you," Richard offered, without apology.

"Did I say that you were?" And Dabny was surprised at how strong her voice sounded despite how torn up and weak she felt. She acted as though it didn't make her one damn bit of difference if he was cheating or not, if he was on his way out to see the slut who'd put those scratches on his back that very moment. She behaved that way, even though her actions from just a moment ago confirmed that she was torn up, that this was ripping through her heart.

"Well, I just wanted you to know that," Richard said, "because I know how your mind works, and you were probably thinking—" He paused, looking guiltily at the floor. "You just needed to know that I wasn't."

He looked back up into Dabny's eyes, as if trying to further cement his honesty, his innocence into her brain, but could only hold her stare for a moment.

"I got to go," he said, seeming unable to continue lying to her, and he was turning to walk away.

"I'm pregnant," Dabny said, not saying it to try and hold him there, because at that moment, she felt she didn't even care anymore. She said it because she knew it was all he ever wanted, and she wanted him to know just how much he was throwing away before he walked out that door.

He turned, a look of surprise shown on his face, joy in his eyes, then a frown of disbelief.

"That can't be. The tests said—the doctor said I can't—"

"I took a test. Got the results today. It's true, Richard. I'm pregnant," Dabny said, and she just stood there, still naked in front of him, but seeming so much more in control. If she would've allowed herself, she could've felt sorry for him, as he stood there looking into her eyes, then lowering his gaze down to her belly, no doubt trying to somehow look inside of her, see the child there, growing within her. It was all he ever wanted, Dabny knew, and he had thrown it away for some meaningless sex with someone who probably meant nothing to him.

But why? Dabny asked herself—wanted to ask him. But she knew the reason, and it went back to that night when he spilled tears on her sweater, the night he seemed to have lost some of his manhood, and she could tell from that very moment that little by little he was trying to distance himself from her. She knew this man, knew that he was thinking that he was probably doing her a favor by slowly pulling away. And he probably thought that even though she still wanted to marry him, he could not, in good conscience, marry her being in the condition he was in, stand in the way of her having a family.

So he would leave her. And he had probably tried, probably stared in her face many times, trying to muster up the courage to tell her that he could no longer remain with her, but his love for her stopped him. So because he could not find the strength to leave her, he did something that would give her no choice but to leave him.

That's what he was thinking, Dabny just knew it, as she stood there looking at him. But something had to have changed; something had to have made him realize that it was Dabny he should've stayed with. That he had loved her too much, that he couldn't leave her if he tried. And as Richard was proposing to Dabny, as the words were softly floating from his lips, at that very moment, he was probably thinking how he would tell whatever woman he was sleeping with that it was over between them. That he had almost made the worst mistake of his life, but he had caught himself, and he would do right from now on.

He would marry Dabny, and even though there would be no children, he would love her with all that he had, and they would be happy. But Dabny was sure that he had never intended on this.

Richard pulled his eyes back up to meet Dabny's and there was sorrow in them, regret, as he searched his mind for the words that would not come. He reached for her, but Dabny pulled away from him, not intentionally, triggered by reflexes alone, as a child would pull away from a filthy, contaminated old man.

That's what Richard was at that moment, contaminated. And as Dabny stood a little further away from him, cradling the arm he had touched, Richard looked hurt. He looked saddened, shamed, like a man unable to touch his own daughter, because he was suspected of molesting her.

"I did not sleep around on you," Richard said, softly, with as much conviction as he could fit into the lie. And then, "I still love you. I still want us to get married."

And it was the same shit over again, Dabny thought. Different man, different year, same circumstances. She wanted to spit in his face at that moment. She wanted to hurt him the same way that he had hurt her, but Dabny wasn't about to find some man to open her legs just to spite Richard. Besides, it wouldn't have been painful enough to him. Nothing could have allowed him to feel anything near what she was feeling at the moment, save for her going to a clinic, having their child cut and sucked out of her belly, and delivering the fetus to him in a jar. But she could not kill their child, for she knew all children were miracles, especially this one, because medical tests had *proved* he could not make her conceive.

Yes, she loved the child too much, and loved Richard too much, she thought, as she looked up at him, seeing the tears starting to accumulate on the ledges of his lower eye lids, threatening to fall.

She still loved him, still wanted their life together, and couldn't bare to let another man go because of one indiscretion. Dabny thought of Tony, his wife, his kids, his *family.* How happy they all seemed. She thought about the wisdom her mother tried to impart to her when she told Dabny that yes, even her father had cheated once, but her mother wouldn't "scrap a perfectly good car, just because of one tiny stitch of rust."

Dabny thought about all that, as she continued to look at Richard. He was a good man, and she didn't know if this was a one night stand, or something much deeper, but that she preferred not to hear. It would be too much.

One of the tears spilled from Richard's eye and raced down his cheek. Dabny extended her hand, smoothing it away with a tender brush of her fingertips, allowing her hand to gently rest there, and caressing his cheek. Yes, she did still love him.

"Turn around, Richard," Dabny said.

"Hunh?" Richard said, seeming surprised that the woman had even a single word for him.

"I said turn around."

He looked at her timidly for a moment, as if she would drive a dagger in his spine the minute he turned away from her, then he obediently followed her instructions.

"Now take off your shirt. I want to see your back."

"What?" and he made moves to turn back around, but Dabny halted him with her voice.

"No. Just do what I ask."

Richard exhaled heavily as his fingers went about undoing the buttons. He lowered the shirt from his shoulders, and allowed Dabny to look at the mess of scars that lined his back. There were three sets, one high between his shoulder blades, one low across his lower back, the other, the deepest, the angriest set of all, right across the middle. There was no question as to what she was seeing. The distance between each scratch was exactly the distance between that of each of a woman's fingers. There was no other explanation. But, again, Dabny told herself she would not throw away what she had with this man, what they could have as a family; the three of them.

Richard turned back around, stood in front of her, buttoning his shirt, a condemned look on his face, when Dabny said, "I was wrong."

"What?" Richard said, shocked.

"I said, I was wrong. I was thinking something else. But it looks to me like you slipped and fell and scraped your back. Is that what you did?"

"Yeah. That's what I did. I slipped and fell," Richard said, not even able to look in Dabny's eyes.

"That's what I thought. I just wanted to make sure we had gotten that straight, because I still want to get married, and I'm going to have our baby, and I'll raise it with or without you. So if you want to be any part of that, there will never be any more slipping and falling, will there?" Dabny said, willing never to speak to him again if he gave the wrong answer.

"No. I'll never slip and fall again," Richard said. "Never."

"Now give me a hug," Dabny said, with as much compassion as she would show a stranger. Richard moved close to her, wrapping his arms gingerly around her bare body. Dabny attempted, but could not find it within herself, to return his hug just yet. But she knew one day when they're alone, in the dark, holding their newborn child, she would.

PAMELA SNEED

Peeping Tom

I recall with intimate and gritty detail
one of my lovers recounting to me
the story of an infamous lesbian poet
getting fist-fucked voluntarily in a San Francisco bar.
What's worse is how this news traveled remarkably quickly
through the mouths of lesbians
from San Francisco's West to New York's East Coast.
As a writer seeing myself in the same position,
I retorted, "I don't give a fuck about what she does,"
but truthfully, I did.
Truthfully, part of me, like a peeping tom,
was curious, turned on by
glimpsing another's world.

For these reasons
I don't write erotica
have fear
imagining my mother reading the gritty details
of how I fuck or how lesbians fuck
(which she says is unnatural) and the shame she'll amass;
or imagining that small circle of lesbians

to which I sometimes belong
and how they'll react,
saying "ooh, that Pamela, she's kinky"
followed by long lists of attributes
they'll attach without ever knowing or talking to me.
This is not paranoia
but like the lesbian poet
happens to any semipublic persona.

As a teenager my first foray into the pitfalls of celebrity came in
seventh grade after writing an erotic story titled *The Adventures
of Brad and Julie*. It was not experienced firsthand but creatively
mimicked after *Playboy*, *Hustler*, and *Penthouse*. Because my
three friends and I were as obsessed with sex as some trekkies
are chasing the proverbial UFO, we exchanged information,
like spaceship and alien sightings—reporting any second- or
firsthand accounts of breasts, penises to the crimson spots of our
first menses. Thus my story was written at school, composed on
graying math sheets, during 2:00 to 3:15 free period, for the
sole enjoyment of my friends and me. However, like escapades
of the lesbian poet traveling by speed-dial to New York from
San Francisco, through some betrayal, news of my seventh-
grade erotic story also spread. For this I received instant and
unwarranted notoriety, which meant stardom in the worst sense:
having complete strangers solicit and accost me in the halls—
junior high school boys would stop me to leeringly inquire,
How's Brad? How's Julie?
Then without warning or a sudden spaceship landing, my
downfall was meteoric—resembling that of Marv Albert, the
prominent American toupee-wearing sportscaster who was
publicly embarrassed for wearing women's panties and other
antics during sex; and the actor Rock Hudson, who was outed
as a gay man suffering from AIDS. My image of virtuousness
and as seventh-grade dating material was destroyed, earning me
a reputation that can only be likened to summer supermarket
fruits ripening too early, that are easily tossed away
or lumped with others of their kind

and go under the labeling:
damaged.

The more curious or investigative side of my nature was actually
piqued at age six, when I gained entry to a new world after
catching my parents having sex. I was confused, had no labeling
for what my father was doing atop my mother—literally with his
pants down. I did not understand how a simple six-year-old's
request for water could cause my father to yell "Get back to bed
or get a beating" and behave so completely uncharacteristically.
I was dismayed, unsure of my wrongdoing, but from then on I
began to ponder, like the mysteries of the Bermuda Triangle
and Atlantis, the secret of my parents' relationship. Were they
like the FBI, blanketing important information? Emulating
Nancy Drew and the Hardy Boys I began searching for clues,
facts, proof of intelligent life, signs of an alien sexual activity:
telltale prophylactics, late night noise, doors left ajar. Finally in
broad daylight I stumbled upon my mother's hidden treasure:
Our Bodies, Ourselves, a book offering explanations to things I'd
always wanted to know.
This only led to more sophisticated questions.
Were my parents practicing positions other than missionary?
    After twenty-five years, did they still have sex?
And in the earlier years, when their fighting was constant and
my father's hands became brutal, was there arousal on both
parts, a story beneath the surface, like Atlantis, or an underlying
dynamic? Was there part of my mother truthfully deep down, in
the darkest recess, enjoying the slap, turned on by my father's
assertion of power?
I remember reading once
in a Richard Pryor biography that he said by beating a woman
    you end up losing
or owning her.

    This is all speculation.
    Perhaps this piece has nothing to do with Atlantis
    but is like a tender fruit
    with its protective layer peeled back

and core exposed
about fear
about my new lover
with greenish-blue eyes
and how she like a deep space explorer
claimed my body
moved across it
without fear
keeps a bedside stock of lube, vibrators, dildos and harness
and how she on our first night
presented an array of plastic dildos
ranging in shape and size
then looked at me in all seriousness
asking which?
Responding shyly I chose
a small, tiny pink plastic dick
which she scuttled away retorting
"that's a buttplug"
which I knew
but my eyes couldn't stop feasting
at a very large, red and black and swirled dildo
that was almost psychedelic
very tie-dye
and reminded me of all places
that arena of lesbian sex
called San Francisco.
That's Champ, she said.
When you fuck me
use that.
Strapping Champ on
I was reticent
wondered if I were man enough
using the same dick
she and past lovers used
if adjusting the harness
I was adept riding bareback
and could without fully
dismantling

like a hungry lover
descend into the unknown
licking the deepest most succulent part
without fear.

With sex, part of me is always adventurous
relishing the occasional slap,
golden shower,
or complete domination,
while the other is hesitant,
unsure
avoids wrongdoing
imagining my father's yell
mother's shame
those lesbian accusations of "ooh, she's kinky"
coming to me like junior high school voices
the damaging labels and gossip
part of me still remembers adolescence
the stiff heavy-handed punishments
that accompany sex
menstrual napkins that I would wrap
then dispose of
like evidence
part of me remembers involuntary abuses
like wanting love and
sucking some guy's dick
behind the high school
being penetrated without permission
and I remember a scenario different
than one expressed earlier
different than San Francisco and New York
where freedoms did not abound
places and times where women could not say
what they wanted
god forbid, publicly fist-fuck
and part of me as an adult
is always stripping off
long cotton underwear, bras and slips I wore

stripping off shame
and the knowledge of hiding
not of sex as a natural process
part of me remembers growing up
in a small town
with blacks few
and girls abhorred
and I can see eyes of an older man
living downstairs
staring at me
in my gangly adolescent body
and for some reason not known
like someone looking to the stars
offered my mother this prediction:
That Pamela,
when she grows up,
will be beautiful
and in this landscape that I describe
his voice above all others
gave hope.

ROBERT FLEMING

Responding to Her Touch

T HE illness of loneliness is upon him again. His lips sting from the mouthpiece of the trumpet, from long sets at the club, from the bruised kisses of a woman who didn't belong to him. What was he doing in Paris anyway? He should have kept his black ass in the States instead of wandering around all over the world, instead of seeking something he couldn't name. Forty years old, broke, no wife, no kids. A nigger without portfolio.

He pours himself a shot of cognac, heaves a sigh, and places a Fats Navarro record on the phonograph. The memory of Fat Girl blowing the trumpet so sweet, so soulfully, sweeps through him as the notes rush up and circle the ceiling in a cone of bright colors. Fats on "Our Delight." He stretches out on the bed again, pushing the empty liquor bottles and crumpled candy wrappers aside to make room for his long legs. There is something about drinking that makes the time go by softly, easily, without the sudden starts and stops that normally accompany the passage of a day. A little scotch, a nip of gin, a splash of bourbon on ice, or a half belly of *vin rouge*. It all gives his existence a veneer of civilization, pretties matters a bit. The stocking cap on his shiny, conked hair itches.

Solange has just left. His Congo cutie. Another man's woman. He replays in his head her arrival two hours earlier, savoring every moment of her time with him. She puts down her purse and without a word takes off her summer dress. She never wears any underwear. She opens her purple thighs wide, pulls back the lips of her sex so he can look down into its scarlet throat. She says she can smell the white woman on her man's penis when he comes home. Her husband, Jacques, out catting. Says the white bitches stink. White women *basali na masoko na maimai,* she says in her native tongue. His sheets smell of her, strongly female, like ripe tropical fruit. Her luminous purple face against the pillow as she urges him to shove it inside, be rough, and starts moving her ass against him like crazy while he reaches under to worry her *amanze,* her clit, with a finger.

Solange says she wants to feel him at the back of her throat and he stops pumping into her so he can apply his tongue to her breasts, teasing the nipples to an aching hardness, and then to her sex. She is tight down there, narrow, warmer than her mouth and moist. She rouses her ass to him and he plunges in her very deep, tearing her with pleasure, but she stops him before either comes. She guides him into position above her head, his legs straddling her as he pushes himself into her pillow mouth. Steady thrusts. A hot liquid flows from her bushy cleft onto her strong thighs, and he reaches around to dip his fingers into the gushing honey and brings them to his lips. Then he works his dick into her afterward slippery with her legs up, riding her bareback, sweat on her face and breasts, until she howls in delight and bites him on the shoulder.

"Jacques doesn't satisfy me," she murmurs in almost precise English. "His thing's too little. But he's a good man otherwise. His friends hate me. His Little Savage, they call me."

"Does Jacques say anything to them about the way they treat you?" he asks, lighting another cigarette. "He wouldn't let them get away with that if he is any kind of man."

"He is like so many Frenchmen, very arrogant about his culture, art, and aesthetics," she says, reaching for the cigarette. "He will not talk to me sensibly about anything. He talks to me like a child. You see, Cole, I know I'm not totally respectable in his eyes."

"Then why don't you leave?"

She folded her arms and rested her head upon them. "I don't know. Maybe I can go to the Sorbonne, take classes and improve myself. He says he'd pay for it. But that doesn't change how his women friends look at me. To them, everyone and everything is more civilized than the African. One asked me if I had any pygmies in my family. Cole, they watch me all the time whenever we go to events, they watch me with a hate that is not hidden. They comment rudely on my makeup, my hair, my choice of clothes, and the size of my ass. I have a fat African ass, yes?"

He laughs. "But I love your African ass."

The mirror is in her hands and she watches herself in it, studying her features intently. "The white women are more prettier, more cultured, yes? Jacques tells me all the time that there is only one way toward civilization and that road goes through the world of the whites. If that is true, then that is bad, yes?"

"Beauty is in the eye of the beholder, someone said, and I believe that jive," he says, taking the mirror from her. It's a shame what their brainwashing can do to our minds, about how we look, about how we think, about what we're worth.

She spins around in a tight circle, nude, her breasts flopping. Two horny French sailors across the way are hiding behind the curtain in their window, getting an eyeful. Unconcerned about them, she continues her strange inspection of herself. "They won't let me be one of them. They accept me only when I play the pagan, the primitive Congo girl." Turning to face him, she says suddenly, "Cole Riley, why are you here in Paris?"

"I ask myself that all the time." He takes a puff on the cigarette. "America's a hard place to live if you are a black man. Jim Crow lets you know it's for white folks. We can't vote, gotta sit in special sections in diners and on buses, can't do a lot of things whites can do. After my brother was lynched in his army uniform in Alabama by some rednecks, I came to Paris after the war and never went back. There's nothing for me there. Not anymore."

She laughs harshly. "The modern civilized man and woman. Jacques fucks my inferiority complex and I think it's love. Now I hate when he touches me. Come here, *cherie*, make love to me again."

"Do you come with him in you?" He needs some rest.

"Never, but with you sometimes." She said that, got up and poured some water into the basin, scrubbed her crotch with soap. And with a quick kiss on his cheeks, she says she'll see him later and leaves.

In the afternoon before going to the gig, Cole strolls over to the Café Tournon near the Luxembourg Gardens, a center of French life now infested with colored artists and writers. The black bohemian life. He has seen them there or at the Monaco. Richard Wright, William Gardner Smith, even that Himes fellow. He missed all of the ruckus between Wright and the little guy, Baldwin, over who was the Man. Or as Henri put it: "Two colored boys biting at each other's ankles." He dug the colored folks here, especially the writers. They'd stake him a drink now and then. They were all over the place, in the Latin Quarter, the Left Bank, even down among the Arabs in poor Belleville.

Yet it would sometimes get to him. So far away from home, from his roots, and the French could be such shits. He didn't mind the snotty French intellectuals who felt they had a monopoly on the finer aspects of thought and style. But the others, the critics mainly, held their own idea of what was black. Much like Solange said. It was the same way in the States. You couldn't escape the bull. You could see it in how they looked at the black guys, the writers and artists, who slept with their women. Somehow it took on a different flavor when the colored boy did it.

Some cats slept with these ofay chicks as a way of settling old scores, getting back through them for the way the massa had treated them back home. He had sampled them but it wasn't a taste that stuck with him. Some of the cats had two, three, even four of them stashed away, but his taste for them was queered by the memory of his brother lynched for making love to a cracker chick who wanted to leave her husband for him. The ofay chick got knocked up by his brother, panicked, and went to her husband and insisted "the nigger raped" her. A few of the local cracker men waited for him to come home, dragged him from his Buick, beat the hell out of him, worked on him with a knife and hung him from an old magnolia tree. The message was clear: nigger boys stay away from the pink at all costs.

Paris looked the other way with colored boys and foreign women, but if a Frenchie chick said a colored boy mistreated her, he was gone, kicked out of the country. No amount of pink was worth that. He didn't want to go back to the States. He couldn't, he knew. He'd die there or end up behind bars.

Weary, Cole finds a seat at one of the little bistro tables outside the place near the Coca-Cola sign. The thin dude who bartends there sometimes chats him up on current events in broken English while he stands at the red copper bar inside and remembers the night when they hung out at Haynes, a joint owned by an ex-GI who also lingered in the City of Lights after World War II. All the jazz cats came through his joint. He went to Haynes for the soul food, especially the jambalaya, but a trip to Café Tournon meant things like chats on spook culture, hometown memories, and fiery arguments about art and music. That was cool.

"Your usual, Monsieur Cole?" the bartender asks flatly, and quickly serves the trumpeter two doubles of bourbon. He downs them one after another while watching a clean-shaven black man in a brown suit sitting at another café table covered with a newspaper, two books, and a notebook. The man stares at the people walking on the street, the passing traffic, and general Parisian madness. Occasionally the pen moves in his hand on the paper.

"Who's that?" Cole asks, sipping coffee.

"Richard Wright, the man who wrote *Native Son*," the Frenchman replies, admiration in his voice. "There is no one with him today. I think he wants to be alone."

When Cole walks out, he gives the writer a quick glance, stepping close to his table so he could see what he is writing. But he cannot and Mr. Wright locks eyes with him for an instant. Cole nods and smiles, says hey brother, which causes the writer to wave him over. The exchange is very brief. They shake hands, Mr. Wright's hand almost limp in his grasp, then he stands at the table. Cole reminds him that they'd first met at the Monaco and again at Haynes's joint. He says he dug *Native Son* and *The Outsider*. Everybody colored knows everybody else in Paris, for the most part. He tells Mr. Wright that he was surrounded by people both times so they barely spoke to one another. The books on the table are Camus' novel, *The Stranger*, a biography of De Gaulle during the war years, and a journal, *Presence Africaine*. He can't read his writing on the paper, a scrawl of letters that covers every line of the page. A photo of Wright, Sartre, and Simone de Beauvoir at the Gaite Bookstore lies nearby.

"Where are you from in the States, my friend?" Mr. Wright asks as he drinks from his water glass, smiles, and rearranges the clutter on the table.

"From New York City. Musician."

"What kind of music do you play?" Mr. Wright asks.

"Jazz. Trumpet like Dizzy. I'm playing at *Le Cave* over in Montmartre until next week," the trumpeter says, and leaves after Mr. Wright promises to come to the club, joining the citizens walking to the Metro. The Underground, is what they call it in London.

That night, Cole gets a nice round of applause when he walks through the club to the bandstand. He holds his horn in front of him in tribute to the cheers. The dimly lit club is only slightly bigger than a jail cell, with every inch of the floor covered with tables. Cole plays brass in the usual kind of quintet with a tenor and trumpet fronting the customary rhythm section, performing a bunch of old standards for the tourist trade and the locals.

Albert, the tenor man and bandleader, clears his throat, stares out at the crowd, and calls out "I Cried Out for You." One of Lady Day's favorites. Cole thinks he wouldn't be there if he didn't need the francs. It is Albert's tune to toy with. The tenor man who thinks he is the next Prez or Bean. Albert blows long, curling lines of sound with his horn turned to the side. Like Lester used to do it. Jean-Paul, the bassist, supports him with a few solid runs, full walking tones. While the pair plays, the others lay out, listening, and finally Cole rolls his eyes at Skeeter, a refugee from Detroit who works the drums. Max Roach is the boy's idol. Then Cole steps to the mike with his trumpet blazing and responds to their lame jamming with chorus after chorus of hot gutbucket blues lines.

Skeeter pats his foot, his hands a blur of motion with the drumsticks, smiling. "Do it, baby, do it."

The trumpeter winks and hears them cheering after each surge of notes, blowing harder and harder. The customers are on their feet, hollering, shouting encouragement. Albert is pissed off, grimacing, holding his tenor and wishing it would all end. This showboating. Cole doesn't give a damn. His solo gets wilder and wilder, hitting unbelievably high notes and sustaining them. As if Skeeter is reading his mind, the drummer crashes the cymbals and does a series of wild rolls on the snare to build the drama. Waiters stop to listen, not a word of chat in the joint, and the cash register becomes mute as a strange quiet sweeps through the crowd.

Tired of Cole's circus play on the trumpet, Albert lifts his horn to his lips and hops into the action. No way this boy is going to run off the stage. He's never copped out of a cutting contest. For four choruses, they chase each other around Billie's tune, one note after another, sometimes quoting from pop tunes, grunts and growls and slurs artfully placed to raise the hair on the back of the neck. The crowd is into it, clapping and whistling.

"Bring it home now," Albert hisses, blowing some low, dark tones from his horn in contrast to Cole's chatty, frisky trumpet runs. He signals to wrap up the number, which they do.

Albert, the bandleader, raises his hand and calls for quiet. "Thank you. *Merci, merci.*" He stomps off the start of the next song, "Night and Day." Cole runs away on this one too, blowing full-out on the trumpet, forcing Albert to follow up with some tricks of his own. He pauses for an instant between flurries, then starts blasting again, a vein pulsing recklessly in his neck. The two horns battle it out head-to-head until they roar through the final choruses to the end. The crowd shouts its approval. This is what they like. Spontaneous invention. Improvising on the edge.

After the show, Albert complains that he is losing control of his band, but Cole doesn't pay him any mind. He watches Solange. Solange, who will later drive her little Saab over to his hotel for some fun and frolic.

"If you don't like what we play, find another gig, Cole," Albert growls. Skeeter the drummer laughs and says the best bands play outside the melody sometimes, stretching out.

"What was that shit you played tonight?" Jacques, the club

owner, asks. Albert frowns and tries to explain while the others laugh. Cole puts on his dark glasses, smooths his glistening conk, lights a cigarette. A husky-smelling *Gauloise*. Then he splits, lusting for his Congo cutie.

Jacques' wife, Solange. His Negress. Miss Congo. A white man's wife. Her purple-black skin, jutting breasts, thin waist, and bubble butt. Long shapely dark legs under her thin cotton dresses. That thatch of black curly hair on her pubis mound, her thumb-sized clit. The knowledge that her man knows about them does not bother Cole too much. Jacques once had them followed to his place. He slapped her around when she got home. She ran back to Cole, all battered. She wouldn't let him hold her nor did she cry. In an odd way, she was proud of the damage the Frenchman'd done to her face. It proved that the white man loved her.

Another night, three of Jacques' imported toughs from Pigalle roughed him up as a warning to leave the African seductress alone. That didn't stop anything. They were together that same night, when she tells him about the day the Belgians from Leopoldville, the capital, came into her village and burned down all the huts and raped the young girls. Her too. A gang of foul-smelling Europeans in her. But Jacques saved her, got her a false passport, and brought her to the City of Lights. Married her and displayed her as his exotic nigger trophy from the Congo.

"Do you know what the Belgians call us back home?" she asks Cole, who shakes his head. "I'll tell you. They call us *macac*, it means monkey. Everywhere you go, someone treats you like a *macac*."

Three days later. It is cold, uncommonly cold for a summer day in Paris. Cole can almost see his breath rise like small vapor clouds. He thinks of a couple he saw the night before kissing and strolling hand-in-hand near the Tuilleries. He watches a wasp crawl across the windowpane. His trumpet sits on the bed amid the two ashtrays full of cigarette butts, sheets of manuscript paper for charts, an overturned bottle of *Pernod*, and an open suitcase. It's an old tarnished Buescher horn his grandpa gave him for his birthday with loose valves and leaks. But he loves its full, rich sound.

A knock at the door. It's Solange. In no time she is naked in all her ebony magnificence, the color of dark bruised plums against the startling white of the sheets. She tells him he is full of shit, for leaving, running away. He laughs. She imagines the head of his dick near her sex and he teases her with it. She imagines him inside her, moving in an easy circular style, the muscles of her vault tightening around him.

"Why do you want me, Cole?" she asks, pinching her nipples. "Do you want me because I belong to someone else?"

He lights another cigarette and continues packing. He is a thin, dark man with a flat broken nose who loves his women purple or dark blue. Once he sampled a *blanc* woman, Aurore, a blond singer from Marseilles, who rubbed his skin like a woman scrubbing a stain from her dress. At other times, she sniffed his underarms, his so-called man scent. She forbade him to use deodorant, and inhaled his scent from the crotch. Sometimes she told him she loved him. Sometimes when he was inside her, he shut his eyes real tight and imagined the actress Simone Signoret or the singer Juliette Greco bucking underneath him—panting, submissive, with her curvy white buttocks hot and wet. That trick never worked.

When Cole crosses the room to Solange, he takes a cigarette from her pack and places it between her lips. He feels her watching him, smoking. She smokes one butt after another until she finally becomes bored and pushes him toward the bed but he resists. She breaks him down by stroking his dick through his pants, feeling it grow into diamond hardness. He realizes she has been drinking, heavily, for her breath reeks of stale gin.

"Jacques says he'll kill me if I see you anymore," she moans. "I think he means it. He'll kill you too."

Cole says nothing, only flips her on her stomach, touches the moisture between her cheeks with his finger and slowly slides into her. He drives into her like her husband would do if he could. He pounds into her for every night he will miss her when he leaves. He rides her like it's the last time, which it is. She screams, screams, screams but he is relentless inside her, twisting and snapping his hips into her, until they come together, crying out as if stabbed in the heart, until she comes once again, lifting up her entire gleaming body, to him, her purple hands desperately clutching the sheets.

The last time. In the time it takes her to smoke four cigarettes, Cole understands that he must leave Paris, leave her softness and the trouble that follows her like a bad scent. When she leaves to go to the window wrapped in his robe, he takes her in his arms and begs her forgiveness. But he must do what he must do.

Solemnly, Cole watches Solange put on lipstick, the rouge coating her ample lips, and powder her cheeks with a white dust. The bed is soaked with their fluids, scents, and their sweat. At the lightest sound on the stairs, he presses his ear to the door, heart pounding, and listens for the men who will come to harm him. He can't run anymore. His Congo cutie finishes the repair job on her face, sits on his bed, and watches her lover with tears in her eyes.

LISA TEASLEY

8 Hours of Mina and Stan

L. A. morning rain. February, two minutes before ten. Mina sits on the cold marble-tiled counter, her red terry-cloth robe in a royal spread behind her. To the right, kitty-corner above the shower, wisteria crawls through the open window. Stan makes delicate circles around Mina's well-defined kneecaps. Goose bumps appear, slightly red in the pale of her albino flesh. Her cornrowed hair is the color of rope, and uncoils like garden snakes as she lets her head drop back to expose the hollow of her throat. Stan rests his tongue there. He slowly licks her collarbone, making a diamond trail up her neck to the four tiny holes in her left ear. Her colorless lashes flutter.

The rain shifts gear from sprinkle to piss-down, spraying through the wisteria in the window, the white floor now glistening wet. Mina concentrates on the bathroom acoustics. Stan pulls her head to meet his face, bites her plush bottom lip, roughly pushes her thighs wider. The cold of the marble and the pad of his round thumb heat her pussy. The goose bumps rise up on her body, flame, then disappear as he caresses, enters, thrusts. Mina almost cums to the sound alone, the sucking hiss of his cock as if inside a membraned microphone and the amplified surge of the rain.

Quarter to eleven. To the living room she follows him. Stan glides the belt through his Levi's loops; she shakes her head. What are you shaking your head at? he asks. She smiles; without her glasses she can barely make out the details of him, but she knows she hates that belt. She also wonders what it would feel like if he whipped her with it.

In the dark yellow kitchen, which is part of the living room, she throws a banana, yogurt, and protein mix into the blender. She turns it on high; Stan screws up his brow. Still on those, huh Mina? he asks, looking for his shoes, which he'd kicked off somewhere the night before. She dips her finger in, licks it, realizes she's forgotten the honey. The blender on, again. Stan still hasn't found his shoes; he looks at her impatiently.

Her hands are on her hips, the bottom half of her hourglass. The smoothie is half full on the counter in front of her. She wears a simple short yellow dress of faded gray flowers, a hint of eggplant colors her lips. Stan's pout appears to her an invitation for a kiss.

Stay where you are, she tells him. He listens. Stan stands. Slowly she walks over to him, her steps measured, calm. She pushes him to sit on the black leather couch and turns on the bright reading lamp; he looks up at it, irritated. She puts her finger over her mouth. Ssssh, he says, in lip sync. She unbuckles his belt, whips it off in one take. She unzips his jeans; he raises his narrow hips, so she can easily pull down his long-legged pants. On the floor she sits for a moment, looking up at him. His dark brown cock is shy at first, then begins to fill itself out under the warmth of the hot light. When the tip touches the cold leather, it lifts a bit, and she smiles. She could barely make this out, the details a blur, but she rises to her knees, and takes his cock in her mouth. Were they thinking of me when they made these? she wonders. Taking him into the base of her throat, she thinks, Yes, they were thinking of my mouth. Stan's head goes back, his lips part enough to see the raw red inside. My god, Mina, he says out loud. My gaahd, he softly growls.

Half past noon. Stan still hasn't found his shoes; and they still have not kissed, tongue-to-tongue, for days.

Are you hungry? Mina asks.

I told you I have a lunch, he says, again irritated, as if she'd hid the shoes, as if she'd turned on the blender once more.

How come I don't believe you? she asks. She's picking up stray articles of mess, a dirty glass here, a two-day-old newspaper there.

Because you never believe *anybody*; the world's against you, isn't it, Mina?

Oh, and the world is *for* you, isn't it, Stan?

No-no, uh-uh, not this again, he says, running his hand over his short clipped hair.

I asked you last week if you would come with me to look at this car, remember? she asks, her hands again on her hips. She has put on her glasses, and feels as ugly and odd as she did as a child. She can see him clearly now, and he is as seductively beautiful as the first time she saw him two years ago. His face round except for the chiseled cut of his jaw, his brows as if brushed in place, the beauty mark at his temple, his dark eyes large with bedroom lids and curtained with girlish fringe.

Well then how about four? How about I swing around then and get you?

I told the guy two! I told him I'd be there at two! How can I change the appointment again? she asks, taking Stan's wrist firmly in her hand.

Well if he hasn't sold the car by now, it must not be worth it. If it could wait a week, it could wait two more hours, Stan says, pulling his wrist away, glaring into her gray magnified eyes, then turning around, heading for the bedroom. Mina throws her body in his way.

It's *me* that's tired of waiting, she says.

Is this all about the car? Or are we talking about something else? Stan asks, staying where he is. Mina says nothing, looks over his shoulder, then tries focusing again, darting from one of Stan's pupils to the other.

You have always taken care of yourself. You know what you want. You have always taken exactly what you want, he says more angrily now, and pushing past her. He accidentally knocks a few books further back into the shelf.

Mina picks up her black-on-white polka-dot umbrella, holds

it tightly around the neck, waiting for him to reappear. When he does, he looks at her with an expression of disgust, a little fear. This makes her livid. She can see he loves her, but this only adds to it. After all, it took him more than a year to realize he did, and even longer than that to acknowledge it.

She points the umbrella at him. How long are we going to go back and forth with this kind of shit? she asks. Why does it always have to be me, waiting on you?

She can see he is shocked, and now her temples throb. She thrusts forward with the umbrella's tip, and as he's raised his palms in the air, the point breaks through the skin. He yells out, then runs, holding the right hand in the left. She saw the blood. And he is out the door. She dashes as far as the threshold, calling after him, but he's gone, barefoot like that in the rain, and he's parked down the hill, and something stops her from running after him, but it is not the rain, which is pissing down again.

You've done it now, she says to herself. She slams the door shut, turns around, stares at her hands. The umbrella is on the floor. Against the dark wood it looks like a clown's prop. She claps her forehead, cups it as if to catch the ache.

Stan was never into pain; Stan was never into fighting. Why do I always push it?

Twenty-five minutes to two. On the couch, Mina lies, staring at the blond peach fuzz on her thighs. She only shaves to her knees, and suddenly this appears to her to be a mistake. She caresses her thighs lightly with her fingers; the goose bumps raise. She looks out the living room window; the lemon tree is green, and so are the lemons. The rain stopped moments ago, now the leaves shine with tears. The sun is peeking out of the clouds and how she hates it for making itself enemy to her skin.

Stan is her mother's color, and certainly her brother's. Close to her father's too, for that matter. If she remembered them all correctly; it had been years, and she doesn't keep photographs. Unlike her brother, her father had never even claimed Mina as his. He'd struck her mother down for giving birth to a curse. She despised him for his ignorance, and she despised her mother even more for being incapable of infidelity.

Runaway Mina. Albino freak. Isn't that what they'd called her back then?

Fuck Stan. And fuck his memories of every other woman, including, and most important, the one she took him from.

Was she sick? Was she empty? Would she feel good again?

Would pride in having raised herself, making her own way, making many men, needing no one, answering only to herself, be enough for her again?

She lies on her stomach, lifting the lightweight fabric of her skirt, letting it gather at the waist. Against the couch she lightly brushes her nipples until the areola gathers in bumps, the tips hard and raised. Her ass in the air, her finger finds her pussy still wet from sucking off Stan. Her gray eyes flit up with the flutter of her colorless lashes, she moans, wanting his dick back inside of her, as she rocks against her finger, the ball of her wrist twisted with her weight against the couch. The whites of her eyeballs have a bluish cast in the dark of the room. She is cumming, and the sun has gone away behind the clouds again.

Thirty-five minutes past five. Mina, chomping on a carrot, stands in the backyard. How is it that this strangely warm, dry wave has caught the air? The sky nearly purple, like the glow of the tiny wisteria bulbs that start by the fence and make their way back to the bathroom window. From out here, she can hear the key turn in the front door. She is relieved but at the same time wonders why she'd ever given it to him.

Mina smells Stan now right behind her. Her cheeks flush, the hairs at the nape of her neck rise. She is embarrassed to be out of control. She wishes she could strangle the rush of feeling within.

I'm sorry, she says, looking out beyond the gray stone patio fence. Stan flattens a dandelion, then with the toe of his new shoes, tries to fluff it back up again.

Four stitches, he says, holding out his bandaged palm.

I'm so sorry, she says, looking down at the grass. The wind whips up a bit, banging the security door shut. I hate Santa Anas, she says.

You think these are Santa Anas, so close after the rain? he asks, coming closer to her, and she looks at him. Stan has such smooth, black, perfect brows, she says to herself, his top lip so full it gives the appearance of resting on the bottom. It also makes him look like a naughty, pouty child. When she licks and sucks and bites on this top lip, it's as if she is molesting a baby brother, or teasing the hurt she used to feel for her fate.

Forgive me, she says, tasting the outline of his mouth, shyly holding the frame of his jaw in her hands. His mouth remains motionless. He will make her work for his tongue. She stops and looks him in the eyes. Without her glasses, they appear to her like a choice between two abysses. If she dives into one, she might find herself; if she dives into the other she might find her death. But he is not looking at her. She turns to follow the line of his sight, and she can just make out a rogue moon.

Down she pulls him into the wet grass. Her breasts are too big for his one good hand and he gropes determinedly as if to make them fit. Her tongue has found the roof of his mouth and he might let her touch his tonsils. His teeth clamp down on her instead. She lets him bite, and she tastes the slightest hint of blood in the mix of their saliva. This kiss is long and slow; a contrast to the speed of their breathing, how fast she unzips, and the quick, desperate adjustments of pelvises and limbs. She has his cock again inside of her womb, and they are moving with the hot, menacing whiz of the Santa Ana winds. She rows and rolls him in, open, found, and listening to their acoustics in twilight.

KWAME DAWES

Deecy and Pheo
A Cautionary Tale

H E expected Kingston to be a mad world of bodies pressing against him, of hustlers harassing him. He did not want to look like a foreigner landing here after several years of being away. He wanted his Jamaican speech to be intact so that he could sound like a man returning to the island after only a few weeks away. He hoped that his scowl, his slow walk, his easy manner, would translate into something local, something homegrown.

He feared that by looking at him they could also tell that he was a man who, at thirty, had failed at love, at making something of his relationships with women, and failed at his many compacts with God. He also hoped that they could not tell that he was now entering the eleventh month of celibacy. After eleven months, he noticed that his body had stopped announcing its sexuality to him. The taste of sex was so stale, so distant that he wondered if he was a man still. Sex was now the disembodied sound of a woman, far away, in another place. He had not touched a woman in a year, not seen the delicate curve of the back of a woman's naked thigh in a year. But he was home and he hoped they could not sniff out this sense of barren disquiet. The sun would heal him—he would make paintings, drink in the thick air of humanity carrying out the rituals of survival that it had carried out for so many centuries on this island.

He expected that the crowd at the airport would come at him—people asking him for his bag, trying to hustle him for money—the moment he stepped into the brilliant, unrelenting heat. He feared that they would see the Yankee veneer on his skin, smell it coming out of his pores. He wanted to feel at home but feared, as he sat in the plane squashed against the side of the cabin by a large African American woman with a hairdo that made her at least eight inches taller, that he was going to land as a stranger.

The landing was gentle. The scraggly grass sped by and the sea was a sharp blue in the sunlight. First the sea, and then the hills rising around him. Above the hills the endlessly open sky seemed to have a depth of meaning—a breathtaking cleanness that suggested that he was somewhere else entirely. He felt at home. He was moved by the landscape, by the way the warm air settled on his body when he stepped out of the plane. He understood at once why some people often fell to their knees on the tarmac on arrival and kissed this island. He himself felt kissed by it, embraced by the gusts of warm air around his face and chest; between his legs its warm tongue welcomed him and he grew wet at once with the feel of the heat.

He was here to bury an uncle he had loved. He had come to make arrangements for his papers and to support his cousins. They had come to depend on him in that way. It was the role he always played. But now, he also knew that he was coming to thaw after the dull and overwrought winter of Connecticut. He had worked too hard trying to make extra money with case after case. There was nothing else to do. Work kept him sane. His routine of loneliness was now properly established.

Standing outside the Norman Manley International Airport, listening to the voices, watching the mad push and shove of the cars, he was startled by the comfort, the ease he felt. It was pleasant to be able to lean calmly against a post and wait for his notoriously late cousin to pick him up without worrying about it. Standing there he did not expect to see anyone he knew.

So when she came up to him out of the blue with a quizzical smile on her face and her voice familiar as pleasant memory saying, "Pheo Hughes, what are you doing here?" he realized that he could not even speak her name. It was Deecy Graham. He had not seen her—her face, her body, her eyes, her short-cropped hair, her legs, those athletic shapely legs, and the full and sturdy hips—in years. He had forgotten her breasts, the even and balanced fullness of them, the way they suggested a certain muscularity even as they seemed succulent and tempting.

"I don't believe this!" he said, as he felt the stretch of a smile on his face. He was suddenly happy. He could not resist the happiness he felt at seeing her. "Deecy, what are *you* doing here? Why didn't you tell me?"

"I told you, but you never listen to me," she said, laughing. Her eyes, oval and full with dark irises, glowed back with laughter. She was happy. They were both quite happy.

He kept repeating, "You look good, you look so good." And she kept laughing and blushing slightly as she changed the subject. She asked why he was in Jamaica and how long he planned to stay. His answers all ended with, "You really looking so good," as he stared down the low cut of her blouse at the deep brown of her beautiful breasts. He knew that they would deepen into a richer mahogany hue after a few days in the sun. She smiled brightly and with such openness and welcome that he felt pulled toward her.

She had come to a best friend's wedding and was staying in Kingston with relatives. She insisted that she had told him, but he had no recollection of it. Sometimes they talked about so many things before she would then tell him that she was wet and she wanted to sing a song for him. He would say, "Sing." And she would say that she loved the way he said "sing." And she would start to whisper his name as she described what her fingers were doing to herself, as she painted pictures of her room, and the small garden that opened out from the French doors. She would describe the way the room seemed full of green light as she lay there talking to him and reaching deep into herself. She always called from her room. In the mornings, she said, she took care of herself.

She called him in the mornings after her husband had left for work. She said the world was a different place when he left. The room was greener. She loved her husband in the same way that she loved her job and her home. They were part of her definition of who she was. He was a gentle kind man who adored her. But she said she never felt the tumbling sensation of entering a world as comfortable as a womb as she did when she was talking to Pheo. She said that Pheo was simply a fixture in her life, a part that she would never want to give up even if what they were doing was wrong. She blamed God for making Pheo the only person who really understood her, the only person with whom she could be completely honest. She said that she had to blame God for making such arrangements and so both she and God would have to live with them.

While Pheo gave her his hotel details her family pulled up in a tan BMW waving, laughing, and shouting. A taller, bouncier version of Deecy ambled up, bag, hair, chains, bangles, keys swinging. Deecy introduced them.

"Pheo? Oh really?" her sister said with a knowing smile, the jewel in her right nostril gleaming.

"Can you imagine we didn't even know . . ." Deecy said, with as much sincerity as she could muster.

"You didn't know, eh?" her sister said, now laughing with playful mockery.

"Really," Pheo said, smiling at this woman who he liked immediately for her humor.

"Well, me would say the same if me was unoo. So you coming with us or . . ." she said, slipping a look to Deecy.

"Don't be silly," Deecy said and then reached and touched Pheo's face. "I will call."

"Hrrmmm. The great Pheo, eh? Well, well . . ." her sister said and chimed her way to the car, her swinging hips adding to the music. She was still laughing. Deecy smiled.

"She alright," she said. "I will call."

"You are looking good, Deecy. God, you look good," he said staring at her—he meant every word.

"You are making me blush," she said.

"You are not blushing," he said.

"I am glowing."

"You are glowing. You look sexy." He said the word in a whisper.

"I am PMSing, that's why," she said laughing loudly. But he knew it was code for her horniness. She always said that she felt awkward when other women complained about PMSing. She looked forward to it. "Hot and bothered," she would say. "Yuh turning Yankee," he would say. And they would laugh.

He smiled back at her. "You are being bad," he said looking across at her sister who was staring at them.

"You make me do that." She smiled again. "I will call you."

Then she left. Pheo stood alone in the hot sun. He felt a terrible happiness, something he could not explain, and the lightness in his head was intoxicating. He was so happy to be in Jamaica.

He decided, that afternoon, to take some time for himself before the madness of family began. He went to a favorite spot of his to think and restore his sense of the island. He drove his cousin's car up Hope Road, climbed up toward the Blue Mountains along the Gordon Town Road, and then turned sharply toward Skyline Drive with its rugged tree-filled stretch of road that overlooked the city. He drove slowly along Skyline until he came to a familiar place where the view of the city was perfect. It was just where a particularly exuberant growth of coffee trees virtually crawled its way onto the road. He climbed out of the car and walked for a few yards, trying to follow with his eye the path of the coastal highway that led along the edge of Kingston toward the peninsula, where the airport was the curved grace of an arm resting on the purple sea.

He was thinking about Deecy, thinking about her smile and the way her body leaned into his when she reached to touch him. He wondered if she would let him touch her, reach his arm around her body and then find his tongue tasting her mango sweetness. He did not want to think about this. Deecy was married, "happily married" in many ways, and they both knew that if they came physically close to each other, if they touched, something terrible would happen—something that could destroy what she had. He did not want to think about touching her, but he was thinking about her and wondering if she was thinking about him in the same way.

He went back to the car, took out his sketchpad and began to write a letter to her. He wrote quickly, feeling the gradually mellowing sun crawling across his body and then over the page, over his hand until it was almost too dark for him to continue. He sat back and took a deep breath. He could feel his penis throbbing. The words he wrote made him drip slightly until he could feel his erect penis slipping against the fabric of his briefs. He reprimanded himself for writing the letter, for his thoughts, and then told himself he would not send it to her. Instead he would go back to the hotel and relax.

He drove slowly along the now pitch-black road, until it dipped into an avenue of streetlights and expensive residences. Soon he was back in the belly of Kingston.

He parked under a copse of almond trees with their fat leaves making grotesque shadows along the ground. He was suddenly tired, very tired. He wanted to take a long shower, and then he would masturbate slowly, thinking about Deecy, and then he would sleep.

He came with his mind filled with Deecy's large brown nipples, her body unfurling over him. He fell asleep uncovered with his ejaculation slippery on his stomach and his thighs. He slept through the night and then for several hours into the day until he was roused by a knock on the door.

He opened the door. It was Deecy in a flowing white cotton dress held up by thin straps. The nipples of her bare breasts were caressed softly by the light fabric. She was a light of startling daylight in the room. She had perspired a bit in the heat. He could smell the faint aroma of her body under her delicate perfume. She smiled. Then she walked past him and sat down. He gathered some clothes and went to the bathroom. He showered quickly and then as he dressed he kept wondering why he was putting on his clothes when he knew that he would probably be taking them off.

He came out, handed her the letter and then sat down on the bed.

They didn't speak. Shaka Demus was pleading with a woman on the radio—his voice a gruff sweetness riding the rhythm.

Deecy stood in front of the French doors, the light outlining the shape of her body through her dress as she read his letter, a half smile on her face. She could feel his eyes on her.

When she had finished she dropped the sheets of paper on the blue carpet and looked at him, her eyes wet. Deecy could feel the flow of wetness between her legs. She could feel her nipples begin to harden. He had taken her so completely with his words that she did not know what to do. She moved toward him, a mixture of sadness and happiness on her face. To Pheo she looked intensely desirous, hungry.

"No," he said. "No, stay there. I want to look at you. I want to talk to you, like in the letter."

"I don't know if I can do that, baby . . ." she said, standing there.

"Please, like in the letter," he said, again.

Pheo's eyes indicated that she should go to the chair in front of the window. Deecy moved to it in strange obedience. But her whole body wanted to reach to him and touch him, to hold him for as long as she could. She wanted to let the scene he painted in the letter happen as he had imagined it, but she also wanted to possess him. She wanted to thank him for writing to her to comfort her at this strange time of the month when her body seemed to dictate everything about what she felt and thought, and yet a time when she was alive to every suggestion, every hint of sensuality.

Right now what she was feeling was not pain, not discomfort, not disquiet—just an intense desire, a horniness that was consuming her, a horniness so refined by this sudden feeling in her that she could lose herself with him. Before she walked into his room, before he had given her the letter, she knew they would touch, would kiss, and she knew that it was possible that they would make love. But she also knew that she would walk away from it all, walk away with a warmth in her body, a slight sense of guilt, but with a freedom to rationalize it as something she needed for now. To her it would mean little else. It was simply a time of being together—the comfort of a familiar understanding friend and a way to manage her loneliness. But now, now she felt something terrible happening. Something too tender, too personal.

She watched as Pheo began to undress. He let the khaki pants crumple to the floor and slipped down his black briefs. She followed the fall of the pants along the bulky muscles of his thighs, down to his ankles—the most vulnerable part of him, a part of him that made her want to touch him the more—to reach to him and hold him. His nakedness—his willingness to be naked before her—turned her on. She liked his body, the way that his muscles seemed to speak in subtle and reassuring ways behind the careless fleshiness around his upper thighs and the slight rise of his stomach. Pheo was distracted by the way her eyes consumed his body. He unbuttoned his shirt but did not take it off. His penis hung, full and gentle in the light—he was getting hard. She looked at his penis, not wanting to, but unable to stop. He casually loosened his balls and brushed his hand against the fattening head. Then he took off his shirt; his stomach and chest were full and round with the hint of undulating abdominal muscles just below the layer of fat he carried with assurance and lack of self-consciousness. She liked his body, its fullness, its solid sturdiness. His nipples were dark and full and she started to focus on them, wanting to touch them with her tongue. He sat down on the bed and leaned back slightly, resting on both hands.

"I want to talk to you, Deecy. To watch you talk to me. Open your dress . . ."

She obeyed.

The only sound was the low mutter of drum and bass—sweet lover's rock eddying like water in the room.

A soft coolness touched her skin as she slowly unbuttoned the front of her dress. Then she slipped the straps from her shoulders and let the dress fall apart to reveal her breasts. She was breathing heavily. His eyes dropped slowly to her stomach, the deep navel, the flesh still there from her two pregnancies, but such a sturdiness to her, he wanted to lick deep into her navel, tickle her, want him as much as he wanted her. Her white G-string cupped the fat softness of her pubis, her thighs, rising to meet her hips, as strong as he imagined they would be. She was naked—full and open to him. He looked at her thighs. Deecy saw his hunger. Now it was hard to tell who was seeing what, whose view, whose mind, whose heart was beating fastest.

She carried his eyes downward to his naked thighs pressed against the softness of the bed, his feet planted on the ground. His penis had grown rigid and his right hand brushed the edge slightly. His body was already feeling that slight stir of pleasure to come. His body was like that. One moment, there was no sensation of sexuality, just the routine rhythms and sensations of a body living in the world—breathing, heart pumping, blood flowing casually—and then he would touch himself, and for a few seconds, the sensation would simply be of flesh on flesh. But after a few moments, after seeing her sitting there touching herself, he began to feel the slow hardening of his cock. He would begin to feel the prick of pins in his lower back and the sharp awakening of his balls—a warmth spreading through his body, spreading deep in his stomach, and then spindling out like shards of light across his groin. He was there now, feeling the warmth and the anticipation of desire. Every time he stroked the bulbous head of his penis, and then ran his hand over the veined trunk of his hardness, he could feel the swirl of sweetness inside his center—it was as if this was all that remained of him, this center where all the blood now flooded.

"Touch your nipples," he heard her say—her voice seemed so far away, as if she were in another country, but yet almost in his ears. Like the whisper of a disembodied voice on a telephone. "Touch them for me, Pheo."

He reached his left hand to a nipple and squeezed it hard. His hips jerked upward. He heard her sigh, "Yes," as she let her fingers slip between her legs.

"I'm so wet," she said.

"I know, taste it." And she did, sucking on her fingers, licking at the taste of her salt. He pumped himself harder, sure that he would be bruised and sore.

And in that moment, staring at the flash of pink and rich brown of her unfolding vulva—the open softness and moisture—he wanted to touch her. He wanted to let his tongue nudge the loose and tender flesh of her clit, to run his open palms over her skin so lightly that he could feel the tiny goose bumps on her flesh. He was hungry. He wanted to lick her nipples, to let his lips gather around the lobe of her right ear that the light from the sun is turning into a glowing orange fruit. He wanted to tongue her and make her tremble into him, make her giggle, laugh, and then moan for him.

He did the next best thing. He spoke to her—making his voice like the soft caress of soft fabric on naked skin. Running his hand over his cock, his voice trembled as he spoke.

"Tell me what you want to do to me, eh?" he said.

"You know what I want yuh to do to me, eh?" She began like that. And while she spoke, he could see that she was now slowly moving two fingers over her clit as she ground herself into the chair. Her eyes were on him. "You know how long I have been wanting this, how long I have been waiting for this. To have you here sitting in front of me. You know what I want to do? My clit is so hard. Let me tell you what I want to do to you. My nipples are hard; my whole body is trying to push out to you. I am letting go everything. I will do anything you ask me to do right now, anything. Because I just want to find a way to crawl into your skin and become a part of you. Look at me. My legs wide apart, my fingers stuck deep inside myself. I want you to . . . to . . . to . . ."

As she spoke, his hand moved to the rhythm of her voice, and he pumped his cock—so stiff, so stiff it pained him with the pressure of blood beating against the stretched skin.

"Say it," he heard himself whisper. "Say it, Deecy."

"I want you to fuck me, please, please, fuck me now," she said, her voice straining against itself.

As she rubbed her clit and let her fingers slip deeper into her body, her voice rose with the sound of the word, while he pumped his cock to the sound of her softness.

"No, no, no . . ." he said, shaking his head, wanting to resist himself. "No, no . . ."

He wanted to come, but he did not want to come. She was now rising to meet her fingers; her left hand had pried her pussy wide open to reveal her wetness as she sank lower in the chair.

The room had grown bright around them and the heat was stifling. He could see her body shining slightly with sweat, and he could feel the drip of sweat down his ribs. He looked at the hills. He knew that sitting here, doing this, hearing her, seeing her, loving her like he was now, he had thrown himself outside of everything he had promised himself—he knew that this was the first time he had allowed himself to imagine something even close to love with a woman. He stared out toward the hills, hoping they would draw him back to what was true, what was valuable, what was responsible. But the hills were unresponsive. Her voice pulled him back.

"I'm scared . . ." he heard her saying. Her eyes were filled with tears; she was fighting the sensations that were causing her body to convulse. "Mi 'fraid, 'fraid . . . I don't know what it is, but . . . I . . . I, mi 'fraid bad."

And he knew that she too was falling, like he was falling . . .

"Deecy," he said to her.

"Yes, Pheo," she said, looking up at his face. It was as if she was in shock, her face was an open question edged with confusion.

"Come," he said. And as he did, he let his hand fall from his penis to his side. She rose smoothly, quickly, and walked toward him. She reached for his erection, moving clumsily in front of him. She squeezed it firmly and he felt his hips reach upward to create friction. She straddled him, and then guided the head of his penis slowly into her. She writhed, and then settled down on him, half-sitting, half-squatting, and then she held his shoulders and looked into his face.

"We can't do this again, Pheo . . . Never. Never—Jesus, Pheo, never," she said, looking at him. His head fell into her open palm, his tongue reaching to lick the salt on her fingers. Deep inside him he felt the strange and painful nostalgia of rain and dark days hidden under blankets, the sadness and sweetness of childhood, and with her enveloping him and squeezing him with her arousal, he began to feel the tears welling in his eyes, as if he could love her forever, and fall completely into her. Her thumb touched his tears. She had a look of total pleasure and sheer un-certainty. She was grinding her body, moving with a slow rhythm toward something too powerful for either of them to stop now.

"Don't cry, baby," she muttered. "Don't cry, baby. Don't stop, just don't stop. Lord! Oh Lawd."

She took a deep breath, held her teeth together and then be-gan making a long whistling sound as she started to come; her grinding movements were now deep and slow, then he felt the burst of his orgasm washing his body.

"Woi, woi, woi, sssss, woi, woi, woi, ssss." Like a girl be-ing burned by a flame or sprinting away from the licks from a belt, she was coming like a Jamaican country girl. "Yes," she said, "Yeees!"—her voice high as a castrati and yet almost bullying, commanding him to come with her. His incoherent response was a throaty deep groan and then a rumble and then something more frightful than that, a sound that made her reach for his face to cradle it, as he fell on his back and jerked spasmodically into her as she held on to him, coming, riding, coming, riding.

They didn't speak after that. They didn't know what language to speak. They both knew that something had been broken and to speak now would mean the beginning of a different relationship, one that amounted to an affair. They knew that if they remained silent, if they didn't make what had happened real by speaking of it, they could survive it. The fear was not of their powerful or-gasms, not of the taboo of their flesh joined, but the tears, the sound of their complete vulnerability and the startling way in which they felt so comfortable with each other, so totally given to each other. They knew that if they spoke about it now, they could never speak to each other again.

They parted with the same prayer in their heads—a prayer for guilt, for the burden of regret to consume them to force them to become penitents, people ready to fall on the mercy of God. They prayed for regret because what they felt was the bright pleasure of discovery, the sweetness of possibility, and none of this was good. Outside the same silent sky watched while inside seethed the contradictory dialect of sin—its delicious liberation and heavy consequence.

She left in her light white frock. He stood on the patio staring at the evening sun coming slowly toward him, reggae music pulsing from the radio behind him. He was thinking to himself that this island was a lovely and consuming mistress.

Alpine County

THE dew feels like wet bugs crawling over my feet. The dark is receding into dawn and an electric feeling like fear but not fear passes through me, causing sweat to run in rivulets from my armpits as I stare across the field at the large gray wolf passing through the dew-studded grass at the foot of the black hills. I had always heard that they are afraid of people, that to come down from the hills they must be sick or old or injured. It looked like it had a knife for a soul, like its urine smelled worse than ten mountain lions', like it would carry off a small child in daylight from a game of ring shout. It, the wolf, did not look afraid.

I turned to the cabin. It was light enough to see the reddish soil I had grown up thinking was tinged with God's blood, "blood" that I know now is oxidized hematite. I look back at Elmira sitting on the porch. Every morning she seems to appear like some ghost while I'm out, barefoot in the grass despite snakes and being sixty-five years old, staring at the sun creeping over the hills. The first time I see her each day I think the same thing.

I know her appearance on the porch is not mystical—she lies there in bed, like she has for years, pretending she's asleep. And when I'm out the door, walking toward the clearing or on the porch if the weather is bad, she crawls out of bed. I look at her long white braids, her worn faded overalls. It's hot, so all she has on is the overalls, no shoes, shirt, drawers. I think what I always think first time I see her mornings—we haven't had sex in fifteen years. I flinch, remembering her hand over the years turning to a fly swatter batting at me. Remember the passion of her drying slowly like a tree stump, the only life in her seeming to be the cancer the doctors say is growing, running a produce farm in her bowels. I feel the light expanding across the sky, the accompanying warmth. I don't know what's different about today, maybe the wolf down from the hills, the understanding of being old, prey, limited, all abstractions that feel concrete under the light expanding across the sky.

I own the cabin, the land. Her father left the land and everything on it to her. She lost it in a crap game forty-three years ago to old, at that time, fast, Stinky Burkes; and ended up marrying Stinky to get her land back. But I bought the house, the land, everything, one night to help him out of a gambling fix. Somebody was gonna kill his stupid ass. But he ran instead of paying the guy. All that's a long time ago. Elmira and I were in love then, I guess. We had whiskey, the moon, a big bed. Two women alone in the country. But that's past—like when the wolf was in the mountains.

We make enough renting out the cabins and the big house. Rent the cabins to summer people and the big house, which you can't even see from here on the porch, to a couple of young women who rent year round and use it as a bed-and-breakfast place. It's all beautiful land we rent cheap. There's a stream but no lake. Summer people love lakes and since we ain't on it we rent for half what the Thomases down the road on the lakefront do. But they don't own it, they way it's set up, don't nobody own the actual lake, so our folks can walk down to the lake, swim and all.

We had started going together way 'fore I bought the house. Her tongue used to turn to blood in my mouth, we used to melt inside each other like butter or ice at high noon. We met each other at a dance with our husbands. Mine didn't last near as long as hers. I don't know why I never gave her back her property. I guess 'cause I bought it making it mine. Or because in those days she was liable to put some perfume on and disappear down the road and not come back with nothing but her life. She had lost everything once, hadn't she: But I would give it back to her now. What difference does it make who owns what, we both old. Mean neither of us is ancient. She's seventy, I'm sixty-five. I could live to be ninety; then again I could go tomorrow.

She knows she still excites me naked in her overalls, the faint smell of her cunt like fresh-killed fish, her roseate-tipped breasts hanging down like cow udders. The feel of her skin is a memory now. I replay the taste, the feel of her. She's poured water into the electric coffee maker; I admit I like some of these gadgets. I break off a piece of cornbread left in the pan from last night. I love the smell of coffee, the feel of cornbread crumbling yellow in my hand.

I look out the kitchen window at her sitting on the porch. The disease, I admit for the first time, is gonna win. I guess that's the way of disease, eventually. Like water, wind moving soil. You can do this and that—plant contours instead of straight rows, al- ternate corn with alfalfa—but sometimes no matter what you do the wind and water and the soil creeps, slides eventually, away, to somewhere else. Erosion, the movement of soil from one place to another by wind, water. It's natural. I used to love her. I used to put one hand on her belly, push down and drive my other hand up her, my whole hand stretched out turning to a fist slowly in her vaginal canal. My arm slippery with Vaseline when we had it, bacon grease when we didn't. She always hated it. But she clung to me. I owned everything, was the man I guess.

I look at her on the porch now, the overalls spread over her body that's spread out itself over the years like a pink-white fan. But she's not pink, white, only her skin is colored like that. We're both colored. You have to look twice but you can tell it 'less you're stupid or blind. We don't have no preference for each other based on our color. That's stupid. It's just how it worked out. Maybe we just knew it would be good for us to be together up here in this ain't nothing really but the Northern Branch of the Ku Klux Klan. We're kinda safe together, being black, but looking white or "other," less like targets. Anyway what would we have done in the city? Been stuck in some ghetto?

Why am I thinking so much about the past when it's over and I usually don't get hung up on how things was; to me things just is—usually that is. I close my eyes, the coffee smell goes up my nose. I see the wolf now. Smell it. I'm in a cave surrounded by fur and feces and damp dog smell. I grab his slick luminous pink doggy penis. His teeth sink into the crepelike skin of my neck.

I open my eyes, remember something I read a long time ago in *National Geographic* about an Indian wolf trap. Where the Indians put a razor in a salt lick and when the killer wolf came with its hunger for salt and licked, each lick would lacerate its tongue. But for some reason the wolf would keep licking till its tongue was ribbons and its life was dripping out red on the frozen white tundra.

I look, my coffee cup is empty. I pour another cup knowing that after it I'll need to pee continually for the next couple of hours precluding a walk or even a drive to town. I look at Elmira still seated on the porch. Then the vision of the gray wolf stalking the hills chokes my brain, sending a torrent of blood out my nose, and explodes like the colors in an early morning sunrise turning into a thousand little clots like drops of dew that begin to arrest the light in my brain. I'm thinking, I own everything, when the last light goes out.

MICHAEL A. GONZALES

Movie Lover

(4 Jana & Jerry)

M OVIE LOVER *opens with a simple white-lettered, black background title card as the electrifying mojo of a Portishead track produced by the Bomb Squad screams louder than spooky synth samples laced with a hypnotic black Moses melody mastermixed with the bitches' brew of Miles Davis's blaster, DJ premier scratching faster, and Burt Bacharach tickling the ivories over a wailing police siren . . .*

FADE INTO . . .

Despite the ultraromantic sentiment of his name, the Bustelo-hued Romeo Blue had never thought of himself as one of the Is-ley Brothers between the sheets. Indeed, Romeo had always been one of those eternal wallflowers gulping shots in his favorite ur-ban juke joint, the Sugar Shack, staring silently at the dancing machine of life. Through a pair of cheap sunglasses, Technicolor images exploded in his mind, giving him a slight headache: sweet swaying brown suga hips grinding to riotous old-school rhythm as Romeo's long-lashed eyes refused to blink. With his shy-boy fears of "coming off" like Barry White rapping, Teddy Bear Pendergrass macking, or paisley wild-child Prince ranting "I want to be your lover," he chose instead to be silent.

In his own reefer-ravaged mind, Romeo resembled the squatting sloped senior depicted in Ernie Barnes's classic finger-popping, high-heel bopping album cover to ghostly Marvin Gaye's *I Want You* (the identical image was used for the closing credits of *Good Times*): content with observing life's bountiful passion, its lustful appeal, and the majestic mojo of exquisite soul sisters through the lens of his camera. While his rowdy friends were living life in the fast lane, puffing Philly blunts and banging out the brains of random wanna-be porn stars, Romeo preferred the semi-darkness solitude of his massive Harlem loft, chain-smoking Newports and studying the cinematic masterwork of Hitchcock's *Rear Window*—the film that made him want to be a director in the first place.

Not that directing cheesy videos for obnoxious rappers—who insisted that female stretch marks were seductive, that every thonged booty sumptuously shake like a bowl of cherry Jell-O, and that each brown nipple be hard as igloos—was how he intended to make his mark as an auteur, but it was a beginning. Hell, it was better than selling sweat socks on *Crooklyn* corners like Spike Lee in his pre–*She's Gotta Have It* phase or dealing with rewinding rental tapes in some kooky video shop as Quentin Tarantino was once forced to do.

Instead, eagle-eyed Romeo spent his brutal days and hellish nights on dreaded sets attempting to locate the entire *fanager* crew ("You know," an associate once said, "when rappers have their biggest fan become their manager!") of Murderous Thug Brothers—two killer-diller Siamese twins who would blast any sucker nigga who dared laugh at their "fuckin' handicap"—for their follow-up shots; or coping with the bitchy temperament of Mary Magdalene, the latest former stripper/sexpot raptress who believed herself more popular than Jesus—not that Christ would have been caught crucified in a pair of Manolo Blahnik sandals and a red-and-black sequined bustier with matching hot pants.

"I'm not sure how long I can work with these bad boys and bratty bitches," he confessed one drunken night after slurping more sake than a Japanese rice farmer. Massaging his thrumming temples to relieve the stress, Romeo frowned. "I went to film school to create art, not babysit a bunch of work-release rejects who call themselves hip-hop artists." He looked on the verge of a nervous breakdown. He looked as though he might burst into tears.

"Yo, Romeo, chill wit dat shit, bro," whispered Leo Nelson, shoveling large pieces of tuna-roll in his wide-open mouth. "We sitting next to a fucking window, have some self-respect." Although most people viewed him as a lucky Long Island wigger who acted blacker than Huey Newton, Malcolm X, and Bill Duke combined, he was also Romeo's former NYU dormmate, drug supplier (he had already slipped a hit of E in Ro's steaming green tea), and current director of photography. Those who knew them humorously understood their bond and balance, because Romeo acted more like an old, park bench Jew while Leo was the Afrocentric honky who could Electric Slide better than the entire wedding party in *The Best Man*.

"How could I possibly have any self-respect when every day I feel more like a nanny to a bunch of juvenile delinquents than a real artist," he whined, draining the remainder of his wine from the tiny cup. "When Martin Scorsese was my age he had already made *Mean Streets* and *Taxi Driver*. All I ever really made solo in my life is a few stupid videos and bail for your statutory rape charges."

"Yo, bro, it was only one charge," corrected Leo, laughing at the memory. "You need to stop acting like I'm Roman Polanski or some motherfucker. How was I to know the bitch was only sixteen? I hope when we shoot in Puerto Rico next week you'll feel better. Shit, maybe if you got yourself a little trim every now and then you wouldn't be so quick to judge a nigga like me."

"A nigga like you!" Romeo screamed, as the heads of the other patrons spun around quicker than pea-soup-spitting Linda Blair in *The Exorcist*. "You know, Leo, one of these cold cruel days you're gonna realize you're a white boy. And I'm sure when that happens you'll be outta the hip-hop world faster than George Jefferson movin' on up. In the meantime, I gotta compete for jobs with people who call themselves Hype."

"You think his mom's gave him that name," goofed Leo, attempting to throw a dash of levity in Romeo's overboiling stew. "Laying in the maternity ward glaring at the funny-lookin' sucker, looking like *It's Alive* or some shit. Then mom duke's said, 'I think we'll name the baby Hype, honey.' Word, I bet any amount of money the nigga's real name is Floyd or Hymie or some ill shit like that."

Always a stylish dresser, Romeo dug in the pockets of his black Hugo Boss linen suit, tossed a twenty-dollar bill on the table. "Throw in the rest, I'll hit you off later," he said, staggering from his seat. "Good lookin' Leo." The moment the cool breeze pimp-slapped his drunken, sagging face, Romeo slunk his sulking self to the corner of St. Mark's Place and hailed a taxi. Indeed, he was shocked to see a fine darling driving the cab. The buxom lady cab driver could have been Liz Taylor's twin sister. Her taxi ID read Luna Starchild. "Uptown, baby," slurred Romeo, leaning his heavy, dazed and confused dome against the window. "We gonna peel for Sugar Hill, at 145th Street and Amsterdam." Moments after the black noise of squealing tires began to screech, Romeo Blue passed out.

Still drowning in a sea of sorrow, slowly rewinding wreaked, melancholy scenes from damaged ego memories, he couldn't help but dream of the doe-eyed, cutie-pie girls from his Catholic school days, tender young virgins clad in tight white blouses (brown, puerile breasts ripening with the changing seasons), gray-plaid skirts that clung to their soft asses, revealing slightly scarred, yet delicate legs. One rainy afternoon, when the class was forced to stay inside, a stacked fast feline by the name of Sylvia Santiago decided that the lunch period would be better spent dry humping boys in the back staircase than catching up on a boring book report.

Although this dazzling Dominican was merely twelve years old, her body was as developed as the bombastic Iris Chacon, the lusty plump Puerto Rican his pop watched on channel 47, always keeping the volume low so Mama wouldn't know. Lying her buxom body down, Sylvia looked like a cocoa volcano on the verge of erupting as she casually parted her legs, gently pulling up her skirt to reveal the lacy underwear she had borrowed from her older sister's bureau. Standing at the bottom of the steps,

Romeo's body tingled with a sensation that was completely foreign, like a sugar rush on Easter morning after devouring a chocolate bunny alone. Lost in the stars and fog, Romeo quickly crashed back to Earth to the roar of laughter.

"Look at the front of Romeo's pants," Sylvia screamed, her obnoxious voice seeming to carry for miles. "My God, he *came* on himself!" For a moment it seemed to Romeo that time was standing still as a photograph, a perverse Mapplethorpe black-and-white 8x10 of a young black boy standing against a white-washed institutional wall, salty tears in his eyes and a sticky semen stain spreading on the crotch of his blue polyester pants. Almost twenty years later, he still relives the ghastly sight of the grotesque faces of his "friends" soaring from the Witch Mountain of his imagination, reels at the memory of their wicked laughter and catty chatter echoing in his ears. For the rest of his wretched time at the school, until graduation two years later, some people still referred to him as Come Boy.

After drifting on a black cloud of memory, Romeo became alarmed when the lady cabby pulled over to a darkened side street. "Miss, I think you're . . ." He could hear a soundtrack of spooky symphony strings laced with a blunted bass as the driver dimmed the headlights. Although in his mind he wanted to be afraid, his body gave him the cue to chill out and enjoy the ride. Leaving the radio tuned to the riotous ecstasy of booming black futurism, swooning Luna was soon crawling into the backseat.

Smelling sweet as a rose, yet shimmering as nasty as an old-school Times Square peep-show ho', in her Frederick's of Hollywood slut-specials, opening her raincoat to reveal a see-through red teddy. Her full-figured body was stacked as a brick house; booty and boobs jiggling like television static. Stroking the front of his pants with her long, red-nailed piano fingers, Luna moaned, "Don't you want me, baby." Her fierce tongue tasted like stardust and coffee. Unzipping his pants, Luna was merely amused that Romeo's once circumcised cock now had the head of a hissing rattlesnake, poisonous venom dripping down her deep throat.

Before Romeo could respond to the driver's voodoo snake charms, the boulevard was bathed in crimson-filtered artificial light and a gang of gorgeous ghetto girls dressed in sheer skintight bodysuits and black snake Vampirella boots (beautiful blow-out Afros crowned their heads like nappy halos) came zooming down the street on their identical noire Ninjas—fiery vibrating motorcycles that these babes rode like thick black cocks, their wide hips straddling the sleek cycles. The bikes' revving motors thrilled their quivering clits (a flood of warmth exploded, brown sugarwalls slowly melting) better than any Mandingo soul brother, especially one who was "down wit da movement" but still refused to go downtown on his woman.

As the commander of the pack pops a burning rubber wheelie on some live-ebony Evel Knievel shit, her fellow Banshee Bitches—that was the moniker custom-scripted on their boss hogs—skidded to an abrupt halt, and jumped from their bikes dancing like Bob Fosse–trained Harlem Harlots as the music began to reach its climax. "Alright you jungle-boogie bitches, let's take this shit back to Africa," screamed Madam XXX, her eyes bright as neon lights, violently ripping the top of her bodysuit: colossal tits begging to be sucked, nipples darker than an eclipse.

Overcome by a lethal combination of passion and chaos, sweat rolled down Romeo's face as he realized that the cool-world motorcycle girls were being played by his favorite blaxploitation queens: Pam Grier—who of course was their undisputed leader—Judy Pace, Tamara Dobson, Sheila Frazier, and Lonette McKee. Looking like a star-studded *Darktown Strutters* wet dream, their sensual "lawdy mama" image burning as fiercely as a Florida forest fire, these celluloid goddesses started shaking their rhythmic rumps, bumping boogie-wonderland pumps as multicolored fireworks began exploding in the darkened heavens the exact moment Luna's flame-dripping tongue had finally burned out. By some miracle, as the music grew more intense, these swaying switchblade sisters gasped as their motorcycles suddenly transformed into mammoth black rockets, which looked more phallic than the Washington Monument.

Smiling with delirious delight, the Blax-pussy posse shrieked in orgasmic bliss as they began to scale the rumbling rockets. "That's mama's G-spot, baby," screams Friday Foster as da diesel-powered dildo finally blasts off.

DISSOLVE TO:

Not long after the hellish Come Boy episode, just one of the many unhappy memories of his cruel childhood, Romeo began spending more hours in various bijous than with boys his own age. "Who needs them fools," he thought, slumped within the warmth of the velveteen vagina of his movie seat. Indeed, before the video revolution killed the trade, the skyscraper jungle of New York City was full of revival houses that specialized in showing vintage films, cartoon festivals (how many young dudes got their first hard-on watching Betty Boop strutting her fine white ass around?), film noir weekends (twenty-four hours of watching cigarette-smoking, long-leg stroking, and gruesome gangsters) and goofy Three Stooges marathons. This is the world that soon became Romeo's life. And, much like his favorite film critic, Pauline Kael, he too had lost it at the movies.

Sitting in the darkness, munching buttered popcorn, Romeo's private universe was soon populated with trips to Casablanca, a jewel heist in the asphalt jungle, dodging bombs with the *Dirty Dozen* crew, and nightclubbing with Pal Joey as they savored the sweet smell of success before it was all merely gone with the wind. Still, no one enraptured his soul-boy love jones more than the wild, wicked, and bewitching Elizabeth Taylor.

Skipping school three days in a row, Romeo sat silently in the Thalia—once Manhattan's most loved, yet most uncomfortable, revival house—continuously watching sweet, big-tittie Liz the Call Girl b-gal bopping in *Butterfield 8*. Showing as a double feature with *The Jet Set*, another flick where Saint Elizabeth was hotter than July, her sadness in *Butterfield 8* made her character even more endearing. It wasn't that Romeo had jungle fever, but Taylor's thick tresses and dangerous curves transcended race; some might say that Liz had a li'l black in her while others will argue that she was a blue-eyed soul actress. Clad in silky underwear and pretty-feet slippers, even playing a tramp Liz carried herself like royalty. If masturbation were socially acceptable, Romeo would have jerked off in his seat without a problem. Instead, he would wait until he got home.

FADE TO:

Still completely dressed, but feeling like he'd been punched in the back of the head with Mike Tyson's fist, he awoke in the middle of the night. Frightened by a nightmare that Romeo couldn't remember, he held on to the sides of the bed as the room began spinning without landing in Oz; then he ran to the bathroom. Shoving his head as deep in the toilet as he could without drowning, his vomit reeked of stale sake and raw fish.

"You poor baby," purrs Elizabeth, dressed in a stylish Victoria's Secret negligee. Stroking his head with her soft fingers, it was obvious that Liz was used to being with men who had trouble with drinking, never quite understanding the evils of the bottle. Turning on the cold water, Liz gently splashed his fevered head. "You'll be fine, I'll take care of you, my sweet Black Velvet."

Collapsing against the side of the battered marble bathtub, it took a few moments for Romeo's breathing to return to normal. "God help me," he mumbled. He felt a slight chill in his brittle bones as the ivory-skinned buxom beauty slowly undressed him on the cold floor. After neatly folding his clothes, Miss Liz helped Romeo stand upright and walked him into the shower.

"Stand in the cold water for a minute; I'll be right back." In the shower his ebony skin looked like wet tar. With his eyes closed, he softly hummed "Theme from Shaft," believing in his mind that he too was a black private dick who was a sex machine to all the chicks. "You feeling better?" asked Liz, pulling back the shower curtain with the funky elegance of Cleopatra. Adjusting the water to a warmer temperature as Gato's lush *Last Tango in Paris* soundtrack floated from the living room, she slowly stepped into the tub wearing a stunning pair of Chanel red-and-black patent leather sandals. Liz's heels were as high as the Twin Towers, her body more booming than a bomb.

Rubbing his body gently with rose-scented liquid soap, he moaned softly at her touch. Like a seductive cat-woman, she licked his ear, running her fingers down his fuzzy back until she reached the crack of his ass. Leaning the warmth of her smooth body against his, Romeo gently held her back as Liz managed to balance one foot against the ledge of the tub, tenderly spreading her pussy lips. Still holding on so she wouldn't slip, Romeo roughly entered her as the shower water fell as delicate as rain. "Harder, honey, harder," screamed Liz, fantasizing herself as a Parisian hooker fucking a Negro GI for chocolate bars during World War II. "Let's go to the bedroom, baby . . . I've brought along a friend."

CUT TO:

Bluish glow of the television washes over the comatose bodies of Romeo, Liz, and an Italian woman who looks strangely like Sophia Loren. The trio is completely nude. Alfred Hitchcock's Rear Window *plays on video. There is a close-up of a lit cigarette dangling in Romeo's right hand.*

DISSOLVE TO FLASHBACK:

Loud, leisurely Puerto Rican men played dominoes in front of the New Yorker Theater, perhaps the most lux-deluxe of the yester-year revival houses on the Upper West Side, as a teenage Romeo Blue aloofly sauntered through the glass doors. Looking more goofy than a Disney character, Romeo wore nerdy glasses that closely resembled comic book ad X-ray specs, ill-fitting polyester pants, and a dirty T-shirt that howled KEEP ON TRUCKIN' louder than Allen Ginsberg reciting poetry.

It was the second day of a Hitchcock festival, and Romeo was fearful that he might miss something. Anything. With his Reese's peanut butter cups and original flavor Wise chips stashed in his pockets, Romeo studied the vintage lobby cards from *The Birds* (a fine, feathered flick he would never quite understand) and *Rear Window*, a movie he was determined to see—after reading somewhere that it was one of Francois Truffaut's favorite films.

With its Franz Waxman score sounding as jazzy as Duke Ellington shooting dice with Charlie Parker and Dizzy on the A train, Romeo was smitten by the complex opening sequence of *Rear Window*. At the tender age of fourteen, it was the first time he realized that the movie camera was moving, lurking, stalking

throughout the cinematic landscape. As the film's credits flashed
on the silver screen (starring James Stewart and Grace Kelly, based
on a short story by Cornell Woolrich, costumes designed by Edith
Head), Romeo was intoxicated by the set designer's imaginatively
recreated view of a faded Greenwich Village apartment building
in full early morning swing: pigeons soaring over countless fire es-
capes as a young composer chills on the piano; a pretty young
thang toils through her morning workout (her ardent ass bending over while her legs spread like butter); a newlywed couple—
yearning let's get it on, sexual healing privacy—yanking down
their pale white shades.

Seduced by the dual ecstasy of Grace Kelly's enchanting
beauty (her slow-mo kiss on Stewart's cheek in their first scene
together was the Disneyland of 1950s screen smooches) and
Hitchcock's own erotic voyeurism, it wasn't long before Romeo
too became obsessed with the private universe outside his own
third-floor window—the prewar brick building only a few hundred feet away. Like watching fragmented television series not
interrupted by silly commercials for obnoxious colognes that
forced one to battle broads in the streets or old supermarket se-
niors freaking out over soft tissue paper, Romeo was entranced
by the multitude of sounds and images that possessed this bustling world he had always been aware of but had never bothered
to acknowledge.

With his bedroom pitch-black, Romeo peered through the
dirty screen, observing the midnight strifes of the aged Hispanic
couple who seemed to be forever arguing, the obese wife dressed
in colorful potato sacks as the bony husband constantly slapped
her. There was the neighborhood's most infamous bad boy,
White Mike, a mush-faced mulatto who fought more than Ali
just to get a rep, stealing loot from his black mama's purse. On
the fifth floor lived the whiny Trekkie George, who spent most
of his free time wearing Spock ears while constructing models of
The Enterprise.

Still, it wasn't until scoping the majestic figure of India—
though he knew not her name; this is what he christened her
in his mind—that Romeo began to understand that shame and
desire were often blended in the same bitter cocktail. Beyond

Romeo's limited naked flesh exposure of Superfly's gal floating in a tub full of bubbles or sneaking glances of his pop's ebony mountain of *Player* magazines (stowed indiscreetly in an old St. Catherine's of Genoa bookbag, stashed inside the small closet outside his parents' boudoir), he had never felt such an assault of emotions.

Kneeling on the firm mattress in his junky, darkened bedroom (one wall was completely covered in four-color *Jet* centerfolds; the floor was carpeted in Marvel comics and orange Hot Wheels tracks) Romeo watched her as though she were a mystic Harlem earth angel; or perhaps a fine-as-grape-wine Puerto Rican goddess who had escaped from the pages of an urban fairy tale.

India, with that luminous Pocahontas hair flowing down her back like an onyx waterfall. India, whose poetic body spoke a secret romance language more ethereal than the stars. India, blasting Jackson Five music while making goo-goo eyes at the group's poster (like most young sisters, she had a puppy-love crush on the pre-ivory Michael), wildly dancing with the wah-wah power of a go-go girl. "Automatic systemic . . ." she sang, as "Dancing Machine" roared from the speakers.

In the darkness of the bedroom, often rubbing the excited flesh of his hardening penis, Romeo stared. Of course, being a Catholic school, altar-boy geek, he felt ashamed of his actions, convinced in his odd mind that it was only a matter of moments before Lucifer (giggling like Richard Pryor, throwing karate chops like Bruce Lee) decided to snatch his black booty and make the freaky nigga serve sausages shaped like coal-black cocks at Klan meetings. Yet, no matter how much guilt he felt by his extreme Peeping Tom perversions, the intoxicating inferno of India's body made fiery demons seem like small children screaming in a playground; while hell was transformed into a heavenly amusement park by the sea.

It was a time of soiled sheets and sticky pajamas. It was a time of vivid wet dreams floating through Romeo's mind like multicolored butterflies: the candy-coated sweetness of making chocolate love to India (*"baby, baby . . ."*) on a secluded beach reminiscent of the passionate love scene in *From Here to Eternity*: cool waves splashing their melting bodies, serious moonlight twinkling in the sky. In a more grimy scenario that resembled the Times Square blues of *Taxi Driver*, Romeo was in a seedy hotel room—across the street stood a church, its lightbulb cross glowing through the cracked window—boning an underage hooker (India) before attempting to save her soul from herself. From Willy Wonka pudding sweet to Martin Scorsese's decadent streets, India was the featured sexy star of each nocturnal production.

So, 'bout a month into his India addiction that was worse than a six-hundred-pound Playboy Bunny on his back, Romeo was standing in a supermarket line with his mom when he noticed India in the next aisle. Dressed in a pair of tight Gloria Vanderbilt jeans and a white tube-top, buying a box of Fruity Pebbles cereal, a gallon of milk, a bottle of Red Devil hot sauce, and three cans of sardines in mustard sauce.

"Jesus wept," mumbled Romeo, not knowing what else to say. It was like his once fertile mind had been wiped clean by A&P aliens: like a trapdoor hid in the floor, Romeo's mouth fell open and his eyes grew wider than Buckwheat's. Of course, it was at that moment that India glanced in his direction. Their eyes locked as though watching God dribble an ill pill on battlegrounds of the famed Rucker basketball courts, kicking Pee Wee Kirkland in the ass with a pair of white high-top Pro Keds. And then, India smiled.

Forever was watching her pretty eyes glimmer beneath the beaming fluorescent white light inside the market. Forever was imagining India clad in a virginal white wedding gown, a laced veil concealing the splendor of her smooth kisser (as the film noir boys would say). Forever was licking the peach nectar of India's dripping pussy, sipping her sticky juice while trapped in a fortress of passion. Forever was sucking her crimson-painted toes, licking salty sweat from her swelling stomach, squirting sugary baby's breast milk down his throat. Forever was the joy of his hands exploring India's body, discovering shadowy boulevards and bittersweet streets, erogenous zones and twilight riots. Forever lasted for about three magical minutes.

"Romeo! Don't let me have to call your ass again," scolded his moms, bursting the pretty balloon of his soulful cinematic daydream, a bubbling brown Curtis Mayfield soundtrack pumping funk in the background. "Boy, if you don't get your head out of the clouds it's going to rain on you for sure." Indeed, how was Romeo to know that those three minutes of forever would be the last time he ever saw India alive?

Recognizing Romeo's face from stealing glances out of her own window, she knew he was the Afroed shy guy who admired her from a short distance. With her supermarket package swinging from her manicured fingers, she hummed Harold Melvin & The Blue Notes' "Hope That We Can Be Together Soon" (featuring Sharon Paige, composed by the daring duo of Gamble and Huff), not paying much attention to the bustling traffic speeding down Broadway. Still humming, she closed her eyes for a moment and never opened them again. A coked-up pimp, hearing the chiller thriller voice of his dead grandma urging him to repent, accidentally killed her with an outta control Caddie. "Fuckin' brakes refused to work," he bellowed to the police. "Man, I didn't even see baby-doll coming across the street."

Staring wide-eyed from the A&P window, Romeo was in a state of shock: blood had splashed on the pavement, her broken body resembled a smashed-up doll. Sweat poured down his bewildered face as his entire body began to tremble and quake. In the distance he could hear the sirens crying as ambulances raced toward the tragic scene. Before Romeo fainted, falling to the floor like a plague victim, chaos had become the name of the game outside the window. The summertime street was soon overflowing with rosary-clutching nuns from a nearby convent, a yelling black wino who claimed, "I done seen the whole thing—nigga was drivin' like a crazy country coon," and a gang of gawkers whose mission was to translate the incident into the poetics of street-corner folklore.

DISSOLVE BLACK TO DA PRESENT:

Romeo is on a downtown soundstage directing a video for the latest D'Angelo clone, an Afroed bro who calls himself Gemini Genius. He is performing a remake of Prince's purple lullaby "The

Beautiful Ones," which now features dark hip-hop textures: wild-styled scratching weaved with taunting melodies and complex rhythms. The clip's concept is a sex subway filled with scantily clad ho's in various buck-wild positions—sliding down poles, gyrating their hips, swinging their phat honey dips. The dancers are dressed in revealing lingerie, silky stockings with garters, thigh-high leather boots, and hooker heels.

Silently staring at the mini-vid monitor as the voluptuous strippers danced to the perfect beat, Romeo Blue was soon sucked into the sexual matrix of the erotic scene. "Who is that girl?" asks Romeo, pointing out one of the fierce beauties whose body blazed like fire. Looking over his shoulder, his bro Leo grinned.

"You got good taste, Ro," he said. "She calls herself Butterfly. That's one of the hookers I found dancing in that underground strip spot I was telling you about. You know, the joint that was iller than Sodom and Gomorrah on a Friday night: wild-child whores sucking dick in shadowy spaces, moaning like puppies in the darkness, taking it doggie style—"

"Alright, Leo," screamed Romeo. "I get the picture. It's just, well . . . she kind of reminds me of an old friend." Swinging her long tresses under the hot lights, Butterfly was dressed in a cleavage-revealing baby-blue teddy (a platinum crucifix dangled from her neck) and a matching pair of Gucci pumps with straps that seemed to climb her shapely legs like vines. There was an exquisite butterfly tattooed on her back. "Doesn't she remind you of India?"

"You're going to drive yourself to the loony bin with this fucking India obsession," Leo barked. "Every other bitch you see reminds you of India's floating spirit. Hell, India wasn't even her real name. You never even really knew her, Romeo."

"She was the love of my life, can't you understand that?" bellowed Romeo, pushing past Leo with the rudeness of a shark. "What do you know about love anyway?"

"Love?" laughed Leo. "You must be on drugs with that bullshit. India was some bitch who got your dick hard as a brick then was too *stoopid* to even pay attention crossing the street. You motherfuckin' never even talked to her. Not once." Slamming his best friend against the wall with the full force of a costumed supervillain smoking Love Boat—a bugged concoction of angel dust, weed, and embalming fluid—Romeo was stopped from hurting this asshole by the powerful hands of Gemini Genius's massive body guard. "You got a lot of shit with you, Romeo. You lucky I love you like a brother."

Regaining an icy calmness, Romeo pulled an Altoids tin overflowing with weed and handed it to Leo. After walking into the production trailer together, they watched the closed circuit monitors (the cameras were hidden from the naked eye) of the cast of freaky females who were now gathered around the food services table. "Roll us a joint," said Romeo, viewing the rouged lipped lovelies munch on chicken wings, collard greens, and other soul food delights (washed down with chilled grape Kool-Aid) catered from a Harlem joint called Lamara's Voodoo Hang Suite. The woman who conjured up the phantom stranger that was India sat apart from the other hungry birds: smooth legs crossed, white light reflected from her crucifix.

Sitting at the console puffing the potent spliff, silently staring at the divine dancer who had no idea she was being watched on the gleaming glass teat, Romeo felt a sexual majesty radiating from the surveillance screen. Her striking video image was the perfect alternative to touching her real flesh, kissing the softness of her real lips, dealing with her real-world blights as a fox living in a world of wolves. In Romeo Blue's moviescape world, this year's India was like a luscious lollipop in a candy shop (just waiting to be licked), a starlet whose sweetness was forever.

Momentarily distracted by Leo noisily opening the door, Romeo moaned, "Do me a favor, yo . . . turn off the lights."

FADE TO BLACK . . .

DIANE PATRICK

Never Say Never

S OME sistas tell me they would never, *could* never, get involved with a white man. The mere mention of it makes them scrunch up their noses and get that "hell no" look on their faces.

In short, race matters.

For me, race *doesn't* matter. What *does* matter to me is height. See, I'm a tall black woman: five feet nine, plus three inches more in high heels. It was no fun as a kid—I was taller than all the girls and most of the boys—but now? Hah! I'm statuesque, baby. Amazonian. Regal. A Nubian queen. And I would never, *could* never, get involved with a man shorter than myself. The mere thought of it makes me scrunch up my nose and get that "hell no" look on my face.

In short (get it?), height matters.

Most women are attracted to men like the ones we grew up with, usually our daddies. Having never known my daddy, I tend to judge most men by my big brother Calvin. He was twenty-four years older than me, a lean six feet two, and a military man. Calvin had the posture and bearing of an African king. Always impeccably dressed and groomed, he never smoked, drank, cursed, or raised his voice, and he always was cheerful and had a joke, military story, or fascinating tidbits of information to tell me. The first man I admired in my life was a tall man.

So I guess that's why I like me a tall man. And romantically speaking, I like to be enveloped in a man's arms, feeling safe and secure. And I'm sorry, but I just can't get this from a brotha under six feet. I made it to my forties without ever waiving this requirement. But last year, everything changed.

It was springtime. Since everybody seemed pissed off with their jobs and bosses, I was plenty busy with my work as a career counselor. Between seeing private clients and conducting workshops and seminars all over the country, I didn't have a moment to myself. And I was loving it.

But you better believe that the career was the only loving going on in my life: in the man department, not a single thing was happening! The previous fall I had broken up a two-year relationship with a very nice English guy because he suddenly became uncommunicative and depressed—not to mention, he developed what we now politely call erectile dysfunction. Though Geoff thought his tongue, fingers, and a drawer full of sex toys were a sufficient substitute, for almost a year I was lying whenever I moaned into his ear afterward, "Oh baby . . . of *course* you made me come!"

But I was quickly getting fed up. After Geoff, I didn't want to have diddly to do with any freakin' man at all. On a tip from my girlfriend Sandra, I checked out a couple of Internet sex-toy sites, and ordered myself a dildo—the Crystal Cock it was called in the catalog. Between that and my trusty handheld shower massage—let the Goddess bless the inventor of that little treasure. Having taken my own orgasm in hand, I declared myself fully liberated from needing a man.

Things were good. Fall turned into winter then winter turned into spring. Then, boom! The day I flipped the calendar from March to April, I suddenly started getting that frisky feeling: I needed a little romance. Yes, I admit that I am the last romantic in this town: parade ninety-nine *foinne* naked men with erections in front of me and, well, I yawn; but substitute one tall, fully clothed nice guy with a kind smile, manners, and a twinkle in his eye and I'm a fawning puppy. What can I tell ya?

Anyway, I decided to place a personal ad. It cost me over two hundred bucks to run in an upscale weekly magazine, but hey, you get what you pay for and I was not looking for no broke-dick muthafucka.

It read:

Statuesque, cheerful, nonsmoking professional black woman with great smile, average build, seeks nonsmoking, world-traveled, professional fellow over six feet, who can come out now and then to play in the big city.

A week or so later, I got my first batch of responses. After eliminating those with badly-photocopied photos, form letters, and those with the second-grade-like handwriting of serial killers (trust me, I know about these things), one stood out:

Hello, Statuesque. I loved your ad. I'm in Manhattan, a very warm, creative, affectionate, attractive 51-year-old white Jewish male who enjoys a tall, solid, strong woman who's full of life and not afraid of being herself. I'm sexy, I'm funny, I have lots of interests: music, sports. So if you would like to meet a warm, attractive man who is adventurous, send an E-mail to Thomas at TLieber@warmmail.com.

Let's see. Jewish. Yeah, so what else is new? If I had a dollar for every Jewish man who was attracted to black women I'd be writing this from my yacht anchored off my island. But this guy sounded friendly and respectful, hadn't said anything about "I'm into black women" or "I love a chocolate queen." He had nice handwriting too.

I sent him an E-mail:

Hello, Thomas. Thanks for your response to my ad! I am indeed full of life and not afraid of being myself. So tell me more about yourself? I have a picture of your personality, but I don't have a picture of you. What you look like, what kind of work you do, and do you like it? So please, send me a photo, or some verbal details. Diane (aka Statuesque).

His E-mail response:

>Hello Diane!
>Well thanks for getting back to me. I'm sorry but I don't have a photo right now, so here's a visual picture: I wear size 9 shoes, 9 and a half. I have nice legs. I weigh 170, 175. I am NOT six feet tall, so I hope that doesn't blow the whole thing— I'm 5'9".

Uh-oh, homeboy's too short, I thought. I positioned my mouse over the "Delete" button and prepared to click.

It was only what he wrote next that saved him.

I'm a lawyer; I do real estate lending work and represent developers. I do enjoy my work; I've been doing it for awhile. I have a full head of brown hair with some salt-and-pepper on the sides. I'm muscular, I run with some friends every morning in the park.

A lawyer, eh? Many of my clients were lawyers, and I enjoyed their mental acuity and insight. Lawyers at least have a command of the language, are thinkers, use their brains all the time, and that has always been a turn-on for me. So I melted a little bit. Thomas, today's your lucky day, I thought, and wrote:

>Well Thomas, I don't know why you're answering personal ads because I'm sure you must meet tons of babes when you're running in the park! But here's my number so you can tell me your story in real time.

He called that evening at about 7:50.

It was 12:25 when we hung up.

Most short men I've known give off a Napoleonic vibe or come across as defensive when trying to rap. Thomas was different. He seemed to be so positive and intrigued by our height difference, and his vibe was so damn secure, that talking about it was almost fun. He asked silly questions: "So, would you let me sit on your lap?" "Will you wear high heels when we meet?" And for the first time, I found a new way to view a rule that I'd previously considered written in concrete. Height had been as big a barrier for me as race often is for some people; but here I was, flirting not only with a white man but also with letting go of my height restrictions.

Although our first conversation, it was quite a comfortable one, a great opening up of and to each other. Thomas explained that he had recently been divorced after a seventeen-year marriage that had "lacked intimacy, passion, and sexuality." Why had he stayed? Family and professional expectations. But for years, he said, he'd tried to find sexual gratification outside of the marriage, mostly using escort services, personal ads, and the like. Finally his wife had discovered it and, humiliated, left his ass. Meanwhile, despite the thousands of dollars spent on purchased female attentions, Thomas had never really achieved his goal of finding intimacy and passion. And here he was again, reflexively repeating the only pattern he knew.

In addition to being serious, Thomas was also extremely flirtatious, in a self-confident and playful way. Normally I would not entertain a conversation with a man who was suggestively flirtatious and admittedly promiscuous, because I considered men like that often disrespectful and decidedly unromantic. But Thomas was downright . . . exuberant, almost irresistibly so, and while I didn't want to admit it, it made me tingle a little. Better go with the flow, gurl, I thought.

We made a date for lunch on Friday, three days away.

The morning of our date was a fine spring day. Thomas called at 10:45 A.M. to ask if I was excited. I told him yes. We had been speaking on the phone for hours every night, so not only was I ready to meet him, I felt as if I was going to meet an old friend.

I arrived at his office at 12:20, ten minutes early. I wore all yellow: clingy V-necked sweater, gold silk skirt, plus gold accessories to highlight my beautiful chocolate skin. My bare legs were accented by low-heeled gold slingbacks. Goodness, I made *myself* horny with my outfit. But boy, was I nervous. I had no idea what to expect but little time to worry about it. Almost immediately after getting the receptionist's call, Thomas arrived to meet me. He was a compact, muscular man about a head shorter than I. Oh dear. He had salt-and-pepper hair and wore tortoiseshell glasses over a smooth unlined face and sharp soulful eyes.

He had a small mouth but surprisingly full lips. He wore a charcoal gray suit, pale gray shirt, black-and-white striped tie, and a very approving smile. As we walked to his office, I could feel him checking me out. Even though I was nervous, I could feel the mutual spark between us.

After an hour-long chat in his office about everything but nothing in particular, we left for a nearby Indian restaurant for lunch. Thomas walked quite fast, frequently ignoring traffic lights. A sign of an abrupt lover, I concluded; he probably *paws* instead of *strokes*. As it was pretty late in the lunch hour, the restaurant was fairly empty so we were seated in a large booth in a dark, quiet corner.

Thomas ate his lunch very quickly, providing me with what I considered another unflattering clue to his lovemaking style. The conversation was an extension of our phone discussions: work, our respective relationships, and a little more flirting than before, but he was still respectful. It was a great chance to observe his expressions and gestures, to assess how sincere he was. And the vibe I got was not that of a slutty lecherous asshole but a man who was very lonely and needed love and affection in his life. Slowly, I allowed myself to imagine touching and kissing him, and I was far from repulsed by that vision.

After the plates were cleared, I excused myself to go to the ladies' room. I was surprised to discover that my panties were wet from just our conversation. I had an idea. I took them off and tucked them inside my purse, then returned to the table with a secret smile on my face.

I sat down and did something highly uncharacteristic of me but which seemed appropriate for the moment and for the man sitting before me.

I took Thomas's hand, placed it under my skirt, and guided it to my center. He smiled; keeping his eyes on my face, he gently stroked me, slowly spread my lips apart, and inserted a curious finger deep inside me, then slowly removed it.

The waiter arrived at this precise moment to ask for our dessert order.

"I'll have the mango ice cream," Thomas said, licking the finger that had just been inside me. Smiling, I looked at the waiter and ordered tea. "Very hot, please."

After the ice cream arrived, he began to slowly spoon the cold, creamy custard into his mouth. I sipped my hot tea, holding the cup in both hands. Our eyes met and held. He read my mind.

"It would be nice to feed this to you," he said, licking the spoon after the last mouthful.

"Where can we go that you *could* feed it to me?" I asked, setting my empty cup on the saucer.

Thomas, not answering, just smiled and motioned to the waiter for the check. Outside, while we waited for the light to cross the street, I dreaded saying good-bye to him. Would we shake hands? Would we kiss? And then Thomas raised his hand in the air and a taxi magically appeared.

"Get in," he smiled. "I have a surprise for you."

I got in.

He directed the driver to lower Manhattan, near the World Trade Center.

"Are we going to walk along the water at Battery Park City?" I asked.

"No, but we are going somewhere where we might get wet," he said, and placed his hand on my leg, sliding my skirt up past my thigh. I noticed a friendly bulge in the center of his pants, and rested my hand on it as he worked his finger gently inside me, removing it only to lick it and place it back inside me.

The taxi arrived far too quickly, at a high-rise apartment building whose doorman greeted Thomas by name. Thomas led us to a single private elevator past the main elevator bank. We boarded, he inserted a key, and the doors closed.

As we ascended to PH1, I began reviewing the situation. I had *never* done anything like this before. What was going to happen in PH1? Would he hug me? Or would he just pounce, poke, and depart? But I had felt the bulge between his legs and God, it had been umpty-ump months since I'd had a hard dick to play with. Yee-ha, I thought. If I get killed up in here at least I'll die smiling.

The elevator opened into a space right out of *Architectural Digest*—I almost came just from looking at it. We were on the lower level of an apartment punctuated by a circular staircase. Huge windows gave views of the skyline everywhere, and sumptuous fabrics covered opulent furniture.

"Welcome to my home," Thomas said, making a sweeping gesture. He studied my face carefully, and he could see my nervousness. He took my hand then, raised it to his lips and kissed it slowly. "It's okay, D," he assured me, still holding my hand. "Let me call my office then I can give you my undivided attention."

While Thomas called his office (to tell them what—*cancel my meetings, I'll be fucking this afternoon*?), I went to the powder room and called Sandra on my cell phone to tell her where I was and if she hadn't heard back from me by six P.M. she was to call the police, his firm, and the city and state bar associations. Then I grabbed a tissue and blotted my lipstick.

I stepped out of the bathroom nervous and tense, expecting to be pounced on by a naked white man. But Thomas was still fully clothed and extending his hand to me to give me a tour.

We started on the upper level of the duplex, where there was a master suite and bathroom with Jacuzzi, and huge walk-in closet. Back on the lower level, he showed me the living room, den, library, and kitchen. A terrace offered a breathtakingly beautiful view of the entire New York harbor, south to Brooklyn and west to New Jersey. As we stood there, Thomas stepped behind me, put his arms around me, and centered that friendly bulge of his in the middle of my ass. I relaxed.

"Do I still make you nervous?" he asked quietly.

"Oh yes, I'm very nervous," I lied.

We stood like that for a moment, taking in the view. Then without a word, he led me inside and pulled me down to sit next to him on the couch.

"You know," he said, "out there just now I was thinking about all the women I have brought here while I was married."

"And what did you do with the women you brought here?" I asked coyly.

"I fucked them," he said, as seriously as if he was explaining a contract to a client. "I just fucked them, and sent them home in a cab." He paused and looked at me. "And then I'd sit up and wonder why I bothered. And I never really came up with an answer—I just kept doing it."

"So why are you here now?"

It took him a few seconds to answer. "Because you made me want to come here. I wanted to be with you. Do you know that in the last few days I have told you things about myself that I have never told anyone else?"

I nodded.

Thomas touched my face, then taking it gently in both hands, he looked deeply into my eyes. He slowly caressed my trembling bottom lip with his thumb. "Such a beautiful mouth," he said. "Feels just as soft as your other mouth."

I closed my eyes. And then he kissed me, a long, surprisingly gentle, deliciously probing kiss.

When our lips finally separated, I opened my eyes and looked at him, smiling. Just smiling. I wanted to hold him then, to put my arms around him for the first time, to feel my face against his. When I did, we just melted into each other. I expected him to grab my breasts or to do some other clumsy-ass thing and so I was surprised when he simply rested his head on my right shoulder. I could feel his heartbeat, his measured breathing. I wanted to consume him, to spoon him up and devour him, to ingest him. I explored his earlobe and eyelid with my tongue, listened to his breathing quicken. Turning his face to the V of my sweater, Thomas ran his tongue very slowly up from the bottom of the V between my breasts to the hollow of my throat and then back down again.

He kept going down, past my breasts, my lap, and my knees to stop at my feet. Taking off my shoes, he nibbled at my toes. Then he slowly ascended to place his hands on my thighs underneath my skirt. Moving the skirt out of the way, he put his tongue where his finger had been earlier, both exploring and creating the wetness between my thighs. Someone moaned. I opened my eyes and realized that the sound had come from deep inside me.

Somehow we managed to stand up, climb that circular staircase, and make our way to the master suite. We very slowly finished undressing each other until there was only warm skin, white briefs, and a hot pink lace bra between us.

I was sitting on the edge of the bed, Thomas standing before me. I placed my mouth on the friendly bulge, playfully lifted his cock, with my mouth, through the fabric, licking the length of it with my tongue. I noticed a spot that was wetter than I could have made it. I pulled his briefs down his hips, releasing his beautiful cock, which sprang out at me. He stepped out of his briefs and stood naked before me for the first time, six good hard inches. Heaven. His eyes were closed, a look of surrender, pleasure, and appreciation on his face. I buried my face in his belly, my arms around his middle. I could feel his cock against my neck, near the hollow of my throat . . . he had made a wet spot there too. I placed a moist kiss on his navel, slowly licking the area around it then buried my face in his crotch. He smelled of soap and a manly musk. Teasing him, I slowly licked all around his groin area; his tummy rose and fell with his breathing, a runner's breathing, strong and measured.

Then when I couldn't stand it any longer, I moistened my lips, and positioning my open mouth over the head of his cock, I gently exhaled a warm breath over it. In slow motion, I wet the entire tip with my tongue, licking underneath from the base to the tip. Then I took his entire cock into my mouth, sucking him into the back of my throat.

Then it was my turn to surrender as he stroked, caressed, and touched me everywhere with his strong hands. It was a very deliberate yet tender touch as he examined me, all over, feeling me for the first time, getting to know my skin, my sounds, my rhythms. His strong muscular arms wrapped around me, his deft fingers and tongue explored deep inside me, until we came, weeping. And still he had not penetrated me with that gorgeous cock. He made me beg him, then he gave it to me good and hard, but slowly, tenderly, and thoroughly all at the same time. After our tumultuous orgasms, we kissed the tears from each other's faces, and locked ourselves around each other for a short sleep.

*　　*　　*

When I got home I sent him an E-mail:

> Well Thomas,
> I want to thank you so much for today . . . it was very sweet,
> just as we both expected. You were incredible, just incredible at
> the art of awakening the sleeping woman within. (Your medal is
> in the mail.) Thank you for your tenderness, thoroughness, and
> kindness.

He replied with one of thanks too:

> Glad you thought I was OK—you ain't bad yourself—a nice
> way to end the day.

It sucks being a woman, though—as independent, professional, ruff and tuff, and all-around bionic as we are, we're
always the ones who get all mushy after we've gotten naked
with someone. It's a genetic thang, what can I say. And this
strong, independent, kick-ass Amazonian Nubian Queen was no
different. We were now in that inevitable gray zone: We Fucked,
Now What?

And so it was in the days following; I couldn't help but notice
a change. Before, we'd talked at least several times a day. Now he
was a lot less communicative and even terse although perfectly
cordial. I tried to rationalize it: well, we'd fucked and it was
great, isn't that the ultimate communication? But of course, the
burning question was, what is he thinking? Either he's finished
with me since he got the pussy and that was that. Or he's so
"full" of me that he's gonna need time to come down.

My instinct told me he was still processing it. I mean, even
the most skillful, educated con artist liar bastard jerk couldn't
have faked the sincerity of his words and deeds of that past
month. (And if he was faking, well then the Oscar goes to . . .)

But of course I missed him. We'd had an intense rapport,
communicated on so many levels, and I wanted to see him again.

But shit, he had been there and just as naked as I'd been. And
at the very least, I was sure he wanted more.

So, I did what so many women find hard to do. I gave him space.

Three weeks later, I received a huge bouquet of flowers—all purples, reds, and oranges. The card read:

> To My Big Girl:
> You have stretched me to a new dimension, and you must forgive me—I have been far away visiting it and comparing it to the old one. You are unforgettable, you have gotten deep under my skin, you have burned yourself into my memory. I wish I could stay away but I can't. This is just the beginning.
> With love and gratitude,
> T.

He called later that night. We talked late into the evening, both admitting that we had been moved by the experience and changed by that afternoon. True, we'd each expected to get laid, but there had been an unexpected bonus of warmth, tenderness, and intimacy that we each had been starving for. To find it under such circumstances was a shock.

And so that was the odd beginning of a very special relationship. Every time I am with Thomas—even after all these months—part of the turn-on is the memory of how we first met, and how he shattered my long-standing prejudice. He keeps a smile on my face, a throbbing in my center, a sweet memory in my soul—by having awakened the sleeping woman within. But more important, he's given me a new outlook on height.

I'll never diss a shorter man again.

JERVEY TERVALON

White Girl Blues

JORDAN arrived at Mary's house having driven recklessly from downtown Santa Barbara over the hills to the ocean, but still he lingered in the car. He wanted to fuck, but now, so near to it, he already felt trapped by Mary, and her mind-warping blow jobs. She took special pleasure in reducing him to a babbling idiot as she sucked him silly. He liked it, but what did she think of him? Some oversexed black man who couldn't get enough of her white girl lips?

She lived right on the beach in Santa Barbara. When they first got together, she said come by, I live right there at the water's edge, like he was sure to be impressed; but the neighborhood by the beach was too dark and secluded for his taste. It felt vaguely sinister; as though Satan worshippers and vampires could be lurking behind the eucalyptus trees. Sometimes he parked a block away; all the rich-ass houses on Cabrillo had high hedges to ensure privacy but also made finding the right address a crapshoot. When he did find the right house, it unnerved him to head down the steps to that ornate wooden door that made him think of the entrances of tombs and crypts in some Hammer flicks.

Something was diabolical about that door and the fancy house in general. He liked lights and noise and people; not trees, more trees, and not some *Dark Shadows* bullshit, even if it was upscale bullshit. He rang the bell and waited, half hoping she had given up on him and had gone to sleep, but then if she had, he knew he would find a phone to wake her and start the process all over again. How did that song go, "Love is the drug . . ."

The door opened, and she stood there smirking in a tight black slip that revealed her ample breasts—but it wasn't her breasts he paid attention to, it was that damn smirk. He wanted to fuck that smirk off her face. She wasn't pretty; but she was sexy and sluttish, and it appealed to him that she knew she was slut-tish. She kept the K-Y jelly and the love oils right on the dresser; she wasn't discreet.

"Why are you so damn late?"

"What do you mean by late?"

"Twelve midnight!"

"That's late?"

"Ten o'clock; that's when you usually bring your ass here."

"I'm sorry. You want me to leave?"

She paused to consider his offer but he knew the outcome. The girl had the hots bigger than all outdoors; one horny-assed white girl.

"Yeah, go home. I don't need the aggravation."

"Okay, cool. I'm gone," Jordan said, turning to head back up the stairs but before the first step Mary jerked him into the house.

"You asshole! You're staying. I didn't wait all this time for you to walk out!"

She pushed Jordan ahead of her through a dark, sunken living room, almost causing him to fall flat on his face.

"Serves you right," she muttered from behind him.

Her room was on the ocean side of downtown Santa Barbara; on the mountain side the owner had the rest of the house. Jor-dan only saw him a few times but that was enough; so blond he looked bleached of color, dressed like a shaman, leading a work-shop of loser New Agers, burning incense, chanting endlessly, and purifying themselves by night swims in the frigid ocean wa-ter. All of that going on below the bluffs while he and Mary were angrily balling their brains out.

Mary pushed him once more into her bedroom and onto her big antique bed; a good bit of the money she made as a technical writer she spent on antiques. A few months ago she was a student of his in a creative writing class he was teaching. He didn't pay much attention to her until she sat next to him and slid her foot up his pants leg. He paid attention to her as she blew him in the parking lot after class.

"Get undressed!" she said.

"I'm leaving my shoes on," he said, to spite her.

"Not on my bed," she said, and slid on top of him before he could unbuckle his pants.

"So what's it gonna be, a dry hump?" she asked.

That did it. Whatever self-consciousness he felt with her was gone. It was all about fucking. She got his fly open and worked him in and rode him.

"Put your hands on my ass!"

"No, your tits," he said.

He held her breasts but she pulled his hands off and forced them to her cheeks.

"Grab my ass!"

He did, as hard as he could. He thought maybe he could squeeze her cheeks until she stopped with the smirk. He wasn't coming 'til she begged.

"Oh, yeah! Squeeze them! Fuck, yeah!"

With all the strength he could muster he squeezed her cheeks hoping she'd scream.

"Oh, yeah! That's the trick!"

He wasn't giving in. She couldn't make him come. Not this sex-crazed white girl. She didn't have the power.

"See, I'm not nutting. I've got self . . . control. Turn you out!"

She could make him come harder than anyone he had ever been with; so hard it made him dizzy.

"Fuck me, you dog!"

Then an unexpected moment of clarity: he saw himself with this white woman he wasn't particularly fond of, sharing a carnal bed and feeling very ridiculous, but like an addict his appetite returned for Mary and so did his desire to fuck that smirk off of her face. What bothered him is that he suspected that he did like her, but it wasn't something he felt comfortable about. He had his idea of what kind of woman he could be serious about, and it wasn't Mary.

"Gonna make you come," he whispered to her.

"Do it!" She shouted back, but he couldn't. He came so hard it hurt. As fast as he came he wanted to go, go so fast she wouldn't notice he was gone until she heard the roar of the Triumph burning out.

She rolled off of him, sighing and rubbing herself.

"Man, you pounded me. Guess you couldn't find someone to give it to, horny bastard."

"Yeah," he said, feeling if she said another word he'd jump out of his skin.

"You're not going to start with that post-fucking depression. That I don't understand. Why can't you enjoy yourself without making everything such an issue?"

"Who's depressed? I'm okay."

Suddenly modest, she pulled the sheet over her breasts and propped herself up with a pillow and stared at him. "Then why do you have your hands covering your eyes like you're facing a firing squad?"

"I'm thinking."

"You better not be thinking about leaving. You leave, that's the last time you leave. You don't fuck and leave."

"That's not what I'm thinking."

"What are you thinking?"

She was right. He wanted to leave more than anything he had ever wanted in his life.

"Mary, I got to go. I have to prepare for my class tomorrow."

She stomped her foot and began to cry.

"I'm not going to argue. I'm not going to get mad at you. But you know you can throw everything we have away if you walk out on me."

God, he wanted to go, but he knew soon as he got home he'd want her again.

"Why don't you face it: you're scared to admit we have a relationship. So you run."

"What are you talking about?"

"You don't want to admit you have feelings for me."

"I admit that. I have feelings for you."

"But you're not serious."

"I can't be serious. I told you that."

"What—that you can't be serious about a white girl?"

"Well . . ." He couldn't bring himself to say more. Instead he pulled the pillow over his head and unexpectedly he found himself starting to drift off . . .

Dreaming . . . He realized Mary was rich, very rich. She would inherit the Black & Decker fortune, or some such thing. He knew he had to marry her. No doubt about it. He'd never have to work again. No, he'd be set; like some lizard in a fucking jar.

He woke later that night, remembering that her parents worked for the county of Los Angeles and were not rich. He sighed with relief; then, feeling her ass pressed against him, grinding slowly against him, so slowly he suspected she might be sleeping and the grind was a horny reflex. Erect now, he twisted a bit until he was inside of her. He fucked her slowly, hoping, fantasizing that she'd sleep through it even though it reflected poorly on his lovemaking skills; but still he was fucking comfortably and effortlessly, rapturous without the effort. No weight of responsibility, just the pleasure of luxurious carnality—but at the peak of the pleasure curve he thought of Sophia and her virginity.

Twenty-three and still a virgin. Did he really want it? And what would be the price? It was obvious that she was a virgin though they had never talked about it. Oddly, the idea of her having restraint attracted him—not because she was fresh or he'd be the first; it was that he imagined she had to be more uncomfortable about sex than he was. He liked it and all, but sometimes the shit was embarrassing, like suddenly all your nerves are on fire, and then they're not, and then you've got to talk to somebody you'd just as soon pay to shut up. Often he just wanted to get a nut and rush off to get some donuts. With a virgin, he could just have the donuts; what could a virgin say? She'd think men just have to have donuts after they come. The nice thing about Sophia is that she couldn't compare him to anyone; he'd be the standard.

Mary, awake now, slammed into him harder and harder, a piston of passion, her ass an alarm clock of desire, destroying his silly notion that they were having sleep sex. He came harder than the first time. Even while gasping for air, the feeling of being trapped like a lizard in a jar returned.

"That was nice," she whispered, turning her head for him to kiss her. Jordan ignored the gesture hoping she wouldn't scream about it.

"It was great."

"Every night. You can come over every night and have me all you want."

"That sounds great," he deadpanned.

A long moment passed.

"Are you still seeing that sorority girl?"

Jordan had forgotten he had mentioned Sophia to her.

"I'm not seeing her the way you think."

"What . . . you're not fucking her?"

"She's a virgin."

"Oh, a challenge?"

"It's not like that."

"So, you're planning on marrying her?"

"I didn't say that."

"Come on, admit it. You found your own kind. A black woman up here in beautiful Santa Barbara, who'll put up with your half-assed ways. She must have a little money. You must feel you hit the jackpot."

Jordan rushed out of bed and dressed so fast he had to stick his underwear into his pocket.

"Jordan, if you walk out on me!"

"Yeah, I know. Don't come back," Jordan said, slamming the door on his way out. He faked all of it. He didn't care enough for Mary to get angry, he just wanted to be home in his own bed, away from all that drama.

Racing over the seaside hills, he felt more relieved with each mile he put between him and Mary and more sure he did the right thing. When they first started sleeping together she said it was purely recreational, but now she wanted commitment and that wasn't in the cards. Next week or so he'd give her a call. She'd see him. She always did. It was on his terms and that's what he needed. It was about sex, but it was also about his schedule. He saw her when he wanted, or not at all. No matter how she nagged or cried, that wasn't changing.

He opened the door of the dumpy duplex on Milpas, hoping his roommate Ned was up, working on another weird-assed painting, so they could laugh about how he ran out on Mary another time. He took four or five steps into the dark living room before kicking something soft on the dirty carpet.

"Oh, man!" a voice moaned.

A light came on and there was Ned in his boxers laughing at Jordan and the crumpled man at his feet. It was a very confused Arturo, another artist, too poor for his own floor to sleep on. Jordan helped him up.

"Sleeping in front of the door? What's up with that?"

Arturo checked himself over, dusting off his suit. His shark-skin suit, with narrow lapels and cuffs that made him look like a kind of Latino *Man from U.N.C.L.E.*

"I was pretty buzzed. Next to the door seemed like a good idea."

"Yeah, he was downing mixed drinks at an art opening."

"Miko was there."

"Miko? She's still torturing you?"

"Oh man, you don't know. Now she's going out with some dumb-ass surfer painter who cleans hot tubs."

"He picked a fight with this big doofus."

"He thought I was some kind of punk ass!"

"He was right." Ned laughed. "He threw you into a hedge."

"Ned had to hold me back."

"Yeah, the next time he threw you over the hedge. Tells me he's gonna say hi to Miko, next thing I know he's charging this big beef-eating white boy. Art's got a lot of heart. He stood up to him and got thrown about ten feet."

Art slumped onto the couch, cradling his head in his hands.

"That's what happened. This stupid couch hurts my back," he said, sliding to the floor again.

"What hurt your back is getting tossed like a beach ball."

"I made my point."

"What's that? You can take a licking and keep on ticking?"

"You nitwits leave me be. I need my sleep."

Ned laughed and headed back to his bedroom.

"I wouldn't have missed it for the world," he said, and shut the door.

Jordan turned to leave but Arturo called to him.

"Hey, you have a spare blanket?"

Jordan nodded and pointed to the sleeping bag on the far end of the couch.

"Oh yeah. Ned put that out there for me. I thought it was a pillow."

Jordan turned off the light.

"Hey Jordan, I never see you lovesick. What's your secret, 'cause I hate living like this."

"I just control my emotions. If things start going funny, I . . . you know, run."

"Run away?"

"Yeah, it's worked so far."

"What if they leave you?"

"I still run."

"Miko likes messing with my mind. She even tells me how surfer boy likes to fuck."

"She told you that?"

"He likes anal action. All the way, like some porn flick."

"She likes that?"

Soon as Jordan asked the question he felt like he was taking advantage of Art. If he was sober Jordan wouldn't be asking Art about the love of his life's sexual likes and dislikes.

"She says she just screams."

"Sound like rape. Too noisy if it ain't. Never did like screamers."

"She says her screams get him excited. She likes that, gets her off."

"Man, she talks too much."

Art started sobbing like a little boy in the darkness.

"Art, I got a half of a fifth of Jack Daniels."

"Great," Art said.

Jordan found the dust-covered bottle on the bookcase without having to turn the light on, but he almost kicked Art again handing it to him.

"You want a cup with some ice?"

"No, it's more pitiful this way. Down on my luck, drinking stale whiskey, crashed out on a dirty carpet."

"That's pretty pitiful."

"Thanks Jordan, you're a real pal."

"Don't mention it."

"How's that cutie pie, Sophia, treating you?"

"We're doing okay."

"Oh man, she's fresh to the game. You can shape her the way you like."

"You sound like a pimp."

"Yeah, being a loser at love makes you bitter."

"Night, Art."

"Night, Jordan."

LOIS ELAINE GRIFFITH

How I Became a Writer

W E were young when we made promises to each other about love. We didn't know what love was. We were twenty-two with hot feelings and knots in the gut when we touched and discovered the hard and soft about each other. I thought we would spend our lives together and have kids and a home that would take fifty years to pay off.

He played the saxophone and knew that he was a musician, but I didn't know what I wanted to be then. I liked to read and kept a journal. I had a dog, a blond cocker spaniel I taught to follow me around. "You better learn to cook," my young lover advised me.

I thought my lover would be my only love. He wasn't my first, but I thought he would be my only—and I would be his only. I just knew we were meant for each other and then he went to play his music and I had to figure out what to do with myself till he came back and we could be inside our love. I was a secretary during the day and spent my nights at home, and he would call in the middle of the night to check that I was there. We talked for hours into the night about his work. His music would grow wings to carry him out into the world of big-time players, he told me.

I had dreams, too, and began recording them in a journal. I went back to school to learn the craft of writing and was told to observe life and describe what I knew. There was a picture I couldn't get out of my head—a naked woman being chased by her lover. She kept appearing in my writings, and my teachers thought I was obsessed. This woman running down a dark, winter street haunted me. Snow crystals clung to her. Moonlight made her skin look like it was covered in glass.

The house directly across the back way from where I lived used to be a rooming house. People were coming and going in this house all the time. The lights in that building burned through the night. There were loud carryings-on and fighting. From time to time police would arrive to settle disputes.

I remember a clear, cold winter night with a full moon. A woman got thrown out the top-floor back window of that house on that night. Her body fell five stories to the yard below. The crash of broken glass, snapped branches, then a thud. Her crying merged with the howling wind. I heard a man's voice wailing: "Baby, baby . . ."

The yards behind the houses in my neighborhood were asleep in winter. Dogs and cats wandered through the dried-up grasses. The bushes became huge tumbleweeds of barbed wire. The trees stood naked, and the ground was hard, cold. The police and an emergency ambulance team came and picked her out of the broken glass, out of the tall weeds and overgrowth of the yard.

Around the neighborhood people said her lover did it because he was a jealous son of a bitch. He got drunk and threw her out the window. The baby daughter she got from some other man was the only witness to the terrible fights. The woman didn't have a stitch of clothes on when she took the dive out the window. She fell near the dogwood tree, snapped off a few branches as she came down, broke her spine and her legs and her skull. She lay in the cold yard, and everybody heard her crying. Even after she hit the ground she was still crying and only stopped later in the hospital when she died.

They took her body away, but I don't think she ever left the

yard. Something of her was still there. Some piece of her became tangled into the life of the tree, because on those spring
nights when you can hear the stir of things in bloom, I'd hear
crying in the rustle of that dogwood. The wind would shake the
forsythia bushes and slap their thin branches against the wood
fence that separated the yards. The fence would creak in the gust
of wind. On those nights I could hear her crying, and the image
of her was pressed so hard on my mind that I wrote a poem
about her—about the hands that could throw a woman out a
window.

I read my lover the poem when he was in town for a minute
before he had to go out on tour again with his band. We hadn't
seen each other in a while. I didn't like this arrangement, but I
appreciated that he was earning a living doing what he loved.
When I saw him he had changed. He was sporting a beard and
mustache and had started twisting his hair into dreadlocks. His
speech was flavored with French words. His voice no longer had
the caress that had held me on the phone in the middle of the
night. I talked to him about the tragedy of the woman who got
thrown out the window and the man who threw her. My lover
couldn't understand why I was focused on this story.

"*Tu ne sais rien*. You don't know their history, Cherie. The
poor guy is probably off somewhere really hurting." My lover
didn't want to understand what was going on inside me. A
strange woman across the way had died, yet every night before I
went to sleep, she had the power to force her cries into my head.

Around the neighborhood people said her lover shouldn't
have thrown her out the window even if she was a tramp and had
other men besides him. Some people in the neighborhood knew
his mother and said the mother was a good African-Methodist-
Episcopal churchwoman and never raised her boy to be shacking
up with tramps. Some people said being thrown out of the window must have been what this woman deserved.

All the yards behind the house where I lived were overgrown.
Wild roses grew in June—deep red dots in the tangle of ivy and
sumac and leaves darkening in green as the summer days played
out. Prickly vines and tendrils of morning glories and dense

clumps of grasses held on to any rain that fell on a cool night, held on to that moisture even when the days were blistering and scorched. The border patches turned yellow but underneath the grasses it was moist when I stuck my fingers in the earth. It was moist under the ivy that covered the rotting fence at the back of the yard—the fence that separated my yard from the dogwood tree.

One night that summer when my lover came home from touring with his band, I had a party in my backyard. I made pounds of potato salad and got some shrimps to add to it. There was to be dancing, eating, and drinking, but the weather didn't cooperate. The night was filled with a misty rain. When it stopped, the clouds parted. The light from the crescent moon and from a couple Japanese lanterns that hung from an old peach tree made shadows that played against the back wall of the house. When my friends and I threw blankets and pillows on the wet grass and flattened the weeds under our weight, broken stalks released a milky green smell into the damp air. We ate and drank. We laughed and told stories and danced to old records.

The last of my guests were leaving when my lover the musician arrived. He had a gig that night and got to the party as light was creeping around the edges of the horizon. There was a mist that chilled the dawn. My lover and I lay together on the damp, cool blankets in the yard. We listened to the sound of foghorns that floated from the East River. That foghorn music filled me with sadness. It made me feel lonely even though we were snuggled against each other.

He lay on top of me, pushed himself inside me. His breath was soft in my ear, but I was listening to the breeze rustle the branches of the dogwood. The woman who had died in the yard was whispering to me. I heard her. Passion was not to be trusted, and I knew that it was only a matter of time before he would quit me. There would be no knockdown, drag-out blowout. Our love would just trickle out and evaporate. In the meantime we held our mouths open, licking the air, trying to taste the flavor of dawn.

He laughed and told me I was being silly. He swore he couldn't hear the dead woman's voice speaking through the tree. When he rolled off me his head was filled with his own music and the applause he'd won that night. The crowd had been warm and receptive when his group had performed at the Blue Note. He was still feeling high off the gig, babbling about the solos he'd taken with his horn. His sax had carried him away that night, and the band was with her all the way.

I listened to his talk. "All the guys got a piece of the action. Baby, I wish you'd been there."

As I watched the dawn with my lover, I told him about the party he'd missed. I was glad he'd missed it. I didn't use my backyard a lot, but after that winter when the woman got thrown out the window, my yard needed some laughing and music. I was sentimental. My friends—Mitch, who lived down the block, and Ben and Tito, who were lovers—teased me and ran a gag about a sky raining women. How big was she? There were jokes about tons of fun and big women falling to earth. My best girlfriend, Janet, remembered a clumsy dancer we all knew who was in an off-off-off-Broadway show that Ben had directed. She was a big-boned, lanky girl who mismatched her clothes. This dancing girl had a routine where she was supposed to spin, then swing her legs over a barstool. In one performance she managed to swing her body over the stool but landed on the floor, but she was a real trouper. She picked herself up and kept going. We laughed, remembering the stupid expression on her face when her ass hit the ground. Women seemed to have a knack for flinging themselves in wrong directions.

I told my lover about the joke my friend Ben ran all night about fallen women. "So you're one of them?" my lover teased.

"Yes, you made me this way." I put my arms around him, covered his lips with my own, filled his mouth with my tongue and tried to force all his smart-ass remarks down his throat. Desire roused in us again and made our hands take possession of each other's bodies. Warmth rose inside me as he pressed his body against mine. We were both paying attention to each other now and I felt like he was a snake slithering between my legs. I wanted to suck the snake of him into myself and keep it alive under my skin.

In the stillness of the first light, before the streets beyond the backyards were fully alive with the sound of traffic and people scurrying into the morning, I heard the song of waking birds and the crying voice of the woman in the dogwood. My lover held me close, pressed my ear against his chest. I listened to his heartbeat and had no chance to feel restless, as he smothered my mouth against his. We rolled on the blanket as a wind shook dewdrops from the trees and released a dank, woodsy smell. The peaches ripening on the tree were still hard, and the cool morning was like satin ribbon on my skin as my lover shot his wad into me. I got up to pee. When I returned from the walk, I didn't want to fold myself back into his arms. I instead sat down to record my feelings about my man and this dawn in my journal.

I was playing with words when my lover came inside and found me at my desk trying to explain myself to myself. He accused me of being selfish and inconsiderate for leaving him alone. I was wasting what little time we had together. He had to catch a flight to D.C. and then to Paris for gigs that were booked. He was impatient, and we both got angry. We argued. If I could understand his moods, why couldn't he deal with mine? Musicians were supposed to be sensitive, but when he started hugging on me like he thought body contact would dissolve our conflict, I threw him out.

After that battle I bought daisies from the Korean grocer and sat around picking off the petals. He loves me . . . he loves me not . . . I lived in sadness until he got back to town and called me. It was three in the morning, but I was so excited to hear his voice, I told him to come over. When I opened the door, he pounced on me, fastened his lips against my skin, and dragged me to my bed. We stripped off our clothes and lay skin to skin. We were hungry for touching and sucked the breath out of each other and forgot our differences.

He was in town with his band for a couple of months. He stayed with me in my apartment so that we had a chance to become reacquainted. He told me he loved me one night, after I made him a fried fish dinner. After we cleared away the dishes, he locked his body into mine. We rolled onto my bed, on the floor against the cool tiles in the shower. The way our bodies fit together unleashed a stream of nasty words from our throats. He had a big dick. I would make him grow thick in my hands and hold him between my thighs. I would tease his fat dick with my wetness. "You can't fuck me unless I say so," I told him, but we both were too loco with desire to hold him off for long.

Those were days when neither of us could keep our hands off the other. Now I realize that our whispered promise of devotion was nothing but sex talk. We were strangers in the daylight. If only he had been smart enough to use his big dick on my head. If only he had slipped it through my mouth to find an opening in my head and fill me up that way. I wanted him to know me in a state beyond words. He should have let me taste who he was before he gave himself to his music.

I didn't know what he expected from me. As I remember those days now, I don't think my lover really wanted me to know him. Sometimes when we were together he would get into a mood and run porno videos on the VCR so we wouldn't have to talk as we lay in bed. We would watch these videos while he played with his dick or practiced on his horn, and I understood I wasn't the essential fire for his sex when he could easily make himself hard enough to cream. But at the time I was accepting, because my lover had been exposed to a lot more of the world than I.

It never occurred to me that he was a dog sniffing at the curve of every leg he saw. I didn't know he had a girlfriend in Paris. I found out about her when she called my house asking for him. She was his overseas rep, and he said their relationship was strictly business. She was from Martinique but lived in Paris, where he had bought a house. An Algerian friend of his, a bass player named Said, needed cash and made a good deal with my lover for this house on some side street on the Left Bank. He never invited me to his house in Paris, but I imagined staying there while he was out following his music. I imagined being in the Parisian house alone, writing down whatever came into my head.

* * *

He answered when his Parisian girlfriend called again. She must have asked him who was the woman she spoke to. I caught enough of his broken French to understand he was explaining that I was his New York rep. When he got off the phone with her, he turned to me and tried to be reassuring. "She's booking gigs for me and the guys over there." When he saw me frown he said: "It's business, baby. You know how I feel about you!"

"No, I don't know how you feel!" I was in a temper. I didn't know how to set aside expectations of building a life with him. I didn't know how to relax and just enjoy the thrill of his big dick. Instead, I felt like he'd thrown me out the window of some tall building along with all the tomorrows I wanted to share with him.

A few days later he left on a European tour with his band, and, in order to make sense of my feelings, I turned to my writing. For many nights while he was away, my sleep was troubled by the screams of the woman across the way who got thrown out her window. The place where she fell in the wild grasses in the yard behind my house was connected to an emptiness inside me. I tried to put this sensation into words.

I worked at my writing. Then, my lover returned from Paris, and he pulled out his snake and tried to use it to separate me from myself. He wrapped me in his coils and slithered through an opening in my head. The snake in him said: Trust me. I put this revelation in my writing too, but I wasn't so dumb that I didn't recognize my lover had the voice of a player when he folded his body around me and said: "Baby, I missed you so much."

He reduced himself to a child who suckled at my breast and had the power to induce a throbbing in the mouth between my legs. I lay trembling in his arms, and although he whispered all kinds of tender words in my ear, I didn't let go my resolve. I had applied and been accepted for a residency in a women writers' colony on an island off the coast of Seattle. I told my lover about my plans. He didn't like the idea of my going away. He got upset and threatened to quit me.

"You said people should follow their passions." I explained I was going there to write and would be staying in a cottage on a hill overlooking Useless Bay.

"You don't have to go to the edge of the world to write." He didn't understand why I couldn't write at home. A good woman didn't go off and leave her man. "You're gonna miss me," he said, and just before I went away to the island he wanted to prove how much a part of him I was. I let him.

He gave me flowers. I dressed up in the lacy underwear that he'd brought from Paris so that he could strip it off me. We danced between the sheets on my bed, and he fingered my body like he knew it was an instrument that would release his music. Afterward he talked about the melodies he heard in his head. I wanted to know what the voices in his head sounded like. "I hear voices too. They give me words to write down," I told him; I don't think he heard me. He kept talking about the suavecito of his rhythms, about his power to color notes and make harmonies with the guys he played with. "We fall into a moment, and none of it is planned," he said. Music was not something that could be calculated. It was something that was felt.

When I left my lover and flew to Washington, I discovered that on clear days in the late afternoon on Whidbey Island in the north Pacific I had a view of Mount Rainier. The natives said this vision was a gift when the sky was clear enough to see the mountain breaking through the cloud cover and the pink fog that coated the air before sunset. From the island in Puget Sound I could see the jagged glacier peaks.

Before I left, my lover predicted I would go away and fall in with men I would meet there. He was right. I made a friend on the island. His name was Brian, and he worked at construction to pay for his house in Alaska. He drank hard whiskey and told stories about the harsh life in the wilderness territory. There wasn't much to do in the Alaskan winter except read, drink, fuck, and wrestle with the elements.

One night Brian took me drinking at a local bar. We sat at a corner table next to the window. I remember there was moonlight spilling over our shoulders as we slugged down a few shots. He studied me. "So you're staying at that place for women scribes working at being a storyteller. That's serious business. If you wanna tell tales you gotta make sense of truth, and that ain't easy." He advised that every good story needed a punch. "If someday you decide to write about your coming to this part of the world, how you gonna let folks know it was worth the time and trouble?"

"I'll write about meeting you," I said, flirting with him.

"You spark me, girl, you really do." He reached under the table and squeezed my thigh. "You ready for some knowledge? A man and woman can only know each other with their bodies." Body talk was the only language that made sense to him. "I don't want you telling lies when you write about white boys like me," he said.

We left the bar, and he drove us to a marshy inlet where the grasses interrupted the reflection of moon on water. We parked and sat hugging on each other in the cab of his pickup truck. I let Brian touch me with his cool hands. He pressed his lips against mine, nibbled at my throat, at my breasts. He reached into my pants, found me wet with anticipation as our breath fogged the cab windows. But that night he had drunk too much, and when he couldn't get hard enough to put himself inside me, he pulled away and leaned back in the car seat.

"Ain't nature a bitch? So, now you got yourself a story about a limp white boy hanging himself out in your face," he laughed. "We're all animals like the rest of the warm-blooded critters on the planet."

Then, he told me a story about a bear and a wolverine in Alaska. Brian was sitting with his legs dangling over the edge of a cliff. Below him white-water rapids turned to eddies against the rocks in the riverbank. A big, black bear ambled along to fish and stumbled into a cave under the cliff where a wolverine must have had a den. She backed him into the shallows of the river. She was growling and snarling to shoo him off, but the bear wanted to find out what she was keeping in her den. He wouldn't go away, so she jumped at his face. When she locked her jaws into his muzzle, he rose on his hind legs, and she hung in the air by her teeth, ripping the flesh off the muzzle to the bone. The bear tried to shake her off. He snacked at her and pulled her to pieces with his grizzly claws, then tossed her body into the river.

"I know anything is possible." I knew he wanted me to consider that maybe cruelty is natural and that maybe some of us are created to be expendable.

"I got a real bad thing for you, girl." He didn't have to say that because I felt his desire in his kiss, in his hands. He tangled my jeans around my knees. He burrowed his face into my crotch and worked on me with his tongue until I was trembling.

At the end of the summer I came back to New York and found that my lover the musician was in town. After two months away from each other, he showed up at my apartment, and we fell into each other's arms. He didn't resist the wild bitch I became who jumped on him to suck every bit of juice out of him. When I let him go, he was shaking and his neck was swollen with hickeys.

"What did you do in that place?" he asked. "You're different."

"My flower holds a color to sweeten a taste under your tongue/Will you let me fill your hunger?" These were lines of a poem I'd written for Brian, and when they fell from my lips as I lay with my lover the musician, I imagined he could smell the musk of another man on my body. I had played him, and he was surprised that I had my own beats. He was so used to picking me up like his horn. His horn was a woman too, only she had a dick. She led him down roads he never knew he could follow. He could blow on her and absorb her into himself—her and her dick—until they became one inside his music.

He was so used to playing me like he played his dick horn. Sometimes when he was on stage I would watch him let his bitch horn claim all his attention. There was no competing with his piece. Sometimes his bitch horn would call my name and dare me to get sucked into his riffs. When I described her in words, my lover said I was mean and jealous. He quit me.

As a kid I went to basement parties where I learned to dance with boys. Back in the day, young girls and boys would throw parties in the refurbished basements of their parents' homes. Couples would hold each other tight as they circled the perimeter of a single square of linoleum tile. Leo Pinkney's father had renovated the basement of his redbrick house on Carroll Street. He kept his family close and worked long hours at the post office to pay for that house. Mr. Pinkney, himself, outfitted the basement. He built the partitions to enclose the furnace. Set wood paneling on the walls and laid tiles on the floor so that his children could entertain their friends and not mess with the rest of the house.

On party nights Leo Pinkney's basement was lit by a red light on the corner table against the wall next to the couch. Couples would be snuggled on that couch, and there was lots of heavy petting going on while Smokey Robinson was spinning on the turntable crooning "Ooo, Baby, Baby." Boys and girls were coupled on the dance floor, grinding pelvis to pelvis. The basement would get warm and humid with the excitement. Musk leaked from under our skins, mingling with the perfume we had used to prepare our bodies for the evening.

One Saturday night Leo had a party. I was there dancing with some boy whose name I can't remember, and his pelvis was grinding into mine. Leo tapped my partner on the shoulder and asked his permission to have a dance with me. Leo and I had always been pals at school, and when he cut into my moment with this other boy, I wondered if he liked me in a special, secret way, or if there just weren't enough girls to go around that night. These two boys seemed ready to square off for the privilege of holding my sweaty body, and I understood the musk that eked from under my skin gave me power over them.

Just before my lover quit me, when he was in town, he showed up at my door in the middle of the night after he finished a gig. His bitch horn couldn't give him what I could. I had been scribbling in my journal, trying to write a poem. I was listening to salsa music and was fired up with its energy. I took his hand and wanted to lead him in a dance, but he said: "Musicians don't dance."

I wouldn't take no for an answer. "Don't look at your feet," I told him. "Look into my eyes and move to the rhythm." But he didn't want to learn to dance, and I felt disappointed that we couldn't share my insight into the music. I stretched him out on my bed and tried to massage the stress from his body, but he couldn't relax. He couldn't get a hard-on.

We saw each other a few more times after that. He would come around in the middle of the night. I would have my Latin music on and would dance around with my journal book in my hand. He watched me without reaching out to draw me close, without making love with me. When he told me he was going to quit me at first I was stunned and thought he was joking.

"I don't know you anymore," he said.

"What did I do?" I asked, and when he couldn't answer, I called him a punk. "I gave you myself and now you want to spit me out your life like some piece of meat you chewed and didn't swallow." I knew he was scared that he didn't have enough juice for me and that bitch horn he played. "We can work this out. You know you're not gonna find any pussy sweeter than mine," I told him.

My language offended him. "You've changed, and I'm not comfortable with you anymore. I keep looking for my old girl-friend. Instead, I've got this person you discovered in the Pacific Northwest." He claimed that pursuing my writing had made me vulgar. "If this is the writer-self you went to discover, I think you should have left her where you found her." He wanted to be folded in the arms of the girl who used to wait for his leftovers after he'd spent the best part of himself on his bitch horn.

I was angry that he quit me. I should have seen it coming, but I hadn't. He showed me a coldness that lived in his heart. I was expendable. He acted like the time we'd spent together had no effect on the man he'd become.

"There's a lethal injection waiting for you down the road. It may not come from me, but some other bitch is gonna shoot fire in your veins," I warned, but he took my words to mean that I was threatening to smash the windshield of his car or wreak some other major havoc on him. I got tired of trying to persuade him that we fit together.

"La Luna Negra" is a song about a new moon night—a night when there is no moon in the sky. Sometimes I write about the things we can only see in the dark. While I was on Whidbey Is-land in the Pacific Northwest, I shared some of my writings with

Brian. I read him a story about a woman who fell out of a window. Before she hit the ground she replayed her life and had to
admit that the man who made the earth quake under her feet
had pushed her.

"It would have been a tragedy if she didn't make sense of herself. The sex was good, but in the end love was no salvation—at
least not what she thought was love." Brian had a smile that crin-
kled his bright eyes into slits. "You know the only market for
that kind of story is other women," he said.

CONTRIBUTORS

Preston L. Allen is a black Caribbean pseudo-Hispanic born in Spanish Honduras on Roatan, an English-speaking island populated with black people. He is the 1998 recipient of the State of Florida's Individual Artist Award in Fiction for his work in *Here We Are: An Anthology of South Florida*. His short works have been in *Writers* and have appeared in a number of literary magazines including *Seattle Review*, *Crab Orchard Review*, and *Asili*.

Jabari Asim is a poet, playwright, and fiction writer. He is a senior editor of *Washington Post Book World* and editor of *Not Guilty: Twelve Black Men on Life, Law, and Justice*, forthcoming from Amistad/HarperCollins. His work has appeared in a number of anthologies, including *In the Tradition*, *Soulfires*, *Brotherman*, and *Step into a World: A Global Anthology of the New Black Literature*. "Rocket Love" is from a work in progress.

Chris Benson is a Chicago-based lawyer and journalist. He has written for *Ebony*, *Jet*, and *Chicago* magazines and has taught magazine-article writing and editing at the University of Illinois at Urbana-Champaign. Third World Press will publish his first novel, *Special Interest*, in the fall of 2000.

Marci Blackman, a staple of San Francisco's spoken-word scene, has performed her poetry and prose at venues across the country. She is a contributor and coeditor of *Beyond Definition: New Writing from Gay and Lesbian San Francisco*, a Lambda and ALA award finalist. Blackman's poetry and fiction has been featured in the anthologies *Signs of Life*, *Lollapalooza '94* (Manic D Press), and *Fetish* (Four Walls Eight Windows). Her first novel, *Po' Man's Child* (1999), was the recipient of the ALA's 2000 GLBT Book Award and has also been chosen as a finalist for the Firecracker Alternative Book Award for Best New Fiction. Blackman is currently at work on her second novel, a historical murder mystery titled *Devil's Backbone*.

Kwame Dawes won the U.K. Forward Poetry Prize in 1994. His seventh collection of poetry, *Midland* (Ohio University Press, 2000), won the Hollis Summers Poetry Prize (judged by Eavan Boland). Dawes teaches writing, African American literature, modern British literature, and postcolonial literature at the University of South Carolina.

Robert Fleming has written numerous articles for *Essence*, *Black Enterprise*, the *Source*, and the *New York Times*, among other publications. He is the author of *The African-American Writer's Handbook* and *The Wisdom of the Elders*. His poetry, essays, and fiction have appeared in *UpSouth*, *Brotherman*, *Sacred Fire*, *In Search of Color Everywhere: A Collection of African-American Poetry*, and *Dark Matter*. He teaches writing at the New School for Social Research. As a reporter for the *New York Daily News* he earned several honors, including a New York Press Club Award and a Revson Fellowship in 1990.

Michael A. Gonzales is a Harlem-bred writer obsessed with black girls, pop culture, and the written word, and he truly believes that D'Angelo's "Playa Playa" was penned about him. In addition to inspiring funky songs, Gonzales has written countless articles for *Vibe*, the *Source*, *Mode*, *Code*, and *Essence*. His first novel, *Platinum*, will be published in 2001 by [S] Affiliated. He's currently slaving away on his blaxploitation memoir *Babies & Fools*.

Lois Elaine Griffith is a writer living and working in New York. She has had plays produced at the Theater for the New City and at the Public Theater. Her stories and poems have appeared in numerous publications. Her novel *Among Others* was published by Crown Publishers. Lois Griffith is one of the founding directors of the Nuyorican Poets Cafe. She also teaches English at Borough of Manhattan Community College.

Reginald Harris is the editor of *Kuumba: Poetry Journal for Black People in the Life*. He received an Individual Artist Award in Fiction for 2000 from the Maryland State Arts Council. His work has appeared in a variety of publications, including *African-American Review*, *High Plains Literary Review*, *Obsidian II*, *Men on Men 7* (Plume, 1998), and *His3* (Farrar, Straus & Giroux, 1999); and on the Web sites of *Blacklight* (www.blacklightonline.com), the Blackstripe (blackstripe.com), and *Blithe House Quarterly* (blithe.com). He lives in Baltimore, Maryland.

RM Johnson has been writing for twelve years. His first novel is *The Harris Men* (Simon & Schuster, 1999), his second is *Father Found* (Simon & Schuster, 2000). The sequel to *The Harris Men*, *The Harris Family*, is soon to be released. RM Johnson was born and lives in Chicago.

Tony Medina is the author of the poetry collections *Emerge & See*, *No Noose Is Good Noose*, *Sermons from the Smell of a Carcass Condemned to Begging*, and *Memories of Eating*, and was named by *Writer's Digest* as one of the top ten poets to watch in the new millennium. He coedited the award-winning anthology *In Defense of Mumia* and was the special editorial director for *Catch the Fire!!! A Cross-Generational Anthology of Contemporary African-American Poetry*. He teaches English at Long Island University's Brooklyn campus and lives in New York City. He can be reached at tonymedina@erols.com.

Diane Patrick's freelancing writing career began with music journalism (*Billboard, Jazz Times*) and progressed to publicity writing for record companies and individual artists. Her most recent book is *Terry McMillan: The Unauthorized Biography* (St. Martin's Press, 1999). In addition, she has authored nine nonfiction books for young readers, mostly biographies of African Americans, and she is a writer and contributing editor at *Publishers Weekly* magazine. She lives in New York City.

Leone Ross is a novelist and short story writer. She has published two novels, *All the Blood Is Red* and *Orange Laughter*. Her short stories have been published in anthologies in the United Kingdom, Canada, and the United States, including *Dark Matter* (Warner, 2000). She is a recipient of a British Arts Council award in 2000 and is presently working on her third novel, *Faith Is Seven*.

Sapphire is the author of *American Dreams*, a collection of poetry cited by *Publishers Weekly* as "One of the strongest debut collections of the '90s." Her first novel, *Push*, went on to win awards in America and Britain and was named by *The Village Voice* as one of the top twenty-five books of 1996 and by *Time Out New York* as one of the top ten books of that year. Of her new volume of poetry, *Black Wings and Blind Angels* (Knopf, 1999), *Poets & Writers Magazine* wrote, "With her soul on the line in each verse, her latest collection . . . retains Sapphire's incendiary power to win hearts and singe minds." Sapphire's work has been translated into eleven languages and adapted for the stage in the United States and The Netherlands, and will be presented in Scotland during the 2000–2001 season. She has been the recipient of residencies at Yaddo, Headlands, and Kunstllerhaus Schloss Wiepersdorf. In September 2000, Sapphire will be Allan K. Smith Professor of English and Literature at Trinity College in Hartford, Connecticut. Currently she lives and works in New York, where she is completing a new novel and beginning a new book of poetry.

Pamela Sneed is a New York–based poet, solo performer, and actress. She is the author of *Imagine Being More Afraid of Freedom*

Than Slavery (Henry Holt, 1998). She has performed at Lincoln Center, the Whitney Museum of Art, the Public Theatre, PS 122, as well as in Berlin, Vienna, and Mexico City. She is the recipient of a 1997 Franklin Furnace Award for performers, and two original works commissions from the Joyce Mertz Gilmore Foundation for PS 122. She has been featured in countless magazines, including *Vibe*, the *New York Times*, *Bomb*, and the *Source*, and on the cover of *New York Magazine*. Her recent publications are *Caught in the Act*, *Tribute to Mumia Jamal*, *Tribute to Pat Parker*, *The Arc of Love*, *Aloud*, *Ikon*, *Black Renaissance Noir*, and *Changing America*.

Natasha Tarpley was born in 1971 in Chicago, Illinois. She is the author of *Girl in the Mirror: Three Generations of Black Women in Motion* (Beacon Press, 1998) and the editor of the anthology *Testimony: Young African Americans on Self-Discovery and Black Identity* (Beacon Press, 1995). She is a recipient of the National Endowment for the Arts Fellowship and numerous other awards. A graduate of Harvard University and Northwestern University School of Law, she is currently a reporter at *Fortune* magazine and lives in New York City.

Lisa Teasley's fiction, poetry, and essays have appeared in the anthologies *In the Tradition: An Anthology of Young Black Writers*, *Women for All Seasons*, *An Ear to the Ground*, *Step into a World: A Global Anthology of the New Black Literature*, *Beyond the Frontier*, and *100 Black Kisses*, as well as numerous other publications. She has won the May Merrill, the National Society of Arts & Letters, and the Amaranth Review awards for fiction. Her work has appeared in the *Los Angeles Times*, *Details*, the *Washington Post*, and other publications. A native of Los Angeles, Teasley is also a painter who exhibits extensively throughout the country.

Jervey Tervalon's acclaimed debut novel, *Understanding This*, won the 1994 New Voices Award from the Quality Paperback Book Club. His latest novel is *Dead Above Ground* (Pocket

Books, 2000). Also an award-winning poet, screenwriter, and dramatist, his work has appeared in the *Los Angeles Times*, *Details* magazine, and other publications. Born in New Orleans, he lives in California with his wife and child and currently teaches creative writing at California State University at Los Angeles.

ABOUT THE EDITOR

Carol Taylor, a former Random House book editor and a book review editor, has been in book publishing for ten years and has worked with many of today's top black writers. Coauthor of *Sacred Fire: The QBR 100 Essential Black Books*, she has been featured in several publications, among them *Ebony*, *Essence*, and *Black Enterprise*. A freelance editor, writer, and editorial consultant, she lives in New York City and is at work on a novel.